TROUBLE IN THE LAND OF COCOA

A Tropical Mystery

Paul Siegrist

This work is fiction. Any resemblances to actual persons are entirely coincidental.

I extend a special thanks to many Americans, Brazilians and Mexicans who are at the heart of this work. Thanks a lot! Muito obrigado! ¡Muchas gracias!

1

Severino

I keep forgetting who I am. That is, I don't exist. But, I once did. I was a victim of stupidity: mine and of others. Some time ago, I held a respected position as an English teacher in Brazil. I was born in Almadina, a miniscule village in the cocoa growing highlands in the State of Bahia. I lost my mother at a young age and my memories of my father consist of vague encounters with a very troubled man. I had the fortune of being raised by my paternal grandmother. If there's anything good or decent in me, it came from her. Her name is Edinalva, but everyone calls her Nalva. I just call her vovó. We're made from the same mold. We both have dark coppery skin, thick black hair, and are short and stout of stature. She and I can talk about anything: god and love, bastards and angels. She always emits the sweet smell of cupuaçú, probably from the juice she makes fresh each day from this tropical fruit that grows alongside the cocoa trees.

My early days were spent like anyone else around Almadina. That is, I learned to walk long distances and did my share of the work from a young age. There were five of us siblings, I being the fourth born. My earliest memories include helping my brothers haul the freshly harvested cocoa-bean pods from the fazenda into town on a carroça, a horse drawn cart that's still much used throughout Brazil. On sunny days, we'd cut the pods open and extract the beans to be dried on straw mats in the street. Back then, cocoa drew a good price and we lived a simple, but adequate life.

As a teenager, I spent many a weekend night dancing Forró. This form of traditional dancing has various roots. The word itself comes from the time during the Second World War when the Americans had bases in Brazil. Several times a month they held dances that were open to the public. When this was the case, a sign that read FOR ALL was hung outside of the base entrance. Over time, the English pronunciation and spelling gave way to the Brazilian Portuguese. It now sounds like *Fo Ho* to a foreign visitor.

I'd generally catch a ride to Coaraci where most of the shows took place. It's about ten miles away and much larger then Almadina. The women of this part of Bahia are graceful and pretty, so life was good.

But that happiness was ephemeral, as I'll soon explain. I had hoped to become the best teacher in this isolated corner of the tropical world. The winds of change and my apparent bad karma were to change my life in ways I could never have foreseen. Nobody lives a life without surprises, but for some, existence itself becomes so absurd that identity disappears and a surreal delusion takes over.

– Severino – my vovó would say, – you can find anything you look for with enough energy, and that includes trouble.

My name is Severino, but she, like all northeasterners, would utter *Sivirino*. She'd be the one that I'd most regret bringing into the mess that was coming my way. I wanted her to know that it was not due to my seeking it. It was a result of the holy hell that history brings in cycles to this sweet earth.

I finished my degree in English in 1969. I had attended Santa Cruz University between the cities of Itabuna and Ilhéus. I'll always have a fond memory of those years, so full of anticipation and excitement. I was never very interested in politics. Like most Brazilians, I assumed that an individual had little say in anything beyond family and friends. Having entered college in 1965, I was unaware of the disastrous consequences that were to unfold after the military coup in 1969. My friends and colleagues were convinced that it was up to the students to stand up to the new president, Castello Branco, who was appointed by the military. Over the next four years at the university, I started participating in rallies to demand a return to what little political freedom existed before the coup. Just my luck, I guess, that in my last year of classes, the student resistance to the authoritative Brazilian regime would lead to the military government that declared a State of Siege and shut down much of the government. Any overt protest was violently suppressed. I'd later learn that it was a worldwide phenomenon. There was student unrest in the streets of Europe and the United States was fighting its own anti-communist delusions in the Cold War and Vietnam.

I never officially joined any of the open resistance groups or the underground ones either, and I assumed that my participation was without serious consequence. This lack of a direct connection to radical groups led to my being accepted as a first-year teacher at a high school in the Malhado district of Ilhéus. It was a dream come true. The low wages didn't faze me. In fact, I felt rich in many ways. The local community met my enthusiasm with positive reinforcement. My students were interested in the subject and it almost felt like I was teaching my younger friends. Life was good. I was in high spirits.

My second year of teaching started uneventful. I had ignored the rising level of violent underground resistance by students at the university. It had nothing to do with me. I felt content with my existence as an unknown instructor of adolescents. During the first years of teaching, I had to document the teaching and community projects that I had accomplished. Each year, I was to discuss my progress with advisors at the university where I graduated. Afterwards, they would come up with suggestions that I was to implement during the following year. I was to document progress on my assigned course of action to the administrators at my school in Malhado. With the military regime looking for subversives in every corner of education, I knew the importance of following through with the requirement.

I had completed the process and only needed to pick up my documentation at the college. They had informed me it was waiting for me in the Departamento de Letras.

I took a bus to the university, where many people congregated at the entrance gates. They held placards and shouted angry anti-government slogans. I paid no attention and went straight to the guard station to request entrance.

– Nobody gets in today! The Army has occupied the university and I've strict orders not to admit anyone – the soldier stated without any emotion.

– I need to retrieve some documents for the courses I teach in Malhado.

– Not today you don't. Nobody is going to pass here... period!

– Could I speak with your commanding officer?

He spoke with another soldier, who left and returned shortly with a Coronel Oliveira Santos. – No one can enter today; we've received bomb threats and are in the process of searching the entire campus.

I felt like my future was going down the tubes. If I arrive next week at the review meeting without the required documents, and with the only excuse being that I wasn't trusted to enter my alma mater because of violent threats against the military regime, the association between radical action and my position would probably be enough to put my teaching position in doubt. Even worse, it could lead to my name being blacklisted by the administration or my arrest by the present regime. That would mean no future teaching positions, nor any other job related to the government. I remembered my friend down the road a piece at the tropical plant research facility, SEPLAC. Ciçero had connections throughout all levels of government in Bahia. I hitched a ride to see if he was working today. He was.

– Ciço, I need your help. – I explained the situation and he laughed.

– How is it that you get involved in trouble that you don't even know is happening?

– It's just another day to me. Can you try to contact somebody at the university?

He could and did, and was soon speaking with a major inside the secured campus.

– Severino Pindoba Jucá. Yes, he's wearing jeans and a blue polo shirt.

After the conversation by phone, Ciço turned to me with a smile, saying that I'd need several Cruzeiro notes to reward the extra service that I was to receive.

– Thanks Ciçero, I owe you one.

I returned to the university and only had to wait half an hour before Major Silva discreetly allowed me to enter the campus. When alone, I slipped him the Cruzeiros and he stated,

– You have thirty minutes. If you remain beyond that, you'll be arrested for trespassing.

I entered and went directly to the Departamento de Letras. The place was in shambles. Every file cabinet had been emptied on the floor. The troops had hastily opened any desk or other place that might hide something. Who knows what was really being procured? I put little weight behind the idea that somebody was actually trying to bomb the university. It seemed obvious that what was going on was a search for names of students, especially those considered subversive. Other than one or two soldiers guarding the outside of the building, I hadn't noticed anybody inside.

After finding my advisor's office and spending around twenty minutes going through the jumble of documents scattered around the room, I struck pay dirt. There is a God! My file with the recommendations for the following year and some letters of approval were intact in the same folder. I tucked the archive under my shirt and quickly headed toward the front exit. Then it happened. Although I heard nothing, I felt a blast of searing wind pick me up and hurl me across the lobby. I didn't stop at the wall, and followed the glass through the windows, and out of the structure.

I tried to inhale, but it was useless. Someone stopped to see if I was alive.

– What happened? – he demanded.

I couldn't speak. He opened my burnt and bloody shirt and noticed the folder. As my breath slowly returned, I begged him not to lose the documents. He took them and said that I shouldn't worry about anything at that moment. Other than a ringing in my ears and a nose that gushed blood, I apparently had survived without major damage.

– Stay right here. I'll get help! –He joined the other soldiers who were looking for casualties and clues to what had happened. They began to look at me with skeptical expressions. Without thinking, I jumped to my feet and ran into the bombed-out mess. I knew the place well and even with the smoke, twisted metal and concrete hanging from rebar, I easily found my way to the far side of the structure. When I emerged, confusion reigned all around. I walked unnoticed towards the back fence of the university compound. Those guarding the fences weren't paying attention to anybody leaving from the inside. I left through the same gate where several military ambulances were arriving.

I circled around the campus at a considerable distance under cover of the thick Atlantic Rain Forest, and hid in dense shrubbery near the highway. Within a few hours, night fell and I could see that all civilian presence had been eliminated. The emergency lights on vehicles revealed a confusing scene: one that mixed loud orders being broadcast, smoke rolling across the tropical landscape and the strange screams of insects and frogs in the steamy darkness. When I was sure that no one was observing my location, I crossed the highway and dropped down to the Almada River. I followed it in the direction of Itabuna. After a few kilometers, I stopped to wash my face. The nearly full moon had come out and I saw my reflection in the slow moving water. It was a different me. The injuries were obvious: a broken nose and blackened eyes. But, what caught my attention was the fear in this face. I lay down to sleep, but the trouble that lay ahead kept waking me up. The night passed slowly and I occupied myself by trying to keep the mosquitoes at bay.

2

Lilly

I don't gamble. I'm a poor loser, and that precludes that profession. So, when I heard that I'd won the contest on the radio station, I felt like I'd won a jackpot in Vegas. The Durango & Silverton Railroad had sponsored a contest to come up with a new slogan to entice more visitors to southwest Colorado. I've always been interested in the Anasazi Indian ruins in the Four Corners region and have worked seasonally for years in the US Forest Service. I put the two parts of my life together and came up with *Southwest Colorado: from the Past to the Top of the Pass.* It later turned out that it was too long for advertising and many of the potential tourists had no idea what it meant. But, at the time, somebody liked it and I won the contest. The prize was one thousand dollars in credit, and in keeping with the travel theme of the contest, it could only be spent with local travel agencies.

I'd already traveled to Europe and Mexico. I wanted to go somewhere different. Peru sounded good. The idea of visiting the ruins at Machu Picchu has always interested me. I was looking for a place that none of my friends had been. Then I remembered seeing the Carnaval parades in Rio de Janeiro earlier this year on television. It seemed as exotic as anything I've seen. I spoke with my sister in Denver.

– No way! – she said. – That's a macho country and you are a woman. They don't even speak Spanish correctly down there!

– Little sis, they speak Portuguese. Why would they speak Spanish? And, I'm a macho woman.

– All those Latin American third-world dictatorships are the same. Do you know anybody down there? Of course not! Please Lilly! Come to your senses. This is such an opportunity for you to go somewhere cultured. Why take off to the jungle? You're a strong woman, but with your white skin and blond hair, you'll stick out like a clown at a funeral. That big mouth of yours could get you into trouble down there and who's going to get you out of it?

– I can handle myself. I'm familiar with macho cultures, remember?

– But you're not Jane and you'll not be running into Tarzan. Even if you do, just how is he going to fit into a marriage plan here in the states?

– I am not in the market. You know that! How many times do I have to say it? And, I don't want to see New York, Paris, or London again. They bored me the first time around. I find more culture on the Hopi reservation than in any of those pompous cities. Why can't you just help me with my plans?

– Have you even checked on the airfares?

– Yes, the travel agent has worked out a package for me. Airfare, hotel with breakfast and two tours around the city come to exactly $720.00. That leaves me with $280.00 to use on car rentals and other expenses when I'm down there. The agent said they would provide me with travel's checks, and that I could exchange them for Brazilian currency in Rio de Janeiro.

– Car rentals? Are you crazy? You don't know how to drive in Brazil! They probably drive on the wrong side of the road. Wake up!

– Rio has four times the population of Denver. What makes you think they don't know how to drive? Besides, I can always pay for taxis or whatever. The point is, I have a chance to go away to see something on my own. I'll never have the money to do this again and the prize is only redeemable in travel expenses. If the prize were for food, would you insist I spend it on steak when I really want bananas?

– OK, I guess you're set on going. Go to the library and see if Durango has any books on Brazil. I'll go to the bookstores here in Denver to see what I can find.

– Elizabeth, would you like to go with me? It would be a real adventure.

– You know John would never go for something like that. Besides, the kids are too young and I'm not much for hot climates. Who knows what kind of bugs you're going to find down there?

So, I found myself with a free trip to Brazil. I was going to spend seven days and six nights in Copacabana. Just the name made me start imagining all sorts of exotic things. What would the people be like? The book I checked out of the library shows many different types of races. The thought of beaches bathed in tropical sun soon had me wondering what kind of swimsuit I would need. A check of the photos in the book revealed that most women on the beaches were using bikinis. I'm not a very effeminate woman. I like hiking, horseback riding and working outside. I'd never considered exposing myself in public like that. But, who would be looking? Nobody I knew anyway. I bought one out of the Sears catalog.

One month later, I find myself peering out of the plane's window at the beaches that line the waterfront of Rio de Janeiro. It's so much different than I had imagined. So green! So hilly! We land and the sweltering tropical heat catches my breath as I exit the aircraft. Christ! It's only 9:00 AM. Customs and immigration take thirty minutes and as I enter the main part of the airport, I see a man holding a sign that reads *Lily*. Hey, there's three L's in my name, thank you. I'm grateful to see him. The travel agent told me that she'd arranged this pickup with the hotel.

– Welcome to Rio.

At least that's what I thought I heard him say. His accent was very strange to me. The Brazilian Portuguese I heard on the flight from the states seems like a combination of French, Spanish and God knows what else. I'm pleased by his gracious demeanor. He has olive colored skin, a quick smile and thick black hair. I love black hair and soon realize that Brazil has many people with all forms of black hair. He loads my luggage into a strange car from Europe. Good thing I packed light. I don't think a large suitcase would fit into that tiny French vehicle.

We arrive at the Hotel Doralina. It's small, but clean. The man at the reception desk helps me fill out the registration and informs me where breakfast is served each morning. The man who brought me from the airport now carries my bags up two floors of stairs to my room.

– There's no elevator? – I ask, somewhat surprised.

– No senhora.

He opens the door and we enter. The room is mostly white concrete, but the floor and some of the walls are covered with tiles. It's spotless and I feel good about being there.

– Senhora, you can use the facilities of the Copacabana Palace across the street. Since you are a *gringa*, they'll assume you are from Europe or America. Just walk in as if you know the place. They also provide added security at the beach on the far side of the Hotel.

The finest hotel in Rio doesn't open onto the beach! I ask the man why that is, and he replies that the wealthier clients would consider that tacky. Instead, the entrance is from the street, Nossa Senhora de Copacabana, on the side away from the beach.

– What's your name?

– Thiago.

I give him a tip and wonder if all of the names here are going to be ones that I've never heard before. I turn on the ceiling fan. It provides more cooling than I had imagined. I hadn't thought to ask about air conditioning. I just assumed they would have it. I go to the open window and look out onto the street below. I can't see the beach. The travel agent said the hotel was just one hundred feet from the beach, but there's no beach in sight here. All I see is a bustling street and the entrance to the Palace Hotel across the way. I'm tired from the overnight flight. At least I don't have to deal with jet lag. I want to take a shower, and notice that there is no hot water. I soon discover that it doesn't matter. The water is refreshingly cool in the warm air. I leave the bathroom and lay naked on the bed. The whirl of the ceiling fan reminds me of an airplane propeller. It cools me instantly and I drift off to sleep imagining myself in a plane in a Humphrey Bogart movie somewhere off the coast of Africa.

3
Lilly

The sun is already up when I awake. At first, I can't remember where I am. Then the flight and arrival in Rio return to my consciousness. I shower and dress in one of the summer outfits I brought with me. I head downstairs, where I'm directed to the room where café de manha, or breakfast, is served. What a surprise! It's an impressive fare. There are many fruits; pineapple, mango, melon, bananas, and others that I'd never seen. I read the names of the juices: guava, caxú, from the fruit that produces cashew nuts, cupuaçú, cajá, graviola, maracujá, acerola and pitanga. I try the graviola and then a glass of Maracujá. They're both excellent. There are sweet rolls, French bread, cookies, biscuits, cheese, cold cuts, cuscus, eggs, meats and much more. A dark skinned woman asks me if I'd like some tapioca.

– Not for breakfast, thank you – I respond. I don't eat sweets first thing in the morning. Then I notice that she's spooning out some sort of course-ground white flour onto a griddle and cooking something similar to a tortilla, but pure white in color. I ask her what it is.

– Tapioca senhora.

She then adds grated cheese and sliced ham. I take a seat at a small table by the window. The street is packed with businessmen, venders, tourists and lord knows who else. The circus is in town and they're all walking down Nossa Senhora de Copacabana. When I go back for more juice, I see the same woman adding banana and cinnamon to the tapioca. She folds the sides of the pancake-like concoction over the filling and adds some thick white cream or something. I decide to give it a try.

– What would you like with it senhora?

I opt for the ham and cheese. I take it back to the table and think how interesting this would be to prepare back home. I taste it and like the dry and almost powdery texture of the tapioca. The flavor is unique and I hope it will be on the menu every day. I later find out that the white flour is made from dried manioc root that's grown in the Amazon region. Although there are several dishes I don't recognize, I like everything that I taste. The coffee is quite strong; it's espresso. They offer cha, or tea, but I decline. The conversations are in various languages.

Obviously, Copacabana is an international place. I grew up in Denver and never really liked it. I always thought it was too big for me. Maybe there were other reasons, but I could never bring myself to figure out what they were. I left for Durango at twenty years old and never thought of looking back. Most of my family still lives there and I like to visit them. Rio is a different type of city. First, it's much larger and the mixture of classes and ethnicities was more exaggerated than Denver. Second, the streets here in Copa were clogged with all types of transportation: cars, motorcycles weaving in and out, bicycles, even horse drawn carts. Among all of this, hundreds of busses accelerated and decelerated at ridiculous speeds. There's even a subway, like New York. The sidewalks are covered with people, some in a hurry and others simply ambling along between the venders who sell all sorts of things from makeshift stands. It reminds me of a carnival setting.

I finish eating and go up to my room. I want to see what Copacabana beach looks like. I put my new bikini on under some shorts and a tee shirt, throw some suntan lotion and a towel into a beach bag and take the stairs down to the hotel reception.

– Can you tell me how to get to Copacabana beach?

The young, almost albino looking clerk tells me that it is one block down from either corner of the block. He notices my bag and comments,

– It's not advisable to take valuables to the beach madam.

– It only has my lotion and towel.

– Have you been in Brazil for very long? – he ventures.

– About 24 hours.

– I hope you find your stay pleasant – he replies.

– So far, I'm charmed.

– If there is anything I can do to help, just ask.

I've noted something about my time here so far. It is this: the Brazilians seem to be honestly accommodating folks. I haven't run into any of the *Hi! My name is bla bla bla, and I will be your waiter* crowd that so turns me off in the states and Europe.

I walk out into the blinding and blazing sunshine. Licença! Someone yells and I jump out of the way just before a cart filled with cardboard boxes comes barreling by me. OK, Lilly! You're in the big city. Wake up! I go to the closest corner and ask a vender which way it is to the beach. Actually, all I can say is praia, or beach in Portuguese, and point in both directions. She laughs and points toward the beach. As soon as she does, I look and see that the beach is easily visible. The travel agent right; the hotel is only 100 feet from the beach.

At first, I am surprised at what I find at Copacabana beach. I expected many palm trees. There are very few and a street, Avenida de Atlantica, runs alongside of it. It's a weekend and the place is packed with every type of person imaginable. I speak of the physical variations. Here on one of the most famous beaches on earth, everyone is reduced to their natural selves. I am quickly offered a beach chair and umbrella to rent. It's cheap and I'm soon comfortably stretched out near the water´s edge. There are groups of people on every side of me. The amount of people intimidates me a little at first. I'm from a place where we maintain much more space between us. I notice that everyone wears much smaller swimwear than at home. Skinny, fat, old or young; nobody worries about hiding perceived flaws. I am so white. I had never noticed it before, but in all seriousness, I'm like a snowman (or snowwoman). I apply the sun tanning lotion.

I can't understand any of the conversations going on around me. Venders wander by, announcing what they're hawking. Some shout out what they're selling. Others have bells or noisemakers to draw attention to their wares. It all blends into a cacophony below the tropical sun. I'm intrigued. I don't want to admit it, but I enjoy it. I always consider myself almost *above* the turmoil that I find city life to be. I'm a mountain woman. A *Rocky Mountain High* cosmic cowgirl. I buy some roasted-in-the-shell peanuts and a large bottle of beer that's served in a thermal case to keep it cold. I'm not sure where they bring it from, but the beer is colder than I'd have imagined. There's music coming from somewhere in the horde off to my right. It's samba, I believe, or maybe bossa nova. I close my eyes and feel the sun heating the blood in my veins. With my eyes closed, I still see a vivid orange glow. So, this is the warmth of the world below the equator. I find everything is real, but nothing is normal. I'm glad to be here.

After a while, I decide to go into the ocean. There are islands off in the distance and the waters are a gorgeous blue-green. The waves are much stronger than my first impression conveyed. After several hard poundings into the sand, I take notice and pay more attention. Like the mountains, the ocean demands respect. I want to learn more about waves. I've always been a good swimmer and have swum in the ocean in Mexico and Europe. Here, along the base of an urban cliff of concrete buildings, I find my curiosity in nature's power activated. I watch others and remember to dive well under the most powerful waves. Then I notice my skin looking pink. Oops, don't overdo it the first day!

I return to my spot on the beach and collect my towel and bag. Out of nowhere comes a young man to collect for the beers and beach gear.

– Volta sempre! – he says as he smiles and waves. – Tchau!

– Tchau. – I say. It's the first Portuguese that I speak with ease and meaning.

I wander along Avenida Atlantica for a few blocks on the shady side of the street. The buildings are similar to others along beachfronts throughout the world. However, the mood here is not like Miami or Acapulco. Why? I can't say. The explanation for that will have to wait until I've spent more time here. As I walk back to my hotel, I realize that many of the folks out on the street appear to live in Copacabana. There are many elderly among the young in this vibrant place. Why would that be?

– Did you enjoy yourself senhora? – the young man at my hotel's reception desk asks.

– More than I deserve – I respond. – Rio is different.

– Where are you from? – he inquires.

– Durango.

I can tell from his expression that he has no idea of where that is.

– Where do you think I'm from?

He ventures – Spain? Italy? Argentina?

– None of those places – I respond and head up the stairs without telling him where Durango is located.

I spend the evening in a small bar and restaurant next door to the hotel. I write letters to my family and friends in Colorado. I'll probably be back home before they arrive, but it's always fun to get a letter from abroad and besides, writing about my adventures in a foreign country always helps me to sort out my feelings and to later remember what transpired. I go back to the hotel and start up the stairs to my room, with plans to turn in early.

– You must be from Switzerland – the young man from the reception says.

– What's your name? – I respond.

– Mauro, and yours?

– Lilly. I'm from Colorado.

He nods affirmatively, but it's obvious he has no idea where Colorado is located. I just love this place.

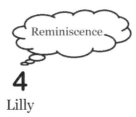

4
Lilly

I remember when I lost my belief in authority and decided that, for better or for worse, I was going to live my life as I wanted. I had been a seasonal worker for the Uncompahgre National Forest for many years. Part of the job required me to participate in fire suppression in much of the Western United States. I was assigned to teams that were dispatched to fires from Alaska to Arizona. At first, it was invigorating. Coming home from a fire always left me with such a macho feeling. Nothing, and I mean nothing, could overcome my ego after one of the big blazes. We put our lives on the line and survived. It was that way. We returned *dick-in-the-dirt-tired*, but tougher than ever.

At least that's the way it was until that day in Northern Idaho. In the steep Bitterroot Mountains, there are always dry conditions at the end of each summer. It's as if the forest was waiting for lightning strikes to set it ablaze. This was not my first time there. The fires along the Salmon River were seasonal occurrences.

One afternoon, my crew was digging a fire line several miles from the actual fire. We were one of many crews that had been assigned to scrape a line about a yard wide, down to mineral earth, in order to contain any lateral advance of the fire. Of course, if the fire were large, it would easily jump this line. Most of the work we did on these Idaho fires was useless. We were there to keep our bosses employed. At the time, large fires in the American West were fought, regardless of the logic or threat to people. If it was a fire, it must be put out. This led to more and more fires each year, but that's another story.

The day was sunny and other than high temperatures and hard physical work at high elevation, it was a beautiful day. The smell of pines has always been one of my favorites. With the sun heating from above, the pine needles radiated their distinctive smell. I was the last person on a twenty-person team that was working its way uphill, digging fire line as we went. To be honest, at thirty-four years old I was pushing my limit just to keep up with the others. I noticed in the distance what appeared to be a rapidly forming cumulus cloud. In the Rockies, summer storms build each afternoon and we sure needed the rain. I recall how clear and blue the rest of the sky was. We had been in the forest for more than a week, sleeping in government issued paper sleeping bags. We hadn't seen the base camp for four days. Up ahead, our crew chief stopped and listened to his walkie-talkie.

– OK, listen up! There is a blow up and it's headed directly towards us. Seek an appropriate place and deploy your turkey cookers!

These were our individual emergency shelters that resembled aluminum foil pup tents. They were for worst-case scenarios, and, other than practice, I had never used one. We just looked at him, waiting for an explanation.

– Do it, damn it! Hell is on its way! – Of course, his words were a little more profane.

I was sure it was a drill. Nonetheless, my heart rate shot up. I was no longer tired. I quickly located a place as far from the towering pines that I could find, scraped a spot free of needles and took out the shelter. It had elastic belts in the corners, to hold down with my arms and legs. I soaked my handkerchief in water, shook open the shelter and assumed a prone position on the ground. The silence gave way to the sound of a locomotive barreling through the woods. The blast of heat preceding it almost took the shelter away. I held on tight and waited for one of the burning tree limbs to come crashing down on me.

The light I saw from under the edges of the shelter was an eerie, wavy orange in color. I thought of my family. So long! I love you. The first burn lasted only ten or fifteen minutes. Then, all was silence. I heard somebody coughing nearby.

– Stay in the shelters you idiots!

Then I heard somebody's walkie-talkie relaying a message from a helicopter above.

– It doesn't look good. It burned directly over them. I see no movement.

Hey! I'm down here and alive!

Then it returned. The winds shifted, and the fire came churning back, feeding on what little was not consumed the first time around. This time, I felt no fear and thought only about getting home. Suddenly it was over. I hear our crew leader shout.

– All clear! Leave the shelters!

I tossed the shelter aside. The world has changed. Completely. Almost nothing of the forest remained. It was a scene of blackened earth and tree stumps, with a white covering of ash. Several of our crew were unconscious and being treated by medics who arrived immediately from helicopters. I'll never forget their mouths stuffed with cinders. Apparently, they had left their shelters and hadn't been able to get back under them before the second burn-over. The scene was triage in what hell had left behind. I would awake with nightmares for years to come.

I never went on another fire.

5

Chucho

I'm known by my nickname: Chucho. I am Zapotec. That is, I'm an Indian from the state of Oaxaca, Mexico. I come from San Pedro el Alto, a small town high in the Sierra Madre del Sur Mountains, a range that lies between the Pacific Ocean and Oaxaca City in Southern Mexico. The elevation here is over 7500 feet, and pine forests surround San Pedro on all sides. The town is known as a peaceful place to stop on the road from Oaxaca to Pochutla or Puerto Escondido on the coast. The only access to San Pedro el Alto is by a dirt road that twists and turns between the coast and Oaxaca City. It's only 150 miles long, but the constant hairpin curves make the bus trip a ten-hour journey. We are located, more or less, at the midpoint of the trip. As a young boy, I liked to hang out with the foreigners who came through town. Little by little, I picked up English. Most of the townsfolk got along pretty well with outsiders. We've been used to them coming through here for centuries.

The area is also renowned for its hongos psilocibios, or psychedelic mushrooms. These mushrooms have been used in Zapotec spiritual ceremonies for more than a thousand years. The federal government gives us special permission to use them. Of course, it's supposed to be only with religious intentions. Last year, several researchers from California visited and studied the effects of the mushrooms. Since that time, many longhaired young people come here to experience them. It gives the Federales a good source of income. That is, the hongos are not legal for non-Indians. The police have checkpoints on the road out of town and use it more to collect the mordida, or bribes, than to control the use of the drug.

As a teenager, I'd often catch the bus to Oaxaca. It's a city of around 90,000 inhabitants, sitting a mile high in a relatively green valley. The ruins of Monte Alban are located on the outskirts of town. The site was established around 500 BC, and ceased to function as a city when the Spanish arrived in 1521. The ancient city attracts many thousands of visitors annually. I had little money to spend, so I'd hang out at the *Zócalo*, the main plaza. It has the cathedral, government buildings and restaurants around a square, landscaped park. The fountains, bandstand and invariable presence of indigenous cultures, both Zapotec and Mixtec, draw tourists in hoards. Oaxaca City has an eternally spring climate. The cuisine is unique. The tamales are the best in Mexico and one can still get a bowl of hot chocolate, with freshly ground cocoa, unrefined sugar and cinnamon to drink in the market. The tlayudas, super-sized tortillas, are sold by elderly women who inevitable have long grey and silver braids. In fact, at least half of the women in this city have long black hair that's generally tied into braids.

Often, I'd sit on a bench in the Zócalo, watching the world go by. Tourists would ask me directions or simply stop to chat. English seems to be the universal language of travelers, regardless of where they're from. One day, a man came up to me and started a conversation. He was interested in the ruins of Monte Alban. He spoke some Spanish, but my English is what allowed us to communicate.

– I'm with my girlfriend and we're hoping to visit the ruins tomorrow. Do you know much about them?

– I've taken the official course to work as a guide at Monte Alban, but I prefer to meet people informally here in the plaza. If you like, I could arrange a taxi to take us up the mountain to the ruins tomorrow morning.

– I have my own car. – the man answers. – Where do you live?

– I stay with my uncle in a part of town called Reforma.

– That's perfect, because we are staying at the campground in Reforma. What's your name?

– Jesús, but everyone calls me Chucho. If you'd like, I can come to the campground at whatever hour of the morning you prefer.

– Do you know where it's located?

He laughs. – There's only one in the city.

– What do you charge?

– Whatever you think it's worth. You decide after the excursion.

– Can you come by around 8:00?

– Sí señor! Oh... what is your name?

– Pablito

We both laugh at this usage of his name in the endearment form. It would translate in English to something like Pauly. He says he has to do some shopping and asks if I need a ride anywhere. I tell him I'm working.

– OK, we'll have some coffee and rolls at the campground when you arrive.

– Hasta mañana! – I say and wave goodbye.

– Tchau!

*****

In the morning, Pablo introduces me to his girlfriend Karina, a good looking and good-natured young American. After some strong coffee, we get into his Jeep Wagoneer and head off for Monte Alban. This site was the pre-columbian center of the vast Zapotec culture. It has many buildings and pyramids, including a giant football court. I give them the typical tour, inventing answers to whatever they ask that I don't know. His knowledge of Mexico's ancient cultures is impressive, but he knows little about Oaxaca. He's a funny sort of guy: eccentric but approachable. We get along well. After dropping Karina at the campground, we head to the Zócalo. We order Tecate beer and some spicy snacks. As usual, the road around the plaza is full of people from all parts of Mexico and the world. The road that surrounds the plaza is closed to traffic and each day is like a constant parade.

Our friendship grows across several years. Each winter Pablo returned. With him, he brought Europeans from the beach areas. One day, we were conversing over some beers, and he asked if I'd be interested in an informal business association with him.

– Chucho, I've been an unofficial tour guide for years. I've reached a point where I'd rather find clients and bring them to the tourist spots where I have local guides who escort them to the sites in these areas. After driving all day, or even several days on the wacky Mexican highway system, the last thing I want to do is be their interpreter and guide when we arrive at a destination. I need to relax and prefer to leave the local tours to the local guides.

– What areas do you cover? I mean, where do you bring your clients? – Chucho asks.

– Here, Cancun, San Cristobal de Las Casas and Palenque. Sometimes, I take a group on down to Central America.

– Do you have guides who work for you in those areas?

– For the moment, only in Cancun. But, I'm working with somebody who wants to do it in Palenque.

– So, how would it work?

– Well, I provide the clients. That is, I would either bring them in my vehicle or arrange their flights in and out of the locations. I'm also responsible for collecting the money.

– What would I be required to do?

– Pick them up at the airport or bus station, transport them to their hotels and give them tours. Also, you'd have to help with any other minor problems that they might come up against, if I'm not present.

– I would use taxis?

– That, or if you can get a driver's license, we could use rental cars.

– What would it pay?

– We'd split the profits 50-50.

That was four years ago now. We've worked together ever since. I now live in Oaxaca City. My job has given me something I could never have imagined: the love of my life.

A little over a year ago, I picked up a group of tourists from the bus terminal. They were a couple from Mexico City and two young women from Paris. I'd long ago grown accustomed to English spoken in various accents from around the globe. On the few occasions when I had Mexicans in a group that included people that didn't speak Spanish, I'd ask them to speak English so we could all understand each other. The Europeans always seemed to know English. I'm not sure if this is because Pablo always arranged it that way, or if it's just that way in Europe. In this group, the two Chilangos (people from Mexico City) didn't speak English and the French girls didn't speak Spanish, so I had to repeat and translate many of our conversations. I enjoy that sort of thing.

Anyway, the Mexican couple, Zully (short for Zulema) and Henrique, was genuinely interested in the Zapotec culture. They were well-read and obviously took pride in Mexico's ancient heritage. The French ladies were out for fun. They had been to the beach in Cancun and had expected to find a beach here in Oaxaca City. They were disappointed, but soon perked up when they saw the majesty of Monte Alban. They also enjoyed the food. Who wouldn't?

The French girls were quite attractive. Zully was more than just eye-catching. She was a goddess. However, she was with Henrique and I'm a professional. So, I noticed, but kept my distance from her, both mentally and physically. With some of my groups, I maintain a formal and distant relationship. With others, we develop a much closer bond than one would normally do in such a short time. I assume this is due to them being far from home, and in a culture and climate different than they're used to. For some, it's a fantasy world here in Oaxaca. Their behaviors sometimes reflect that. I have friends who were clients that still write me from time to time.

The day before they were to leave, we went to the artisans' market. The Chilangos and the French girls were quite good at bargaining down the prices. Here, the majority of the venders are Zapotec. When the French girls offered a price, the venders would speak to each other in Spanish before replying. That way, they could discuss the amount they'd be able to get from the women. Of course, this didn't work for the couple from Mexico City. When Chucho and Zully haggled with them over prices, the vendors spoke Zapotec among themselves. I could understand everything they said in either language.

– Do you think this is a genuine piece of pottery from a Zapotec ruin? – Zully asks Henrique.

I'd just arrived to the venders' stand from arranging to have the car washed while we did the shopping, and had missed the first part of the conversation.

– Where are the French women? – I inquire.

– Over there – replies Henrique, motioning towards the collection of small eateries where I see they're sipping hot chocolate.

– Chucho, do you think this is a real relic from a local ruin? – Zully asks.

– Probably not, but let me speak to them to see if I can find out.

I speak to the venders in Zapotec. – Look, I've known this couple for a week now and they're honest Chilangos who just want to know the truth. I think they'll buy it whether it's a copy or genuine. They just don't want to pay too much.

– What do you care what they pay? If you can help us get more for the piece, we'll give you ten percent.

– I can't do that. My job depends on my honesty. I understand that you need to make a living, but much of my business comes from word of mouth. If for no other reason than the fact that Zully is painfully beautiful, you should give her and her husband a break. After all, they're compatriots

They start laughing. – Yes, they're not rich gringos, but you don't know your group very well.

– What do you mean by that?

– They're not married. She told me that the guy is her cousin.

Whoa! I started thinking. I guess I never really asked. It just seemed that they were with each other. Come to think of it, they were always together. But, I never saw them embrace. I look and see no ring. All this time I could have expressed my feelings toward her. I return to the conversation with the sellers.

– OK, is it real or not?

– It's a copy, but a good one.

– Zully, it's a copy. Nonetheless, it is quality work and not only is it a beautiful reproduction, but you won't have to worry about breaking the federal antiquities law.

– They want 120 pesos, – she replies. – I will only offer 80.

I turn to the venders and say in Zapotec. – She will only pay 70.

– We can let it go for 100, no less.

– OK, I'll pay you the difference of 30 pesos, but don't let her know.

– Fine with us.

– Zully, I convinced them to sell it to you for 70 pesos. I think that's a very good price.

– So do I! Thanks Chucho!

That night we all go out to a local disco. I'm the salsa and cumbia king. Thankfully, Henrique has two left feet. After a couple of dances with the French girls, I ask Zully to dance. She accepts and is a very good dancer! The scent of her hair immediately has an erotic effect on me. God, help me with this, please! As the night progresses, Henrique dances with one of the French girls. The other has latched onto an Aussie traveler. Zully and I take a break and walk outside to get some fresh air.

– You're quite the dancer Chucho! I bet you have plenty of women in your life.

– No. I'm quite alone in life.

– Do you live with your family?

– No, they live in a small town in the mountains. I have an apartment here... Zully?

– Yes?

– I'd like to get to know you better.

– Why did you wait until the last night to say that? I had a feeling that you wanted to tell me something, but you kept yourself so distant.

– I guess I thought you wouldn't be interested in a part-time tour guide. I know you're a nurse in Mexico City. What does your family do there? Have they lived in Mexico City for a long time?

– I have no family. My parents were killed in a mudslide in the state of Guanajuato when I was a child. I was adopted by a family in Mexico City. They're my only family. But, we're not as close as I would have liked.

We turned to each other. Nobody was near and only the crescent moon observed that first passionate embrace. From that moment on, all of my energies have been directed towards doing everything in my power to make Zully's life as pleasant as I can. I'll always feel that way. We visited each other for eight months before we decided to get married. My family helped me pay for a wedding in the cathedral in Oaxaca City. My wealthy uncle volunteered to pay for our honeymoon.

6

Chucho

That morning, not a cloud was in the sky. My friend and I had set out from the town plaza in Oaxaca just as the first light of dawn was visible to the east. I remember the coolness in the air and the dew starting to vaporize on the still quiet streets. We walked for half an hour to one of the local bus lines that were located in various parts so the city at that time. As we ambled through the purple shadows cast by the mountains, I heard roosters crowing and donkeys braying.

Both of us had the distinct feeling that today was going to be different from any other. The lack of clouds was fueling our excitement. We were on our way to observe, if luck held out, an event that had occurred throughout the history of the earth, long before humans arrived on the scene: a solar eclipse. Without a doubt, the Zapotec civilization that had populated this region used shamans and astronomical observers to explain the spiritual significance of solar eclipses. Perhaps some had even figured out the astrological configurations that bring them about. It didn't matter much to the sun and moon; they were simply participating in their day to night to day interplay.

I was psyched. This might be the only chance to see a full solar eclipse in my life. I had hoped for clear skies and... so far, so good.

The bus was full of locals and foreigners. Most of the tourists from other countries were staying in town with plans to attend the extravagant celebration of the event at Monte Alban, the great Zapotec city that sits on the flat top mountain above Oaxaca. I had decided to experience the event on my own terms, in a less hectic setting. This was my landscape and my time and space. I wanted to be part of it.

I descend from the bus where a dirt track leads from the highway up a steep slope on the side of a mountain. There are dozens of people walking the same route. I had never seen so many folks on this road. The sun was now above the ridgeline and birds were singing in the bright light. We pass many venders taking advantage of the foot traffic. They offer water, beer, tamales, chile rellenos and a variety of food and drink. The item that draws my attention is different: a small white cardboard box with nothing in it.

– What is this? – I ask. – How can a box of nothing be worth five pesos?

– It's worth nothing at this moment amigo, but in a couple of hours, it'll be worth the price of not going blind.

He then gives a better explanation. On one side of the box, there is a small, pin-sized hole.

– You hold the box so that this little hole is pointing towards the sun as the eclipse begins. You don't look at the sun, as it'll blind you. You look inside the box, at the white side across from the hole. There you will see a miniature version of the eclipse, as it evolves. When you see the entire corona with a dark center, it's safe to look at the eclipse directly for a few minutes.

I wonder about the whole hole-in-the-box thing. Still, I'd heard about people in other places who had lost part of their vision by looking at an eclipse without protection.

– How about four pesos?

– Mano! I only have several hours on one day of my life to sell these. You only have the same amount of time to buy one. You couldn't go back to town and get one for three times the price. It's up to you.

Several people are buying the boxes after hearing his rap. I decide to do the same.

My friend and I walk on up the road. We've chosen to view the eclipse from Yagul, a small Zapotec city known for its observatory on a rocky point high above the valley. When we arrive at the ruins, there are already hundreds of people sitting on walls, standing on temples and others are wandering about, seemingly without rationale. I had already picked out a place on the far side of the mountain where I was sure we would be alone.

Several scientists from Europe had set up telescopes and other mechanized equipment. I wasn't interested in those. Whatever they recorded could be seen later on TV or in the print media. I spot something that does draw my interest, but I couldn't understand what purpose it could serve. A half dozen or so people had spread out white bed sheets on the ground. I speak to a woman who sits on one of them.

– What's up with the sheets?

– After the eclipse starts, and just a few moments before it goes total, a wavy patterns of lights flows across the ground. Supposedly, it's easier to see this with a white background.

– Why would that be? – I ask.

– Just before the changeover from direct sunlight to the darkened light from the corona, the last bits of light from the sun are irregular. The light is broken up as it flows between the craters on the surface of the moon. This produces a wavy, zigzag pattern across the ground. It is said that the patterns in the stone lintels that adorn many of the buildings at the ruins of Mitla are representations of this phenomena.

– Really?

– Well, actually I've no idea if it's true or not. I saw that on a program about eclipses last night. – the woman replies with a laugh.

I notice that she's having trouble with other people stepping on the sheet.

– Say, my friend and I are going further up the mountainside where there'll be less congestion. Would you like to come with us?

– Thanks. This crowd is getting larger by the minute. I was about to give up on the idea. My brother and sister are with me. Can they come along too?

– Sure, but, nobody else. If we start inviting everyone, it'll be as crowded as here.

She agrees and folds up the sheet. The five of us start the climb up the steep trail that leads to an ancient observatory. Others are also heading up this trail. About two hundred yards up the path, I turn off and follow a small ledge. The others tag along. We walk silently for a few minutes. Then, I start a direct ascent up a talus slope. We all start laughing. For every two steps up, we slide back down one. As we reach the ridgeline, we find ourselves waist deep in shrubbery.

– Keep with me – I yell to them.

We arrive on a flat promontory that overlooks the far side of the valley. Nobody is there. The others spread out the sheet and we sit down on a ledge to take in the view.

– Wow! How'd you ever find this place? – the brother inquires.

– I like to wander around and find new things. I've too much energy for my own good.

There is no shade, but we're used to the sun here in Oaxaca. My friend and I have brought sandwiches, wine and water with us. The others also have food and drink. We share what we have and the hour of the eclipse approaches. We find all of us were born in small villages in the state of Oaxaca. The three of them are from the Mixteca side of the state, and my friend and I are from the Zapotec highlands between the Oaxaca city and the Pacific coast.

The first hint of the impending eclipse comes when flocks of birds settle into trees and cactus, preparing for night. The sunlight starts to fade. Cool winds whip the outcropping. It's eerie. The sun is directly above us. I bring out my white box and the others chuckle.

– What's that?

– A sort of sundial for solar eclipses... I think.

I position the box like the vendor explained, and to our amazement, it works. The interior side of the box shows a mini-sun. It's easy to see where part of the sun is disappearing. My anticipation grows.

– Hey! – the woman's sister calls out. – There are pieces of pottery all over the ground here.

– Yes – I reply – I think this area was used for some ceremonial purpose hundreds of years ago.

– This is so cool! – she adds. – We're sitting on top of remnants of the ancient past, where the previous indigenous peoples probably watched an eclipse.

– Who knows? – I say. – You might very well be right.

The sky darkens quickly. Then a strange reddish glow seems to flow across the land. We're mesmerized by the sight of this reddish light producing a pulsating series of zigzag lines moving across the sheet. Nobody speaks. All eyes are wide open.

Just before the eclipse becomes total, I look directly at the sun. In a moment, the ring of light around the sun appears like a wedding band, with a brilliant diamond on one side. A few seconds later, the diamond disappears. The darkened center within the sun's corona seems like a tunnel that runs between this world and another dimension elsewhere. At least, that's how I experience it.

In the distance, we hear cheers from the crowds below. Some are singing. The brother pours each of us a glass of champagne. We laugh and toast each other. I'm elated. The whole event has turned out to be more than I had expected. As the sun reappears, birds start singing as though it's daybreak. They seem overly emotional, but that could be my own sensation of excitement.

As we walked the long road down to the highway to get in line for the buses that would take us home, I realized that I had seen something that would be a part of me until the day I die. It made me feel so alive.

7

Yoko

I was pondering my good fortune of being born to normal, healthy parents. Then I realized that normal is just a description of what one accepts with ease. My father always said that the most precious gift that comes with being human is free will, and more importantly, the courage to use that free will to change things. He should know. He used his to kill others voluntarily. In Italy, he often saw a look of surprise on the faces of the Fascists just before he killed them. What was a Japanese man doing in Europe? It didn't matter to him, however. Dead was dead and he never gave it a second thought.

Here is how it all came about.

My great grandfather on my father's side of the family was one of thousands of Japanese who immigrated to Hawaii in 1899. They were the last to do so freely. In 1900, when the Americans took possession of the Hawaiian Islands, contract laborers were banned. My father was born in Hilo, Hawaii and moved to California in the 1920's. My mother's family left Japan and moved to São Paulo, Brazil in 1915. Eight years later, they moved on to California. Mom was born the next year.

I'm ethnically Japanese, with short and shiny black hair, above green eyes that reveal my ancestry. I only speak English, and have never visited Japan. In fact, I've never been out of the United States. I'm like any other *Baby Boomer* that was born to a parent that had served in WWII, with one difference; my father and mother were placed in an internment camp in Arizona in 1942. In 1943, when Roosevelt signed the order to permit Japanese-Americans to serve in the army in Europe, my father served in the 442nd Infantry in Italy. They were the most highly decorated regiment in the history of the United States. He was a hero like anyone else who put his or her life on the line in that madness overseas. Shortly after the end of the war, my parents moved to Oregon, where I was born.

I recently graduated and received my teaching certification from Southern Oregon State College. I will start teaching history at a small middle school in La Grande, Oregon next fall. That leaves me three months free. What are the three best things about being a teacher? June, July and August. My mother has always wanted me to visit Japan. To be honest, I'm not interested. I'm not a great traveler. Going from Ashland to Portland is about as adventurous as I'm willing to be. So, when my folks presented me with their idea of the perfect graduation gift, I balked at accepting it.

My father had said,

– We hope you will accept this gift in the spirit that it's offered

I, like all others my age, was glad to be moving out from their protective oversight and into my new adult life. I love my parents and they're the most intelligent people on this planet. They have given me so much: unlimited love, moral guidance, appreciation for value of education and respect for the rights of others. They provided me with the best gift parents could ever give a daughter: self-discipline.

– What? You're giving me something that you have to convince me to want? Somehow, I feel it's not the tune-up and new tires I need.

– Yoko, we want to give you something that will last far longer than anything you might use for your car or new apartment. – My father said this with such devotion to me that I felt a growing lump in my throat. They had both taken such good care of me for so long. Someday I'd take care of them. I'll make it up to them, when the time comes that I'm stronger and they'll be the ones that need protection.

– We'd like to see you learn more about your ancestral roots. We thought the best way to do this would be a journey to discover what your family went through to get you to this point in life.

Uh oh! I didn't like the sound of that. I already know the stories and am more than proud of my linage. But, I am who I am. I don't want to live in the past. Mom and dad have extreme bonds to their unique and, at times, tragic past. I don't.

– Mother! I'm a history major and will be teaching it soon. I don't need to be told what my interests should be! I'm an adult. Please treat me like one.

They hand me an envelope. A scarlet envelope.

– If it's a ticket to Japan, I'm not going to accept it.

– It's not a ticket – my father softly states.

I open the envelope and notice the tears flowing down my mother's face. Inside are a credit card and a small card that reads:

**$3,000 – to be used to visit
your ancestral homeland**

I feel my face flush. How could they be so self-centered? Where are the parents who always encouraged self-assertiveness? What happened to free will?

– And, if I don't use this?

– Give it time. You have three months free and we know you've been preparing to leave next week to look for your new apartment in La Grande. You'll find it in your heart to use it.

– How about a trip to see my uncles and aunts in California?

My father displays his usual expression of gentle astuteness.

– You may use it to visit anywhere that any of your predecessors have lived and died. You are very gifted intellectually. We're sure you'll not belittle the meaning of the gift by only going down the road a piece to see your current relatives. It is up to you to decide. I trust your abilities Chiyoko. You are the gift we send into this world, the results of all we bequest to the future.

My father only uses my full name when he's dealing with something essential between the two of us. I've learned to accept this as a sign of grace in our relationship. The respect they both offer me lies on my heart like a newborn on its mother's breast. It only awaits nourishment.

– Give me time to consider it, OK? – I kiss them both and go to my room. It will soon be a place of past memories. The bed seems like it belongs to an adolescent I knew only yesterday. I've lived in this space for most of my life. Would some young woman in the future have a parent that wants her to know what my life was like long ago... back here in the 1970's? Are we both future and past? Do those that lend us their genetic makeup really matter?

I put on a Cat Stevens record and recline on the bed. I fall asleep with visions of Samurai warriors wandering through a blizzard.

The next morning was one of those infrequent days in Oregon when the sun comes out after days or weeks of rain. A mist rises over every field and the towering fir, pine and spruce trees glisten in the bright sun. I live for mornings like these. Apparently, that's not true for everyone. The northwest has more than the average number of suicides, due in large part to the extended lack of sunshine. Some say it's the rain. But, it's the prolonged cloudiness that enters the psyche of everyone up here. Grey-tones cover the land. Fog is a common occurrence.

I like the rain and fog. I remember my cousin visiting us when we were still quite young. He was on his first trip to Portland and had never seen the little bumps that separate traffic lanes on the freeways. Sometimes it's hard to see the lines on the road due to fog and drizzle. He asked my father what they were.

– They're to help blind folks when they're driving.

My cousin sat silently in the back seat of the BMW. His face was full of wondrous discovery. I could see him imagining a blind person staying in the lanes by using the vibrations from the bumps.

– How do they know when to exit? – he asks.

We all break into hysterical laughter. I shout,

– they listen to the others in their car.

He socks me in the shoulder and with flushed face, he laughs with us.

Oregon is an exotic place. It has everything, good or bad, that one might want in life. The beaches are wide, seemingly endless extensions between forest-covered headlands. The currents are too cold for swimming but the bracing temperatures, the sound of the awesome surf, the endless birds, the majesty of some of the largest trees on earth hovering atop the cliffs and mountains that surround the beaches make them thrilling places to walk. The state also has grand rivers and mountains. This abundance of natural and accessible features is why I have never wanted to travel elsewhere. I was born a part of this landscape and I feel a kinship with it. Why would I want to go to an overpopulated island far across the Pacific?

Still, my parents were seldom wrong in their advice for me. In important matters, they were always correct. That has been both a blessing and a curse. The benefit of meaningful guidance can't be denied. I'm a better person for it. However, there is a downside. Some lessons in life are better learned the hard way. My folks have always told me this, and their lives reflect it. They learned firsthand how maintaining dignity in the face of adversity could bring an inner grace that most never achieve. That's my point; if you're never forced to confront calamity, and always heed the logical recommendations of others, how can you end up wizened by experience? Little did I realize, at that point, that I was soon to get an opportunity to confront fear and self-doubt.

That afternoon, during a walk on Land's End beach with my dog Rowdy, I remembered something that would open a door for me. Some of my ancestors had come to America after spending time in São Paulo, Brazil. As a history major, I was well aware of the unique circumstances of Brazil's history. São Paulo has a population of more than twenty million people and that's a little scary in itself. Brazil is also famous for beaches. I started wondering what it would be like to walk alongside an ocean beach, and actually be able to swim in the waves. Then the floodgates of my mind opened. Would there still be relatives of mine there? What would the food be like? I'd never met anyone from Brazil, although my university had some volleyball players on scholarship from Brazil. I started singing in my mind. *The girl from Ipanema*, which I love, and then another song lodged in my mind for days, much to my consternation: Barry Manilow's *At the Copa*. By the time I drove home, winding through the coastal range, I was convinced. Mom was right; something in my ancestral past awaited me. I was going south of the equator.

That evening, at the dinner table, I let the cat out of the bag.

– I've decided where I'm going to visit.

Mom and dad froze and waited for my words. Their faces were a mixture of apprehension and curiosity.

– I'm going to find out why mom's family went to Brazil and then left for the United States, just eight years later.

My father gently embraced my hands with his. At times, I saw in him a gentle manifestation of the Dali Lama, his spiritual leader. His expression was one of pride and confidence.

My mother simply uttered
– at least it isn't California.

She looked relieved.

8
Yoko

Here I am, the history major that spent four years in the university, and I've learned almost nothing about my own genealogical background. Look, I'm young. I can't help having a sinking, almost repulsive reaction when I hear others start speaking about how hard their life was in the younger years. I'm as compassionate as anyone. I realize the world is filled with those who can and will use others to further the material and psychological domination that defines their lives. Whether I like it or not, this is how most human animals function. It's in our genes. People fear what they don't understand, like a wolf that guards its fresh kill. She wants to eat in peace, but consistently looks around to assure herself that nobody is going to take what she has. If danger appears, she becomes defensive. For the wolf, it's nothing personal. For the human, an over complex mind makes it personal. Challenges to one's existence are attributed to some rationale that often expresses itself as ethnic, gender, age, spiritual or an endless variety of other manifestations. We're not a species that grazes peacefully on the hillside like a deer. We possess the genes of the wolf that stalks the deer. It's the self-control of these impulses that we call civilization. It has come and gone, like waves across historical waters.

I understand why so many lament the injustices in the world. I do too. I live in a society that openly values self-control and compassion for others. I'm living in one of the civilized cycles, at least in this part of the planet. I've studied the lessons from the past. I think I've learned to avoid participating in the behavior of destructive societies.

I'm young and want to neither be saved, nor be required to save others. I never told my parents my true feelings. That is, I prefer to forget the personal effects of their history.

– Yoko, you don't have any idea how good you have it! When I was your age, the world was getting ready to tear itself apart. I was the outsider who had come from within. Life is too easy for the youth of today.

My mother often spoke in this manner. I secretly hated her when she lectured me like that. My world is doing just the opposite; it is confronting wrongs and coming together. It's the Age of Aquarius. Love is in the air. Tomorrow holds so much promise.

– Look for your place in the here and now Yoko. Everyone has her own reality, especially the young. Be aware of yourself. Get ready for your future and don't concentrate your energies on the past.

My father understands me well. He and my mother are so unlike each other. How could two people, so much in love, have such divergent philosophies? It's not surprising that many young people are confused. How are we to balance and comprehend the Ying-Yang upbringing that we have to endure?

*****

– Have you made any specific plans Yoko? – my father asks.
– I'm going to finalize the trip itinerary tomorrow. The travel agency is preparing several possibilities for me to consider. – I reply.
– I've been doing a little research on Japanese immigration to Brazil. Did you know that São Paulo has the largest expatriate colony of Japanese outside of Japan? There are more people of Japanese descent in Brazil than in the United States.
– Why would that be? – my father asks, – There are so many more opportunities here in the States.
– Well, the end of the agricultural based society in Japan at the start of the twentieth century, and the rise of industrialism left many rural peasants without a means to sustain themselves. Meanwhile, in Brazil, the end of slavery created a shortage of workers in the coffee plantations in the state of São Paulo. The elite ruling class in Brazil had attempted to "whiten" the population by luring Europeans to replace the newly freed slaves. Until 1892, Africans and Asians were not allowed to immigrate to Brazil. Low wages and dreadful working conditions for immigrants became a political issue in Italy, and it prohibited subsidized immigration to Brazil. Then, Japan and Brazil signed a treaty that permitted Japanese migration. Not long after, our family arrived in Rio de Janeiro.
– Yoko, have I told you how much I respect your curious mind? – Father replied. – Your mind is like a sponge.

Mother assumed her usual disapproving stance.

– Yes, my dear, it's about time that you directed your energies toward something more meaningful than that hippy music and the latest styles in England. Rolling Stones, Animals, Elton John, Beatles... I'm so tired of hearing about those European drug fiends. –

*****

The overnight flight from Portland was tiring to say the least. I wanted to go first class, but my mother had forbidden it.

– You can use any extra money when you return. If you need it in South America, you'll regret squandering it on ten hours in an airplane.

I attempted to sleep in a sardine can. How can some people do that? I slept very little and now found myself gazing out the window at a city that seemed to have various downtown areas. How strange! The countryside surrounding São Paulo was as green as Western Oregon. For some reason, I felt a strange combination of dread and curiosity welling up inside of me. I forced myself to feign excitement at the idea of going to a foreign country while saying goodbye to my parents at the airport in Portland. My father was so proud of me. I didn't want to disappoint him, so I let on that this was my dream come true. In reality, I'd wondered if it was going to be more like a dream or a nightmare. Now, an unexplained excitement was indeed overcoming my lack of sleep. I found myself breathing slow and deep. What would I find in this megalopolis so far from home?

We land in a light mist. As I exit, I'm surprised at how warm the rain is here. It felt good and smelled fertile. Mom had helped me contact the Japan Foundation in São Paulo. They'd recommended a hotel near the airport in the Congonhas neighborhood. I took a taxi to the Hotel Santa Maria. I had heard of the Latin American laid-back attitude. There was none of that here. This is a city of action. My room is on the fourteenth floor and I've a view of the endless urban landscape. Impressive! It dwarfs Portland. It may not be the big apple, but it definitely is the big mango.

9

Severino

– Bem te vi! Bem te vi!

I awoke to several common birds shouting their greeting. It means *I saw you well* in Portuguese. The morning sun was bright and the green light cast on my skin from the canopy above made me feel like I was part of the surrounding jungle. The river's babble was soothing, like waves on a beach. I am always more at ease in the forest than in the city. But, my pain from the accident and the night spent on rocks and plants reminded me that today was not going to be a day to commune with nature or anything else.

– Bem te vi! Bem te vi!

– Yes, and they did too – I muttered to nearby birds. – Not only that: they have my records to identify me.

I started sorting out the previous day's mayhem. I had given my name and shown my face at the scene of a crime. Who was the cretin who planted the bomb? There were ambulances. How many were injured? Did anyone die?

I crept back to the highway. The university entrance still had plenty of activity: police activity. I waded across the river and followed it upstream for a few hours. I needed a place to lay low awhile. I have a friend in Itabuna who I can trust. I needed to clean up. I tossed my bloody and torn shirt aside. It would be better to ride the bus shirtless. Itabuna is a mixture of everything odd in this part of Bahia, and I won't draw attention. Another kilometer of walking and I stood at the bus stop. Fifteen minutes later, I knocked on Ramalho's door.

– Oi! Tudo bem? – he greeted me. – To what do we owe the pleasure of this visit?

– Trouble – I mumbled. – Let me inside and I'll explain.

By then he'd noticed my physical appearance and his negative reaction was starting to spook me.

– Oxente! What happened to you? Get in the car! We're going to the hospital!

– Wait, it's not that easy. Do you have any water? – I was parched and my face was starting to pound out a painful rhythm to my brain. After a few liters of water and some bean stew, I felt better. I explain that a bomb had exploded at the college and I needed to distance myself from the event.

– I'll contact Waldemar Chianca. He's a doctor I've known most of my life. – Ramalho reaches the doctor on the phone and he tells us to come over immediately. We jump into his Ford pickup and tool across Itabuna to a small clinic on the outskirts of this city of about 100,000. I've a love-hate relationship with Itabuna. I'm endlessly fascinated with its collection of tropical characters. They are at times stunningly beautiful and every possible point on the ethnic spectrum is covered. Brazil is unique in its deep-seated acceptance of different ethnicities. Especially in Bahia, it's rare to find racial prejudice; everyone has several prominent tribal groupings within their genetic history. The infinite mixing of Indigenous, African, European and other cultures is obvious everywhere. Here in Bahia, the people are of a rare beauty. They are attractive and accessible, a breed of people who are open to all. Here, it's acceptable to stare at anything that might interest you. People live their lives openly. This sometimes produces a crass honesty that can make outsiders uneasy.

On the other hand, Itabuna is also endlessly chaotic. The juxtapositions of rich and poor, clean and filthy, sun and shade, order and mayhem are ubiquitously present. The odors one encounters in the streets run the gamut from tropical flowers to septic stench. The place is growing like mad and the arrival of marginally economic peoples places a strain on all services. Corruption is not lacking. It's best to take the good with the bad or just stay away.

We enter the clinic and Ramalho speaks with Dr. Chianca, who immediately brings me to a room and examines my face.

– Any other injuries? – he inquires. – What did you tangle with?

– A friend of mine threw gasoline on a barbeque and the result was an explosion that threw the grill into my face.

He sets my nose in one quick and excruciating snap. – Jesus Christ! You could have warned me!

– You would have felt it more, and if you had tensed up, it might have taken several tries. Relax! You're lucky that no bone damage occurred. Nonetheless, we need an x-ray to verify this.

After examining my vision and taking several x-rays, Dr. Chianca gives my some prescriptions for pain pills and something to reduce swelling in the face. As I leave, I turn to ask what the cost is.

– This is a favor for Ramalho. Just take it easy for a week or two and get a hold of me if you have further complications.

– Obrigado doctor. Tchau!

We leave the air-conditioned office and the sultry midday heat reminds me that my life is not going to heal as quickly as my face. On the way back to the house, Ramalho asks me why I hadn't told the doctor what had really happened. I explain my encounter with the soldiers.

– Did they recognize you?

– The military police know who I am. They found the archive with all of my personal information in it. I was carrying it with me as I left. Have you heard anything about the university on the news?

– Christ! It's the only thing on the television. Several university employees were badly injured, and worse, an army sergeant was killed. They have taken scores of militant students into custody. You can't let them get to you until you can prove your innocence.

– Prove my innocence? I was the only one who entered the building before the explosion. I bribed my way in, and they caught me leaving the scene of the blast. They're going to think I was trying to remove evidence of my name from the crime scene before the explosion. Just how the hell am I going to explain that?

We arrive at the house and I'm offered a place to rest. I hit the bed and am asleep within seconds.

I awake with moonlight coming through the window. I grab the clothes Ramalho has loaned me and tiptoe out of the room. I leave a short note of thanks to him and his wife Maria. I'll be in touch with them when the time is right.

– Cuídam-se amigos. I whisper as I pass their bedroom.

The sun is just starting to illuminate the horizon as I slip into the street. I walk the few kilometers to the bus depot. There's a bus leaving in an hour for Almadina. While waiting, I read the local paper and find that, indeed, several were injured in the university explosion. Nothing is mentioned about a death. Suspects are being sought.

    – Severino! Where you headed? Going home to see your family? – Toninho, a friend from Almadina inquires.

    – Yes.

    – What happened to your face?

    – Bicycle wreck. I'm going to spend some time with my grandmother until I heal.

    Toninho tells me to look him up and heads to catch the bus to Ilhéus. I recall that many know me in Almadina and if I'm to remain incognito, then I'm going to have to come up with a place to hide out. Then I remember the farm that my family abandoned long ago. It's barely standing. As a boy, I spent time there. Although I lived with my grandmother, I visited the farm on weekends. My father lived there, but he rarely spoke with me. In all honesty, I hardly knew him. He was a loner. My grandmother told me that something inside of him broke when my mother died. He never recovered. He was damaged material before I became conscious that I needed a father. He meant well, but some people should never fall in love. For them, when love ends, they continue life as though they have some form of terminal disease. They never love again. Depression and alcohol await their inevitable acceptance. He existed another five years before the consequences of his drinking took him out of the picture.

    The bus pulls into Almadina about 6:00 AM and all is quiet. This place is always calm. It's surrounded by steep hillsides and rock outcroppings that are covered with rain forest and cocoa plantations. Below these, cattle ranches occupy the lowland valleys. My grandmother is still alive. She's 84 years old, and more thoughtful and humorous than most people are at half her age. I go directly to her house on the edge of town.

    – Bom dia querido! Finally, you come to visit your vovó! Give me a kiss.

    As I embrace my grandmother, I feel the urge to tell her that I love her more than ever and that I may not be around to see her off into the ever after. But, I simply mumble

    – You know vovó; I love you more than anything on this earth. Nothing could ever separate us for long.

    She mentions nothing about the incident at the university, so I assume it hasn't become common knowledge that I was there: at least not with her. She asks if I've received word on my contract for the following year at the school in Malhado. I tell her they have decided not to hire any permanent teachers, due to financial troubles in the district.

– I'm going to take a year or so off to figure out who I am and what I'm going to do.

– Ai filinho! At least you're going to spend some time with me.

– Actually, I'm hoping you'll give me permission to fix up the old homestead. I need a place to reflect on what I'm going to do with my life now.

– Filho, you can stay there for the rest of your life for all I care. Nobody wants to be bothered with that remote place. Somebody staying there will at least keep it free from squatters. But, why on earth would you want to be so secluded at your young age?

– Vovó, maybe I've been chasing the wrong dream. My father worked that fazenda and I'd like to see what he was up against in his younger years.

– He was up against a problem with drinking. He kept trying to make a plot of land fulfill his dreams during the worst drought this area has ever seen. It broke my heart to see that he couldn't or wouldn't face the fact that he was never going to make up for the loss of your mother by burying himself deeper in his useless illusions than your mother in her grave.

I was ten years old when my mother died. She had a heart attack at a young age. She smoked herself into her last resting place. I remember when my siblings and I received the news. I couldn't accept it. I remember a night of sorrow beyond what any ten-year-old can comprehend. Life went on, and in time, the memories became sweeter and gentler. Ultimately, time arranges everything with its endless harmony.

– Vovó, I'm going to ask that you not mention my plans to anyone. I want to start this venture with as little attention as possible. I have no idea if I'll have more luck than dad did. To be honest, I'm a little humiliated by the fact that my job was not extended. I need time alone to reflect. Can I count on you to keep this a secret for the time being?

– Of course, you can. I don't like the idea of you staying alone up there, but I'll respect your wishes. You will visit me from time to time though, won't you?

– Com certeza vovó. You're the only one I feel close to and I'll visit whenever I can. However, I want to spend the first few weeks entirely by myself. I hope you can appreciate my reasons.

– I don't agree with them, but you're a grown man now and at least you'll be closer. Promise me you'll be careful and return to see me as soon as you feel comfortable.

– Don't let anyone know that I've arrived and, more importantly, that I'm up in the highlands.

I spend the day and night with her. The next morning I head out on the road that leads to Floresta Azul. A bus travels this route several times a day, but I don't want others to notice me. It takes until noon to walk the five miles to the turn-off that leads to the old farmstead. I walk up the deeply rutted track that leads into the highlands. This part of the road has been washed out for years. I'll leave it that way for now. I arrive at the house, but it's not livable anymore. The roof long ago caved in. The walls are broken and sagging. Still, something in me stirs when I view the surrounding green pastureland backed by the Atlantic Rain Forest. My spirits start to rise for the first time since the bomb went off in my life.

10
Lilly

In the morning, the phone rings. When I lift the receiver, I hear:

– Bom dia senhora. It's seven o'clock.

– Obrigada – I reply. I'm getting good at using one word to express myself.

Today I'm going on an excursion to the giant Jesus statue that sits atop a mountain overlooking the city. The tour leaves in an hour and I head down to breakfast with everything I think I'll need for the tour: jeans, hat, camera (I brought six rolls of film from the states) and the Cruzeiros from the dollars I exchanged before leaving the airport yesterday. I still didn't understand exactly what they were worth, but I was glad that I had them, as it's not like Europe or Mexico; American dollars are not accepted here.

In the breakfast area, I notice it's more crowded than yesterday. I request the banana and cinnamon tapioca. It's sweet, but I like it. As I drink coffee and wait for the tour operator to arrive, I hear at least four different languages being spoken. I can speak a few words of Spanish. What American can't? But, I hear none of that being spoken. Most visitors to Rio are from Europe. That probably explains why nobody here guesses that I'm American. In Mexico, it's taken for granted that anyone as white as I am is an American.

The tour bus pulls up outside and two men enter the hotel. They announce that those who are going on the trip to the Christ the Redeemer statue should line up beside the bus. Almost everyone in the room heads for the door. I follow. The bus is different from any I had seen before. It's a Mercedes and looks to hold about thirty people. They verify who we are as we enter and I hear one couple speaking English. I think they're from England. I sit next to them and find they're from Bristol.

– I'm Veronica and this is Mark. – The woman states. – Have you been in Brazil very long?

– I arrived the day before yesterday. And you guys?

– We came to Brazil last year and stayed in São Paulo for ten days. "This time we are touring Rio."

The bus traverses the mayhem that is Rio's street traffic. Elizabeth was right. I could never have driven here. It seems like nobody has any idea of where they're going, or how to stay in a lane. After a half an hour or so, we pull over at the base of the road that goes up to the statue. The driver's assistant exits and returns shortly with our passes to the park. The ride up the mountain is a thriller. I'm used to steep inclines in Colorado, so that doesn't bother me. What I find a little disconcerting is the limited space on each hairpin curve. The bus is in a low gear, grinding upwards and at each curve, we see other buses barreling downhill and slamming on their brakes to let us pass within an inch or them. Nobody stops and it all seems quite natural. About half of the passengers in the bus are Brazilians and none of them takes notice.

We leave the bus in a parking area and walk through the sunlight and brisk wind to the base of the Redemptor, as the big Jesus is called in Portuguese. It's much larger than it appeared from below. The Brits and I were glad the tour guide spoke both Portuguese and English. Like most tours, the facts behind the creation of the monument were not that interesting. The statue, however, was inspiring from whatever angle. Set against the bright blue sky and the undulating city landscape below, it was perfect for photos. I took out my camera and made sure it had film. I took several shots, including one or two of Mark and Veronica. Then I heard a voice ask,

– Would you like me to take a photo of you and you parents?

I looked around and saw a young man looking at me.

– They're my friends. – I reply and then add – Yes, that would be kind of you.

He takes several shots of us together, and then asks if I'd like a few of just myself with Jesus. I agree and he positions me for the photos as though he were a professional photographer. I go to retrieve the camera and he suggests we go to an extended concrete section that overlooks the city, beaches and ocean far below. In the back of my mind, I'm thinking that I need to be careful with strangers. But, I had noticed him before. He's with our tour, and I figured it would be safe. After all, there were hundreds of people surrounding us.

– Stand right there. I can get a shot with Copacabana and Ipanema beaches in the background.

I do as instructed. He returns and I notice how easily he smiles. He asks my name.

– Lilly, with three L's. What's yours? – I venture.

– I don't understand.

– What is your name?

– Oh! It's Aritana. Aritana Santiago Pinto.

Another name I've never heard before.

– I thought that all names in Portuguese that end with the letter "a" are for women.

– That's generally correct, and I often have Brazilians tell me the same thing. My name is indigenous. My mother is Indian.

– Oh! Sorry...

– Don't worry about it. Where are you from?

– Take a guess.

– Well, I heard you speaking English with your friends, so I'm going to guess Australia.

– Ha ha. Not hardly. Try the other side of the globe.

– You are an American?

– One hundred percent.

He asks if my friends and I would like to have lunch at a small cafeteria that overlooks the city below, with the Jesus above. Apparently, it will fill up fast, but there's still space if we go right away. Mark and Veronica decide to stay and hear a spiel about the miracles that started to happen in Rio after the construction of the colossal prince of peace. I ask them to let me know if the tour operators decide it's time to leave. They nod in agreement, obviously fascinated by the spiritual transformation that the Redemptor had caused in Rio.

Aritana is around twenty-five years old. He has dark eyes and a slim but muscular build. I realize that I'm enjoying looking at him. His skin is the color of ripe avocados. His hair is jet black and shiny, reflecting the bright sunshine.

– Where do you live Aritana?

– I'm from Maceió, a city far to the north of here. Have you heard of it?

I reply no and tell him that, other than Rio de Janeiro, I know nothing of Brazil. I ask him what he does for a living and he tells me that he's a Military Policeman. I assume he's an army cop, but he informs me that in Brazil many ex-soldiers go on to become law enforcement officers that function in all states. I guess it's sort of like the National Guard back home, but with local police powers. Later, I find that they do most of the major crime control and investigations throughout the country.

– Do you have a family? – he inquires.

– Yes, my parents and two sisters in Denver.

– You're not married?

– Not hardly! I don't need a protector in my life and most of the men I meet are looking to do just that.

I see his face contort a little and I feel that I really didn't have to state that so bluntly. He hadn't, in any way, come on in a macho manner. I touch his hand and quickly add,

– Don't get me wrong, I'm not saying that I'm not interested in meeting men. I've taken a break in the dating scene recently. It's too much of a competitive game for me. I'm sure that, in time, Mr. Right will come my way.

– Say Lilly, I'm going to a place tonight that I don't think most foreign tourists know. My father told me about it. It's a cultural center that presents much of the food, music and other aspects from Northeastern Brazil, where I am from. Would you like to come along?

I hadn't come to Brazil to find romance, but neither was I against the idea. Aritana seemed pleasant and well mannered. I'd have to check him out first and see if this cultural center was know by other Brazilians.

– Can I let you know this afternoon after I get back to my hotel?

– Of course. Are you staying at the Doralina?

– Yes, how'd you know?

– That's where most of the tour members were picked up.

– Oh, that's right. – I add, wondering if he had noticed me from the start of the tour.

– I'm at the Hotel Apa, just a few blocks away. Here's the phone number; it's room 402. Let me know if you can make it. Another couple will also be going.

I jot down his number and we finish eating the mixtos, as grilled ham and cheese sandwiches are called in Brazil. The tour operators announce the departure of our bus. By the time I'm dropped off at the hotel, I'd begun to hope that the evening would be as interesting as this jaunt around the Jesus had been.

11
Lilly

At the hotel, I call my folks in Denver. I don't mention Aritana. Colorado seems like a planet away from here. All is well at home and everyone wants to know what Brazil is like.

– Different. – I reply. – It's far more urban than I had imagined.

Most of the time, I can't understand what is going on around me, but I keep that thought to myself. No use giving my mother an excuse to worry about me.

– The music is diverse, and unlike anything I've heard before. The sun and beach are as fine as I had hoped.

I couldn't tell them much about Brazil, as it was still a mystery to me. I tell them that I'm doing well and have plans to visit a cultural museum or something like that this evening with some others in our tour group. My father cautions me not to go anywhere alone.

– That city has ghettos and you don't know the bad areas of town. –

I promise not to do anything foolish.

– We love you Lilly – they both say. – Call us every day, OK?

I decide to go to the Hotel Apa and see what I can find out about Aritana before I speak with him again. I ring the front desk and request a taxi, and when it arrives, I head over to his hotel. It's only a five-minute drive. I enter and walk directly to the reception counter.

– How can we help you today senhora?

I'm a very informal and direct person. Some take this attitude as an affront, but it has served me well in life. I like to think of myself as simply honest, but some describe me a brutally honest. I get straight to the point with the hotel clerk.

– I've met a gentleman on our tour to the Redemptor today. He has asked me to go to a cultural center with him tonight and I'd like to know if you could supply me with any information about him. He's staying at this hotel. The man turns and speaks with another older man, apparently the one in charge. The elder man asks me for Aritana's name.

– Aritana Santiago Pinto.

He has opened the registrar, but does not look at it.

– I know his father well. Aritana is a policeman from the state of Alagoas. His family stays here often.

That was better than what I was hoping to hear.

– Do you know anything about a Northeast Brazil Cultural Center?

He laughs. – It's know by everyone here as the *Feira de Paraíba*, or the Paraíba Fair in English. If you are not going to travel to Northern Brazil, it's a good way to see some of the unique customs from there. Many tourists enjoy it.

I thank him and exit the hotel. I don't want Aritana to think I'm distrustful of him. I decide to walk back to the Doralina. The street scene of Copacabana is in full swing. I notice that many elderly people here have an attendant helping them go about their tasks. I've always thought that one of the measures of a society is how they treat their older generation. The sidewalk is packed with people from many walks of life: tourists in swimwear, businesspersons in formal attire, street urchins looking for handouts, shoppers, street venders, and me.

Not that anybody notices me. I'm a small dot on this canvass of life in Rio. Back in Durango, I'm known by many. I can't walk down Main Street without stopping to chat. Here I'm incognito. It's both unnerving and invigorating. At this moment, in this spot, I simply exist. I've no history here. I'm both vulnerable and entirely free. I return to a thought that's not new to me. That is, most people in this world have never been completely alone. Most people have never spent more than a few days, at most, without being in the presence of family, spouse, friend, boss, colleague, or somebody they know. In my work for the National Forests, I used to do a lot of backcountry patrol. I checked out trails at the beginning of the summer season. At times. I wouldn't see a human for up to a week at a time. It was great.

I think of my sisters. I love them dearly. I've always felt like they were with me spiritually wherever I roamed. But, it's true. They have always lived near our parents. They have never spent more than a day or two away from their center of support. Even when Barbara went away to college, she lived in the dorms until she became engaged. After they married, the interrelationships became even less individual, and more interdependent. I don't find anything wrong with this. To the contrary, I assume it has many beneficial aspects. I simply think that my reality, that of living without a safety net, is something they *can't* appreciate. To each their own path in life, of course.

And, mine now brings me to my hotel.

– You have a message. – The clerk says.

He hands me a piece of paper. It's from Aritana and he has repeated his invitation. I call him and ask what time we will be leaving. He says that they will pick me up at 8:00. That gives me several hours to rest up and get ready.

I'm waiting in the lobby when Aritana comes in. He's accompanied by a man and a woman. He introduces them to me. They are Alex and Lizandra. They are also from Maceió. We all pile in their rental car and head to the São Cristovão neighborhood, where the Feira de Paraíba is located. It's a huge complex that's in the shape of a mammoth boiadeiro, the traditional headwear of the Northeast cowboy. Upon entering, I find the place is full of stalls that offer food, music, crafts, liquors and god knows what else.

– Let's get something to eat – Alex suggests. – I'm famished!

Everyone agrees. Apparently, Alex and Lizandra have been here before. We follow them far into the complex to a restaurant called Olinda. I let my new friends order. We are served a large meal that includes carne de sol, a type of sun-cured beef. It's served with fried manioc root called aipim. They also bring plenty of side dishes and salads. One learns early in Brazil to order as little as possible, because they'll always bring too much.

– Can I drink the water here? – I ask.

– Sure, but I thought you said you like beer. – Aritana says.

He's right. I order some Bohemia beer and we share it amongst the four of us. The waiter brings several other bottles during the meal. Afterwards, we decide to split into two groups to see what is being offered in the booths. We agree to meet at one of the bandstands in an hour. Aritana and the others have offered to teach me a little forró dancing. I've no idea what they're talking about, but I like to dance.

Aritana and I stop at a nearby shop that sells music. He says the music that's playing is forró. I like it from the start. It's somewhat like a cross between country and rock, with a little salsa rhythm thrown in. He starts to dance right in front of everyone. I'm a little embarrassed, but later learn that one can dance whenever and wherever in Brazil. The same can be said for singing. I had already noticed some people singing on the sidewalks, even those who voices were not so melodious.

Next, we come to a booth that's offering samples of several types of cachaça, a uniquely Brazilian liquor. It's made by fermenting the sap from sugar cane. The process is simple and each region of Brazil has distilleries of varying sizes. I quickly gulp down a shot of Rio de Engenho, a cachaça from Bahia. It burns! But, I like the taste. This is not a smooth tequila, but more like a the cruder mescal that's produced in Mexico in a similar manner.

– Be careful Lilly. It's strong and can creep up on you – my new amigo informs me.

I insist on trying another shot from another distillery. This time I go for Serra Limpa from Alagoas. It goes down like fire. As before, I like the taste: raw, but real. I buy a small bottle to take back to Colorado, and we walk on down the aisle. During the next hour or so, Aritana explains a multitude of artisan works, homemade candies and cheeses, bottled hot peppers and clothing. I try to imagine what Northeast Brazil is like. Maybe it's somewhat like our western states, with cowboys, regional music and plenty of open spaces. He states that Brazil, like America, is so large that it has regions with marked cultural differences. He tells me Brazil is almost the size of the USA. I find that a little hard to believe, but after getting back to the states, I find he's correct.

We meet the others back at a bar beside a large stage. There's a band setting up to play. Alex and Lizandra are drinking caipirinhas, a drink made from cachaça and lime, sort of like a Brazilian Margarita. Sounds good to me! I order one and find it's a little too sweet for me. Lizandra tells me to let her have this one and she orders one for me with less sugar. That's more like it! She speaks little English, but with Alex's help, she communicates adequately with me.

The band starts up and it's loud. The music is forró. The stage has several women in skimpy garb who are dancing to the music. I ask Alex what that's all about and he states that many forró bands have dancers on stage. Why not? People flow out of the surrounding bars onto the large dance floor in front of the stage and start to dance. I watch and feel the beat of the music enter my psyche. I want to go out and try it, but am not sure enough of myself. Aritana appears in front of me and takes my hand, urging me out onto the floor. He gives me a quick lesson on double steps for each movement. I see many of the dancers have sophisticated and coordinated moves, but he stays with the basic steps.

– Let the rhythm take you wherever you want. Just enjoy and don't worry what others think. – He tells me with his disarming smile.

The caipirinhas are having their effect on me and I find it easy to go with the rhythm. I learn another thing about Brazil. When a band plays, they don't take a break between songs. The next number starts immediately after the preceding one. After a couple hours, another band starts setting up.

– How late do they play here? – I ask.

– In Brazil, the music goes until dawn. – Lizandra says.

It did, and I danced much of the night with Aritana. By the time we drove along the Avenida Atlantica to drop me off at my hotel, the sun was coming up over the ocean to my right. Joggers and bicyclists were moving along the sidewalk and bike path along the beach. I felt good: exhausted but happy. Aritana walked me to the entrance to the hotel.

– Good night. That is, Bom dia! Thanks for a great time. – I said in a half-asleep voice.

As he turned to leave, I stopped him and gave him an embrace. I wanted one more chance to smell his hair. What was it that attracted me so much to him? We kissed lightly, and went our own ways: I into the muted, florescent-lit lobby, and he into the soft morning sun.

12
Zully

I wanted to speak with Chucho about something before I'd be able to give him an answer to his marriage proposal. I phoned him and he asks,

– What is it baby? You know you can tell me anything, at any moment. I want our relationship to be open. I may not agree, but please; feel free to express whatever opinion or doubt you might have.

– Jesús, I don't have any doubts about our abilities to communicate. You're the only one in my life that I can tell anything and everything. I want to talk with you in person about something that I've said that is untrue.

– OK Zully, go ahead. I'm ready.

– I can't speak about it on the phone. I have the weekend free. Can I come down to Oaxaca and meet with you?

– Sure baby, let me know when your bus will get in and I'll be there to pick you up.

The following Friday I take the ten-hour trip from Mexico City to Oaxaca. It's always good to get out of the big city. I was born, and spent the first six years of my life, in Hidalgo, a small town near the capital city of Guanajuato. I like Mexico City, where I live, but I always feel more at ease in smaller communities. The trip from Mexico City to Oaxaca passes through the Valley of Mexico, on to Tehuacán, known for its mineral springs, and traverses a pine forest at 10,000 feet of elevation before dropping into the dry, semiarid Valley of Oaxaca. Chucho is waiting for me at the bus depot.

We go to his apartment. It's actually just one room with a bathroom off to the side. I've spent various nights here with Chucho and I've no qualms about sleeping with the man I love. Our intimate life is one of the strongest aspects of our relationship. Tonight, however, I don't want to sleep in the same room. I need to gather the strength to speak about something I've not allowed myself to dwell on for years.

– Chucho. Please help me with something tonight. You know I love you more than I love anyone, but I have a request. It's this: I need to find a place to stay by myself tonight. It has nothing to do with you. I need to find a part of me that I've hidden away for much of my life. Can you handle that?

– Ai, Zully! You didn't mention that before. If there's something I've done wrong, let me know. If you need peace, I can sleep with my uncle and let you stay here alone. Or, I could stay and not speak, if that would work for you.

– No! – I quickly regret throwing that word out so strongly. He's done nothing wrong. – I need to be alone in order to think things through. In order to find where I am in relation to something I left long ago.

He looked hurt and worried. I couldn't tell him any more at this moment. He asks me if I have eaten diner. I tell him that I have and that I'm not hungry.

– I had thought we could visit the ruins at Yagul tomorrow, – he says. – It's a special place for me. There are many places where we can talk in private. Would you be up for that?

– That sounds perfect. What time will you be here?

– It's best to leave early. At that hour, the sun isn't so hot and there will be few tourists at the site. Can you be ready by 6:00?

I agree and find it hard to look directly into his eyes. I stare at the silly piñata that he has hanging in the corner. It is a copy of Elvis Presley's head. As usual, I find it oddly fascinating. It's the only thing interesting in the room. Chucho has a bookshelf full of maps, English-Spanish dictionaries and other assorted reference materials that he uses when he's working as a guide. This is a simple man with a profound understanding of time and culture, and a boundless heart. I hope he accepts me after tomorrow.

We say our goodnights and I kiss him as though I might not see him again. Perhaps I'm over dramatizing this whole thing. Still, down inside, I realize there is a deep-seated denial that I cannot bring into a marriage. I must confess it before I can give my life freely to another.

– Adios.

– Hasta mañana.

*****

Chucho knocks and opens the door at dawn. I'm already up and ready to go. We walk out to his uncle's Volkswagen bug. Chucho has prepared a picnic lunch. I love this man. He's always so prepared. We drive through the colonial part of downtown Oaxaca and take the Pan-American Highway that heads to Central America. We're only going a short distance. Less than an hour later, we pull off the highway onto a steep and straight road that takes leads to the foot of a small mountain. He parks the car and we pay the small entrance fee. The guards know him and they exchange small talk as we enter.

– Who is this with you? – one asks.

– It's the love of my life: Zully.

– Mucho gusto en conocerle – the guard says to me in a friendly manner.

We wander among the Zapotec ruins. Chucho explains the periods of development and how this was a center of spiritual importance. The ruins are not visible from the road, but they're extensive. After touring the main part of the ancient city, Chucho asks me to wait atop a small pyramid. He returns shortly with the basket of food and drink that he had brought.

– I thought we could eat up on the mountainside. It was an observatory of sorts and it has a splendid view of the entire valley.

I agree, and he leads the way up a steep path. After twenty minutes we arrive, sweat pouring down my face. He shows me an observation point and explains how this area was used both defensively and as an astrological observatory. I follow him to the far side of the mountain. We climb to the top of a rock outcrop. From there, we look out on a great valley below. The whole area is backed by rugged mountains. It's beautiful and I imagine that this view has changed little in a thousand years. All civilizations seem to have revered distinct natural formations, but few had actually depicted it in their art. The Zapotecs were no exception to this rule. Their art highlighted the human figure, architecture, clashes of war and images of perceived gods. Other than a few seascapes and snowy bamboo scenes from the earliest Chinese artists, extensive portrayal of landscapes in nature was unknown until European and American artists filled canvases with exaggerated, almost mystical panoramas of the natural world. Perhaps they were still too much a part of the landscape to consider it a separate entity.

We sat down on the rocky edge of the overlook and let our legs dangle in space. Far below, the dry riverbed coursed through cornfields. Hawks soared below us. Chucho had brought tamales to eat and agua de horchata, sweetened rice water, to drink. As we started lunch, I decided to just blurt out my secret and expand upon it as necessary.

– My parents didn't die in a mudslide. That's a story that I made up long ago and have repeated so many times, I've come to believe it myself. It's always been easier that way. No one ever questioned me about it. You will be the first person that I tell the truth.

Chucho finishes his tamale and turns his gaze from the valley to me. He says nothing. I feel my strength wane, but continue.

– My memories of mother and father are vague. I was four years old when I last saw my father and six when I last saw my mother. We lived in a small farm outside of Hidalgo. I only remember that we had little or nothing to eat. My father was an alcoholic and I've disturbing memories of violence: his violent fights with other men, the violent arguments between him and my mother and some frightening confrontations between him and the police.

Chucho reaches out and places his hand on my knee. He knows that this is not the time to embrace me.

– My mother was not well. She had mental problems. She was cruel. She loved to humiliate others. I don't know if she was even aware of it.

I could feel the sobs starting to surround my words, but I could not hear them and I wasn't going to stop until it all came out. Chucho remained silent.

– We were a large family. My father was a complete failure. He spent his time in town and it was said he had other lovers. I'm not sure. – I paused to breath. – I remember the night he came into the room where I was sharing a bed with my two sisters. I couldn't see him in the darkness, but when he inhaled his cigarette; his face was illuminated with a soft red glow. It was the last time I saw that face. Of course, there are a couple of photos to remind me. To remind me of a man I never knew. I do remember his words. He said he had to go away and that he would return for us as soon as he found work and a place for us. He vanished from our lives.

Chucho touched my arm, but I turned away, gazing into the open valley, and focusing on the birds soaring below. My face was wet and I knew I was crying, but I didn't hear anything.

– My mother tried to keep things together. I believe she never had a chance. She grew up with little support in her own family. She had no formal education and no real skills in life. Rural Guanajuato was as poor as it gets in Mexico at that time. I remember a constant parade of men in our house.

I dropped my eyes to my lap. I was destroying a paper napkin that I had in my hands. It was moist and shredded. My mouth felt the same way. I was glad for the mountain breeze that cooled and somewhat dried my face. It felt like steam was rising from my skin.

– There were just too many challenges for her. Too many of us and too little strength on her part. She did her best for several years. One day, she took all five of us down to Guanajuato City. She bought bus tickets for us to the main terminal in Mexico City. She paid the driver a generous amount to watch over us for the nine-hour trip. When we arrived at the bus terminal, there was no one to meet us there. I can't remember exactly what happened next. Eventually my brothers and sisters drifted apart. I occasionally hear from them. Some live in Mexico City, some in Guanajuato and I even have a brother in Texas. I missed them more than I ever let them know. Each of us had to carve a life out of the nothing that lay before us. Ultimately, a couple who could not have children adopted me and I grew up in Mexico City. My new parents always treated me well, but they never showed much human sentiment. I was raised much like a favorite pet.

The wind and sun felt good to me. Chucho waited.

– My mother was never seen again. Some said that she committed suicide, but in the end, nobody knew and it didn't matter.

I let my tears flow, and the sobs echoed down the valley. Chucho held me close and tried to dry my face. I looked into his face and added the last thing I had to say about those bitter memories.

– I can't remember if she kissed me goodbye. I needed that last kiss and I think she left without giving it.

Now I turned to Chucho and opened my arms. I was so relieved when he responded the same way. We sat on the brink of the precipice, and held onto each other for quite a while. Then we heard other people approaching. We grabbed our food and walked away. Only Chucho returned their greetings.

On the way back to town, we stopped at Teotitlan de Valle. Here, the best tapetes, or hand-woven blankets, are sold outside the homes where they're made. The local women weave them from wool with natural dyes made from plants and insects. We buy one small blanket and then sit down at an informal bar outside of one of the houses that sell blankets. We order some Tecate beers and a shot of Herradura tequila. I soon feel the weight of the conversation leaving me. I realize that I feel more honest than I have in many years. I no longer have to hide anything. I do not intend to reveal those truths to anyone else, but I'd no longer hide them from myself.

– Baby, you know none of that makes any difference to me. What I love in you has nothing to do with your past. To the contrary, your suffering explains why you are so considerate. The sensitivity you always demonstrate now has a logical basis. I'm not going to say that I understand it all. I haven't walked down that path. I can only state that I love you without reservation and you'll always have someone to count on if you choose to spend your life with me.

– So, you still want to marry me?

– As soon as possible.

13

Yoko

I find the hotel and its employees a little impersonal, but nonetheless accessible. My room faces the airport, but I can't hear the planes due to the thick glass that can't be opened. A door gives entry to a balcony, high above the street. I'm shocked by the vast difference between the refrigerated air inside the room and the heat that engulfs me the moment I step onto the balcony. The Santa Maria is like any other business-oriented hotels in the world, clean, modern, well run and full of uninteresting men and women in suits. I grab a quick shower and take a nap for a couple of hours.

Upon awakening, I descend to the lounge. It's almost empty. I eat a large lunch, known as almoço. In Brazil, the main meal of the day is served between noon and three in the afternoon. Afterwards, I call my parents from my room. They seem glad to hear my voice.

– Why didn't you call from the airport? – my mother inquires.

– I was unable to get the pay phone to work. I didn't have any Cruzeiros. The money exchange wasn't open.

– I told you to call collect young lady! You can be as meek as always with anyone else, but I'm your mother, and you will call.

After assuring them that I'm lodged in a good hotel, and that I'll call them every day, we say goodbye and hang up. I turn on the TV, but can't understand any of the Portuguese programming. Still, it's interesting because the products being advertised are unfamiliar to me. The slapstick manner of hawking goods seems a little surreal. Would I find Brazil to be an amusing reflection of the country and culture from which I come? Around eight in the evening, I descend to the lobby and ask the front desk manager if it's safe to go for a walk around the neighborhood. I'm anxious to see what this city is like.

– No problem, if you stick to the main streets between here and the airport. Don't walk alone after 10:00PM! Call a taxi, even if it's only a short distance. – He gives me a card with a taxi company's number on it. – They're honest and know our hotel.

I had decided to stay close to the hotel today, and will start the search for my family history tomorrow. While strolling down Moaci Avenue, I'm reminded of downtown Portland, but the buildings are a plainer, unadorned concrete. Just a block away is a restaurant-bar that has many patrons laughing and chattering openly. It's well lit and I'm invited in by a man who holds a menu on the sidewalk. He explains in English that the specialty of the house is espetinhos, skewered meat or cheese grilled over coals. This is a popular place where young people congregate. I'm not particularly hungry, but I decide to go in. I choose a small table in the back where I can observe the crowd in relative seclusion.

The waitress comes by to take my order. Most here are drinking beer, but they also have a large selection of juices. I don't recognize any of them by name and follow her recommendation. I'm not sure what the name of the juice is, but she's right; it's good. After bringing the pitcher of juice, she states,

– We have servers circulating among the diners and they carry trays of espetinhos and some other side dishes. When you see something you like, let them know and they'll mark it on your bill.

I watch plates loaded with skewers of barbecued beef, chicken, sausages and cheese pass by. Interesting, but I'm not hungry, at least, not yet. What I do notice is that the people here vary widely by color. I'm surprised to find that quite a few of them are obviously of Japanese ancestry. Maybe this search for the past is going to be easier than I had expected.

Near the entrance, a group of young men and one woman are putting their chairs in a circle. One has a guitar, another plays a single snare drum on a stand and the woman holds a tambourine. A waiter brings them a bottle of beer. The man with the drum starts beating out a soft rhythm. Little by little, the others join the music. Eventually, one male starts to sing. They take turns singing. I think back to the parades of spectacular floats I had seen on TV of the Carnaval in Rio. I assumed it was samba, but later learned it was pagode. Funny! Listening to music live can be so appealing. This could become addictive. I love music and find most musicians are committed, hardworking people that put in the time to reap the benefits of a job well done. The music continues, and seems completely spontaneous. A tray is passing by with what appears to be hamburger on a stick.

– What are those? – I ask.

– Kafta. They're quite good. Would you like one?

I nod my head in agreement. He quickly sets a plate in front of me with the espetinho on it. I notice that others are putting sauces on them. There are hot pepper, garlic and other sauces in small bottles on the table. I see one that's familiar: Tabasco. He returns with farinha, sautéed manioc flour that I later find is served throughout Brazil. He also brings vingrete, made from chopped onion, tomato and vinegar. I like everything except the farinha; it seems too dry. The sound of mixed laughter, pagode, conversations and traffic passing on the street make me feel less alone in a foreign place.

After a while, I head to the bathroom. Like most places in the world, I find women chatting in front of mirrors while adjusting their makeup and hair. Do men do the same? I mean, do they make small talk in front of their own reflections in public bathrooms? Somehow, I doubt it. A Japanese-looking girl asks me something. I don't understand and reply that I don't speak Portuguese. She asks where I'm from (something I do understand in Portuguese).

– I'm an American.

– You have a strong accent. But, not an American accent. Where did you grow up? – she asks in English.

– I grew up in the United States, but my parents spend their time among almost exclusively Japanese friends and relatives. Maybe some of their pronunciation rubbed off on me. – I was unaware that my accent was that different, and wondered if this young woman simply didn't know what an American accent sounded like.

– Your English is quite good – I comment

– Thank you. My parents insist that all of their children learn it. They think it's prestigious and will help us in life. They're probably right.

We leave the restroom and I return to my seat. I was deciding whether to order more juice when the girl from the bathroom comes up to my table.

– Are you alone? That is, if so, would you like to join us? – She points to a table where five or six people seated. Several of them appear to be Japanese.

I'm a little tired this first day in a foreign land, but hey, I'm here to find out about Japanese that have left their homelands.

– Thanks! That would be great. – I reply.

I soon learn that these Japanese-Brazilians haven't left any homeland. They're like me: born and raised in a different country than their ancestors and have completely embraced the culture of Brazil.

I'm introduced to everyone. The girl who invited me is Márcia. All four of the Japanese-looking people in the group have Brazilian names. For some reason, I had expected them to be like me, with Japanese names.

– What brings you to Brazil Yoko? – a man called Felipe asks.

– Well, to be honest, I'm here to satisfy a request of my parents. They feel I should look for what it is to be Japanese, other than in America. I don't have much interest in going to Japan, so I selected Brazil, since some of my relatives once lived here in São Paulo. I hope to find something about them. For some reason, they only lived for a few years in Brazil. I would like to see if I have any family who still live in São Paulo.

– Are you traveling alone? – another asks.

I'm not sure if I should tell him too much about me.

– For now, I am – I respond.

Not all of them speak English, so I limit my conversation to Márcia. She tells me she's twenty-five years old, and lives at home with her parents. She's finishing her studies to be a physician. She has one brother, Robson, who also lives at home. She asks me if there are many Japanese descendants in the US.

– God, there are hundreds of thousands of us.

Márcia seems surprised.

– I've never hear much about you. Are you allowed access to all levels of education and other aspects of American life in your country?

I'm surprised at the question. I never imagined there might be people who thought Japanese Americans would be limited by their ethnicity in the US. To be honest, I had never really thought about it. I've always had the respect of my teachers and others in our community. Few of my friends are Japanese. Why would these Brazilians think a thing like that?

– We see the black people rioting in California and other cities on the news. And, Mr. Martin Luther was assassinated last year, right?

Ah! At least I knew where they were coming from. There really was trouble in the streets and campuses of America. My country was at war in Vietnam and things were changing at a pace that had many worried about where the future would take us.

– It's a complicated issue – I reply. – But I don't notice any animosity directed towards me.

They're all drinking beer and other drinks. They laugh and sing along with many of the songs. They seem to be like any other group of young people back in Oregon. I'm at ease and feel fortunate for having been invited into their group my first day in Brazil. It gets late, and I've plans for tomorrow. Around two in the morning, I tell them that I must head for my hotel.

– Where are you staying? – Márcia asks.

I tell her where and state that it's only a block away. They all know the Santa Maria. When I ask them if the restaurant would call a taxi for me, they tell me that they're leaving and will walk me home. I accept the offer. As we leave, a small boy in the street extends his open palm to me.

– What does he want? – I ask.

– Coins – somebody answers.

– I don't give money to anyone who has not earned it – I state. I hate panhandlers. I notice that Márcia gives the child something. Why would she do that? Children should not be out at this hour of the night, much less begging.

As we walk along under the streetlamps, one man in our group starts singing. They walk with me into the lobby and they all take turns giving me a kiss on each cheek before they turn and leave me alone in the hotel.

– Tchau Yoko! Cuída-se! – they say almost in unison.

I get the key and head up to my room. It has been a good day. Márcia gave me her phone number before leaving. She said her university is on break for the next several weeks and that she would be glad to help me with my investigation if I wished. I fall asleep with the news in Portuguese on the television.

14
Yoko

After breakfast, I find a message waiting for me at the front desk. It's from Márcia. She wants me to give her a ring. In my room, I dial her number and she answers.

– Bom dia Yoko! Tudo bem?

– Tudo! – I reply.

She seems full of energy and her upbeat disposition, along with the radiant sun and blue skies outside, cancel the trepidation I was feeling about the chore ahead of me today.

– My mother says I can use the car to take you to Liberdade today.

– What is that?

She laughs. – It's a neighborhood. I believe you would call it something like Japan Town in your country. I thought it would be a good place to begin your search.

Márcia tells me to be ready in half an hour.

– You are so lucky. It's Sunday and there's a fair.

Exactly half an hour later, she phones from the lobby. I exit the elevator to find her smiling face. She takes me by the hand and leads me into the street, where a boy is watching the car. She gives him some coins and he stops the traffic and directs her into the street.

– Today, you will learn how important we Japanese are in the culture, economy and history of Brazil. It's so much better to see for yourself than to have somebody explain it.

She says that it's easier to take the subway, but she loves to drive. and on Sunday, downtown São Paulo is not too crowded. I ask if she knows when her family immigrated to Brazil.

– My mom has all the facts. I believe it was in the nineteen twenties. I'm proud of whom I am, but I don't keep track of all that family tree stuff. Brazil is a country of immigrants. Other than the Indian tribes, all of us descend from immigrants.

I look into her Asian eyes. They could be mine. Her words are mine. A thought crashes into my brain. What if America had been like Brazil and there had not been any World War II internments to leave a scar on my mother's heart?

    – America is also a land of immigrants. We call it a melting pot. It seems like every ethnic group has had to fight for acceptance there. And, the process is far from over. Many are tired of waiting for equality. My father says one of the problems we have is that there are too many waiting for economic equality. They want the government to force it on the people. He's convinced that what we need is equality of dignity. He believes that, as humans, we can never be equivalent; it is not attainable. He thinks that if we learn to give dignity to everyone, equality will not be necessary. He's the wisest man I've ever known.

    We park near the Sé subway station. Márcia says it's considered the center of the city. It's filled with tall buildings and wide streets: nothing new to me. We descend into the subway and she buys tickets for the ride.

    – It's best to go the last part by subway. The fair is very popular and parking is a problem.

    We travel until the next station, Liberdade. As we come out into the bright sunshine, I feel like I've emerged into another country. The buildings have a Japanese appearance. Even the streetlamps are Asian. Most of the signs are in Japanese. Márcia points out a newspaper machine that sells Japanese language newspapers. Around the metro station there are booths selling all things Japanese. I'm overwhelmed. I didn't expect this. Márcia beams with pride.

    – I love my city. – She states. – It's so diverse.

    Her statement makes me realize that I'm enjoying this city also. Portland has a Chinatown, but this is larger, and more authentic for some reason. I had read before leaving Oregon that São Paulo has the largest population of Japanese emigrants in the world, but I'm still surprised at the completeness of this neighborhood.

    We wander around the booths. I'm familiar with much of the food offered here, as my folks and I often eat Japanese food. The selection goes far beyond the Sushi and Sashimi that most in the states take for Japanese food. But, food is only secondary here. Márcia leads me to a small shop that sells plants. She says many are native plants from Japan. Her favorite is one called the *happy plant*.

I learn that both the male and female plant must be cultivated side by side. If planted alone, either one will die.

– They die of loneliness – a woman states. I think of my parents and wish I could buy a pair to take back to them.

I enter another shop. It has a large bamboo tree with colored ribbons tied all over it. The small and elderly man standing nearby sees the curiosity in my face and explains.

– We are preparing for the Sendai Tanabata Matsuri festival. Some call it the Festival of Stars. Legend has it that two lovers became stars that were separated by the Milky Way. They're united for one day each year. On the seventh day of the seventh month, they're reunited. The festival encourages love, hope and peace.

– What do the colored papers tied to the bamboo represent? – I ask.

– It is said that if one writes a wish on them, it will be fulfilled on the date of the star's reunion. – He replies.

Each color represents a different meaning. I choose red, for passion. I quickly write my request and tie it to the tree before anyone can read it. I ask what happens after the stars meet. He says that the bamboo and messages are burned in a ritual of decorum.

I buy some candy made from beans. I realize that I don't know Márcia's last name.

– Omatsu, Márcia Omatsu. What's yours?
– Koga, Chiyoko Koga.

She suggests we visit the Historical Museum of Japanese Immigration. It's located nearby. I'm up for it, and we walk the couple of blocks to the entrance. It has two stories of displays that reveal the drama of the Japanese that ended up in Brazil. Liberdade means freedom. It was the center of the Japanese immigration from the early twentieth century. Liberdade slowly developed into a community of wealth and stability. There were Japanese schools, newspapers and businesses. Baseball was played on weekends.

Then came World War II. In 1941, the Brazilian government prohibited any printed materials in Japanese. President Getúlio Vargas broke relations with Japan in 1942. Shortly after, all Japanese in Liberdade were evicted from their homes. They were only allowed to return after the end of the war.

I left the museum more informed, and surprised about the treatment of the people during the war. I shouldn't have been surprised. I'm a history major and know that history is often paralleled by similar events in other areas. I had not expected to find this to be the case in Brazil. Human limitations are not a secret to me. Márcia notes the difference in my demeanor.

– Something wrong?

– No, not at all. I'm just surprised to find such similarities between Brazil's history and ours.

We go to a churrascaria, a restaurant that serves barbeque, and eat lunch. As usual, the quantity of food is ridiculous. I'm hungry and eat several platefuls. Márcia tells me that she has a friend that works for the Japan Foundation.

– Would you like me to call and find out if he can do some research on your family name?

I reply yes, since my parents had no idea if any of our family were still in Brazil. The only information we had was a family belief that some relatives on my mom's side had lived in Brazil before going to the United States. My parents think they were in Brazil from 1915 until 1923.

She phones her friend and afterwards tells me that he would try to find something out for me tomorrow, since nothing is open today. We head back to the subway station. I'm pleased with the day. I feel like the lesson I've learned today is this: my mother is wiser than I had believed. We are more than the moment we live in. It's not the brutality of history that separates humankind; it's the ignorance of it. Dignity is not found in pretending that we don't have different stories that add up to our unique presence on this planet, but rather, in incorporating these multidimensional realities into our conscious acceptance of the frailties of our species. To forgive and never forget.

On the way back to the hotel, I thank my new friend. She has helped me experience an awakening that I had not expected. Before dropping me off at the Santa Maria, she tells me she would like to introduce me to her family tomorrow. Could I come for almoço? I accept and feel like this Brazil trip has worked out better than I could have expected.

– Did you enjoy Liberdade today? – She inquires.

– More than I can say.

15

Severino

The small fazenda has one hundred and fifty acres, most of it in overgrown cacau, or cocoa trees. It's so remote and marginal that even squatters don't want anything to do with it. Back in the heyday of cacau production, in the nineteenth century, all available acreage in Bahia was planted to meet a seemingly insatiable world appetite for chocolate. Then, the market collapsed. It's still grown around here, but the money it brings in is minimal. Not to worry, that's not why I'm here. I'm here to save my ass.

The small house is still standing, but only barely. The red roof tiles have long ago caved in. Two walls still stand. The rain forest has reclaimed much of the area. A tree that I imagine is about ten years old stands somewhat stately in the middle of the house. I've brought several rolls of black plastic sheeting to erect a temporary shack. In the first few days, I build a shelter that's waterproof and ugly. Fortunately, I've saved much of my first year's salary. I had hoped to put it down on a house in Ilhéus. It will come in handy. I bought several of the tools I need to start clearing the land: a machete and an ax.

The hillside provides shade from the sun during the morning hours. I awake at dawn and start clearing an area around the collapsed house, leaving anything that can be seen from the road in disarray. I want others to think the place is still abandoned. On the third day, several hours into the sweaty and hot work, I realize I'm enjoying it. The fertile smells of this tropical forestland are pleasant. The more I work this land, the less I want to go back to the city. I find this landscape like a good book, and wonder what the next chapter will bring.

The well has filled in with soil and rocks. I rig a system to collect the rainwater from the roof of my makeshift hut. It provides enough water to drink, cook and bath, as long as I use it efficiently. The cacau trees are in better shape than I thought at first glance. I remember drying the cocoa beans in the sun during my youth. Good memories. The sounds during the day are mostly from birds. They come in all colors, and the parakeets are the ones I most admire. I'm colorblind, but the yellow and blue ones catch my eye. At night, a chorus of frogs goes at it from dusk until the wee hours of the dawn. I pass the days alone. This is the first time in my life that I've spent over a week without hearing the voice of another soul. At first, it seemed odd. By the end of the first week, it seemed comforting. Nobody had come around looking for me. A good sign.

At the end of the second week, I go into town.

– Vovó, tudo bem?

– Thank God you're OK! I was so worried about you out there in the middle of nowhere. Severino, come give your grandmother a kiss!

It's good to be loved. It's even better to love somebody. Simple things are starting to mean more to me. I'm more aware of the pleasure that being with my grandmother gives me. She has become my lone focal point since I moved out on the fazenda. When I lived in Malhado, she was a link to my past, something from which I was growing more distant. Here, I found myself wanting to be with her more often than I could. I ask her if anyone has inquired about me and she says that no one has mentioned my name.

–Did you tell anybody what I'm up to?

– No, but I was plenty worried. Why don't you just stay here in Almadina with me?

– To tell you the truth vovó, I'm enjoying my work on the land. Did my father ever talk to you about his feelings about working the place?

– Severino, he spoke in almost reverential tones about that worthless piece of property. What he saw in it, I don't know. He felt more at ease out there than anywhere else. He was more like a hermit with each passing year. He said God kept him company and that I was mistaken if I thought I could find God in church. He thought the priests were trying to trap God in the place he least wanted to be found. Can you believe that? He never went to church, except during the festivals of São João and Christmas. Poor Zé Paulo, he found more beauty and truth in the shape of a tree or the colors of a butterfly than in the art in the cathedral in Ilhéus. Imagine that! He lost his mind up in the hills, I tell you. I wouldn't want to see the same happen to you Severino.

While in town, I ask around to see if anybody has a motorcycle for sale. I find several, and after some intense bargaining, I buy a used, almost abused, Yamaha. It's tattered, but runs well. I need it to avoid taking the bus out to the fazenda. The less time I spend with people from around here, the fewer questions I'll be asked. After spending the night with my grandmother and eating as much as she could force on me, I load my backpack with as many supplies as possible and head back home. I like the sound of that word: home. I never had one of my own. I make sure that nobody sees me leave the main road that leads to the steep and mostly washed-out track that ascends to my place.

I had watched the news on TV at my grandmother's house. There was student unrest and problems reported from Rio and São Paulo, but nothing more was mentioned about the problems at the college in Ilhéus. It was as though nothing had happened. But, I knew the investigation was still going on. I had called from a pay phone to my school in Malhado. A colleague informed me that a couple of Military Police had come by and wanted to talk to me about some files I had left at the college. They said if anybody saw me, I was to report to the police station in Ilhéus or Itabuna. Sure, and say goodbye to freedom forever!

After four weeks of getting the place organized, my thoughts turn more and more to restoring the cacau orchard. I start thinking of where I might want to build a new house. There is a low rise out back of the old house that I imagine would be perfect. It is surrounded like a horseshoe with Atlantic Rain Forest above and cacau below. It has a view off towards Floresta Azul. Beside the campfire one night, I find myself speaking aloud.

– Estou feliz.

Early the next day I prepare the motorcycle for a road trip. I stash what little possessions I have in my hut and load some clothes and a few other necessities in my backpack. I put my money for the road journey into safe places, some of it hidden on the bike and the rest in my shoe. Before the sun comes up over the ridgeline, I set off on a journey that I hope will help me find peace in my life. With any luck, I'll be back within a week.

16
Lilly

In the morning, I awake early. It's a Sunday and at six o'clock, the street is almost deserted. I decide to go for a walk. I head towards the beach and Avenida Atlantica. I'm surprised to see so many people out walking and jogging this early. The avenue is a divided boulevard and today half of it is blocked off to traffic. I'm told this is to accommodate the thousands of people who will be arriving to soak up sun, jog, or stroll along the closed section of the street. I walk along the sidewalk that's composed of thousands of black and white stones, arranged in a pattern that's unique to Copacabana.

After half an hour or so, I decide to head away from the beach, back into the city, into the tranquil and quiet concrete canyons. I had my mind set on finding a coffee shop for espresso and some sweet rolls. I walk down Rua Xavier de Silveira. After a couple of blocks, I pass by the Cantagalo subway station, and notice a young girl sitting on the stairs outside. She looks around twelve years old. Her eyes are focused on some far away and nonexistent place. Her clothes are just scraps of cloth. The face is streaked with tears, but she doesn't make a sound. I pass by and keep walking. When I reach the next corner, I turn and look back. Nothing has changed. She's lost in space.

A few minutes later, I find a small coffee shop. It has tables on the street, and is just opening. I'm the first customer. I take a table where I hope to watch the morning unfold. Rio is a great people-watching place. My cappuccino arrives. In Brazil, a cappuccino always has chocolate in it, and generally has several chocolate bonbons served with it. My thoughts go back to the girl on the sidewalk. What was her story? I think of my aversion to cities. It's exactly these impersonal and brutal realities of the urban scene that turn me off. I admit to myself that it frightens me. It reminds me of a lonely and difficult time I had in Denver quite a while back.

The waiter brings the rolls and I ask if he could keep them a few minutes for me.

– I've forgotten something. I'll be right back.

As I walk back towards the subway station, *The Boxer*, a song by Simon and Garfunkel, is playing in my mind. She's still sitting in the same spot. I stop and observe. Many are entering and exiting the station, but nobody notices her. And, she doesn't seem to notice them.

I sit down beside her. She barely glances at me.

– Oi. – I say, hoping that a simple hi would bring a response. Nothing.

– Do you speak English?

She stares ahead.

– Say, I'm having café de manha. Would like you to join me?

Her eyes meet mine. I pantomime my invitation. She seems to be evaluating me. I imagine a film clip of us from far above, everyone around us involved in the swirling, urban action of the subway entrance, with the two of us remaining motionless. Eventually, she speaks.

– Who are you? What do you want?

– I thought you looked like you could use a friend.

– I don't need friends. – She states, using the word amigas. She's afraid of something. Of me.

– I'm eating at a restaurant just down the street. I'd like you to come eat also.

I'm not sure if I'm getting this across, but she gets up when I do and walks alongside of me. She could use a bath. We are soon seated at the same table. The waiter eyes her and me suspiciously. To hell with him. I order a complete breakfast for her. This means she can eat as much as she wants from the smorgasbord that's set up inside. She silently enters and returns with a plate heaping with a little of everything. I let her eat in peace. Afterwards, she goes back and returns with several glasses of juice and milk. When she finishes, I ask her name.

– Marina.

I use my hands and voice to get across to her that I'm thirty-seven years old. She tells me she's fourteen years old.

– Where do you live? Do you need a ride to your home?

– I am home. – She states without any emotion.

– But, where do you live?

She starts to say something, but it's drowned in a choking sob that seems to embarrass her. Others around us are staring. I ask if she would like to go to another place. She declines and asks if I'd be willing to pay for a sandwich for her to take with her. I order several to go.

– Desculpa senhora. I don't mean to trouble you with my problems. It's been a bad week for me. But, I'm OK now. I'm OK.

– You live on the street? – I ask.

– Sim.

– For how long have you done this?

– Two years.

I ask her why, and she mentions a mother with drug problems in another state and a father in prison. She says it's not as bad as one might think. But, everything changed for the worse last week.

– What happened?

– My brother and I used to sleep at night in front of a side entrance to a bank. They know us there, and as long as we were gone by early morning, there was no problem. They even let us store the large cardboard box we sleep in behind their trash dumpster. Occasionally, we were hassled by vagrants, but the street gangs knew we were harmless and let us be.

I think of my camper near Durango and vow never again to think I'm poor.

– What do you do during the day?

– During the morning, we collected aluminum from trash containers in Ipanema and Leblon. They throw out more cans there than in Copacabana. In the afternoon, we'd go to various restaurants asking for something to eat until somebody gave us something. Generally, it didn't take too long. At night, we'd collect cans from tourists in the beach stands on Copacabana. I also asked the gringos for coins.

– You talk as if this has ended. Have you come up with another way of getting by?

She looks away and starts shaking.

– I don't know what I'm going to do now. I'm afraid without my brother. He kept me safe. But, it's getting better. I've found another place to sleep with girls a little older than I. They know what happened, and treat me well. I'm still collecting aluminum and have started to speak to the tourists again.

I'm not sure what has happened to her and am not sure if I should ask. But, I do.

– Did your brother leave?

She looks down and then directly into my eyes. With a voice as devoid of emotion as I've ever heard, she tells me her story.

– My brother and I were sleeping like normal last week. I awoke with the sound of a car stopping near us. I couldn't see anything outside of the box. Somebody started yelling about vagabond trash, and how we're responsible for the drugs and crime in Rio. I was scared, but my brother told me to keep quiet and not move. After a few minutes of horrible insults, it grew silent. The car's motor was still running, so we knew whoever was outside still remained.

I was suddenly reminded of a time when a friend of mine and I had pitched our tent alongside of an interstate highway in Texas, as we were working our way back to Colorado from Mexico. Our money had run out and we were hitching home. During the night, somebody stopped and started screaming about hippies and that our kind of trash should not be allowed in the state. They left without incident, but I will always remember thinking that they were going to do something.

– The last thing I remember was a loud voice shouting "filhos de putas!" Then the night lit up. Flames were everywhere. I clawed at the cardboard and it finally gave way. Outside, I looked for Victor, and saw that he was still in the box. He was screaming and trying to get out. Then all was quite. The flames slowly died down. I can't stop remembering the smell, a combination of gasoline and burnt meat. I ran into the night, my hands in pain.

She showed me her hands. They'd been burnt on the palms. I hadn't noticed it before.

– You need to see a doctor for those injuries.

– I did. I went to a clinic the next morning and they bandaged them.

– And Victor?

– I never saw him again. I was told he was buried the next day. I've visited his vault once. I can't go there anymore.

I couldn't speak. I wanted to take her and hold her. To make everything all right. But, it would never be all right. I felt so helpless.

– Did you call the police?

– Call the police? The police did it!

I wasn't prepared to hear that. I later found out that some of Rio's law enforcement officers had taken it upon themselves to start cleaning up the city. That is, eliminating the street urchins. I also learned that more than fifteen thousand children sleep on the street on any given night in Rio. At that moment, I felt like screaming. Instead, I asked Marina if she would like to stay with me for a while and that I'd try to find her some permanent housing and care. She laughed.

– You don't know what it's like here. I don't want to be under anybody's control. I trust no one, including you. If you want to help me, just leave me in peace.

We leave the restaurant and when we reach the street, I put what little money I have with me into her hand. She takes it and gives me a kiss on the cheek.

– Obrigada. – She says as she turns and walks away.

I walk back to the beachfront. The happy people walking, jogging, bicycling, tanning, drinking, swimming and enjoying life seem distant from me. I stop at a barraca, the term for the small beach stands that function as mini-restaurants. The sun is now high in the sky and it's hot.

– Do you have any cachaça?

– Sure, you want the cheap stuff or something better?

I order the cheap stuff and down various shots and a few large bottles of beer before I realize that I've no money to pay for it. I leave my watch for the owner to keep until I return with the money.

17
Lilly

I call Aritana in the morning. He's still sleeping and his voice sounds like an old vinyl disk playing at slow speed.

– Oh, it's you Lilly! No, no, it's fine. Can I call you back in ten minutes?

– Yes, I need your advice on something.

– Anything wrong? – He seemed to be waking up fast.

– Nothing that can't wait ten minutes.

I hang up and stare out the window. The sunshine is bouncing off the windows of the buildings outside. Nothing has changed from yesterday. Yet, it's not the same Rio. I need a break from this endless action. I think about Marina and then about the enormous hangover that's hammering my brain. I had woken up with my clothes on and sleeping in the easy chair in front of the television, which was still on. I felt embarrassed. I hadn't pulled a night like that in many a year. I laugh out loud.

– You're still alive girl. Still capable of surprising yourself.

The phone rings.

– Aritana?

– No senhora, it's the front reception. We received a message from your mother. She would like you to call.

– OK, thank you very much.

– Senhora? – the man replies in a hesitating voice.

– Something else? – I inquire.

– Are you doing all right? – he ventures.

– Yes, why do you ask?

– Well senhora, the night crew told us about your incident with the taxi.

I had no idea what he was talking about.

– Yes, and...? – I replied

– The driver returned this morning. He said he regretted not being able to find your watch when he dropped you off at the hotel, but he needed to finish his shift in the taxi. And...

I remembered the watch at the barraca on the beach.

– And what?

– He hoped you wouldn't phone his supervisor, as you insisted would be the case this morning.

I had absolutely no idea what he was talking about.

– I don't remember saying anything like that.

– Senhora, it was quite a scene. You were screaming at him on the sidewalk, claiming he had stolen your watch and that you weren't going to pay and would call the police and his boss. Our doorman helped you into the building and the bellhop helped you up to your room.

Oh no! Stupid in Rio. I thanked him. As I put the phone in its cradle, it immediately rang again. It was Aritana. I tell him about Marina, and how I had reacted by making a fool of myself.

– Everyone plays *good-night-Cinderella* at one time or another. – he reassures me. – What can I do to perk you up again?

– I need to get out of the city for a couple of days. Any ideas?

Aritana says he has a friend in Lumiar, a town located in the mountains nearby. He could call and see if his friend's house was available for the weekend. If so, we could leave by noon and be up there in three hours. I quickly answer that I like the plan.

– OK, let me call Nelson.

He calls back in five minutes. The place is available for the next two weeks. We can stay as long as we like. He says he'll pick me up in two hours, and mentions I should bring warm clothes.

– I only have one sweater and some jeans.

I'm waiting in the lobby when he pulls up. The hotel staff is treating me with kid gloves. God knows what all I said and did last night. I had called my mother and told her I was going to another beach area and would phone her tomorrow from a pay phone. She didn't like the idea at all.

*****

Aritana and I pull into the chaos that is Rio's traffic at midday. He's a good driver and has a funny looking Peugeot. The cars here seem like toys. It takes us an hour of crazy driving before we reach the outskirts of Rio. Along the way, I see another side of this sprawling metropolis. The slums, called Favelas, extend up every steep incline. Many have stairways that ascend upwards toward ramshackle concrete dwellings. Graffiti is extensive. Still, the people that occupy every sidewalk are exquisitely beautiful. I again wonder how this limitless mixture of humanity came about. I remember what a friend that I worked with in the Forest Service in Utah had told me. For over half of the world, home is built from what others throw away.

The highway we take out of the city starts upwards, towards the highlands. The ascent is gradual, but consistent. I'm reminded of the interstate that climbs into the mountains to the west of Denver. I now feel the same relief that I've felt so many times on leaving the urban pandemonium for the pine-covered mountains. I've always marveled at my family members' inner strength that allows them to live among such confusion. How do they do that?

The temperatures drop as we keep rising and we soon enter a lush forest. Aritana looks at me. I notice that I'm staring out the window like a child. I had hardly said a word during the trip. He asks if I like the view. I tell him that I've never seen a forest like this before.

– It's the Atlantic Rain Forest – he says. – The Amazon rain forest is the most diversified on this planet, if you include flora and fauna. But, if you only include plant life, then the Atlantic rain forest is the most diversified woodlands in the world.

I'm pleased by what I see and what Aritana says. I've worked and spent time in Rocky Mountain forests for years. I still find myself amazed by the diversity of life in Southwest Colorado. I want to see more of this rain forest. My head starts feeling better. My mind clears. The feeling of dread is gone. We pull off the main highway into a twisting and narrow road that leads between towering trees and radiant green pastures and meadows. I note the banana trees, growing under tall pines trees. It's a mixture of conifer and tropical. The road continues uphill, following a river. People wait at rural bus stops and traffic is minimal. We cross a small bridge, enter the town of Lumiar and stop in front of a small plaza.

– Nelson left the keys with the proprietor of a restaurant here. It's a good place to eat. I hope you're hungry.

– I'm famished.

The plaza could be in Germany. It has a wrought iron bandstand and the surrounding buildings are in a style that mimics Germany. We enter a restaurant and the people eating could pass for Germans, Austrians or Swiss. They speak Portuguese with a Brazilian accent. We sit at a table on the veranda overlooking the plaza. The surrounding hillsides are verdant grassland topped with thick forest. Birds sing in the cages that line the ceiling of the veranda. We inquire about the key to Nelson's house. The waiter brings it and some beer. We order chicken stroganoff. Aritana says that the region was settled mainly by Swiss immigrants and that many of the people here are their direct descendants.

After eating, we jump back into the Peugeot and Aritana gives me a short tour of Lumiar. It's small, around a thousand inhabitants. Soon, we drive out of town, and eventually, up a small gravel road. At a cemetery full of concrete crypts and no vegetation, we turn onto a dirt path that weaves steeply up between pines and bananas. We follow a tributary of the Macaé River. We park under a high canopy of treetops. All is silent and the light is tinged with green. Aritana motions me across the road. I find an orchard of banana and tangerine trees, with steeply sloping basaltic mountains in the background.

We return to the car and grab our suitcases. A path twists between a jungle of trees, vines, flowers and statues. It's a fantasyland. The house is tiny, like something out of a fairytale. Every room opens out to decks and balconies. Inside I discover a fireplace. To the rear, an elevated porch overlooks a green wall of bamboo and the jungle beyond. Standing on it, I hear the river flowing, below and beyond the thick jungle.

– How do you like it? – Aritana asks with a smile on his face.

– It's enchanting! – I turn to him and we wrap our arms around each other. It's my first jungle kiss. His skin smells like the ocean. We stumble up the ladder-like stairs and find two tiny rooms. In one, a mattress is leaning against a wall. We knock it to the floor and passion engulfs us. Fertile smells and the sound of the river blow through the open windows. We mount each other in a flurry of tossed clothes and linked eyes. The room is full of sparks of electromagnetic passion. It's the blending of pine and tangerine, mountain blizzard and tropical downpour. It's over far too quickly.

I lay beside him, a little embarrassed by the rush of it all.

– Thanks – he tells me. – I needed that.

– De nada.

We both laugh. I'm glad he's not ashamed of his male lust. No games, just desire and fulfillment. We shower together and he asks if I want to go down to see the river.

– Of course!

We climb down the trail that leads through the towering tropical forest to the river. A flat spot beside the water has a place for barbeques. Beside it, a stone walkway juts into a large pool of swirling water. Waterfalls above and below us gush between giants boulders. On the far side of the river stands the ever-present bamboo and banana trees of this area. I walk down the stone path, where the clear water is deep enough to swim. I slip into the water, but it's too cold to stay there. Aritana finds this amusing.

– It gets warm enough to swim in the afternoon, after the sun has heated the water.

We stay beside the rushing waters, telling each other who we are and what our lives are like until it gets dark and the crescent moon comes out. I'm cold. We start up the trail. In the dark shadows of the jungle, we scale the steep slope to the house, using our hands as much as our feet. Fortunately, the house has electricity. The light seems strong after the ascent in darkness. Aritana plugs in the refrigerator and leaves to get some things out of the car.

When he returns, he carries several bottles of wine and cheese, olives, bread and salmon. He leaves again and returns with dried pine boughs. He takes me by the hand and we go out to the back porch and then down to the area below it. There he asks me to pile firewood on his outstretched arms.

– Lilly, can you bring up some of the smaller kindling?

I grab what I can hold and follow him into the living room. I watch him prepare the hearth for a fire. I'm known as an expert in fire building back in Colorado. I think this isn't going to work, as the pine needles are not very dry and the firewood isn't either. But, the oils in the needles burst into flame instantly and eventually the kindling ignites the logs. I prepare the food and bring it out on a tray. We curl up by the fireplace. I find it so odd. This morning we were in a steamy madhouse of a megalopolis and tonight we are huddled beside a fireplace, trying to stay warm.

The night and the next day drift by unhurriedly. We grill meat by the waterfall, lay naked in the sunshine and mist from the falls and explore more of each other's bodies. I examine many of the trees and plants around the house. I'm unfamiliar with any of them. I envision working for the Brazilian Forest Service. We eat tangerines off the trees. On the second morning, we prepare to leave. Aritana knows the neighbors up the road. They prepare a breakfast for us on their wood stove. I don't want to leave, but he has to get back to work.

– I was supposed to be back in Maceió today. I told them that my mother needed help getting to a medical appointment.

We drive a different route back to Rio. We go over a dusty pass and drop down to the ocean at Rio de Ostras. We follow the coast to Niterio, where we cross the nine-mile long Rio-Niteroi Bridge into Rio de Janeiro. The bustle of the city doesn't bother me so much now. I'm glad to be with Aritana. He parks in front of the Hotel Santa Maria. I no longer care about the taxi incident. No big deal. After we bring my things up to my room (including bananas and tangerines), I go out to his car with him.

– Did you enjoy your trip to Lumiar?
– More than I can put into words.

18
Chucho

Don't ask me why Mexicans would choose to honeymoon in Rio de Janeiro. Hey, why not? We arrived last week from Mexico City. This city is both magic and tragic. The verdant tropical forest tumbles over black basaltic outcroppings, eventually giving way to the sandy beaches of the Atlantic Ocean. We were lodged in a small, but gracious hotel in Copacabana: the Gladiator. It had nothing roman in its ambiance, but it did have a great rooftop pool with a view of the bustling Copacabana community and the distant panoramas of Sugarloaf Mountain and the surrounding hills, with the Redemptor, or statue of Jesus, on a peak visible far in the distance.

My name is Jesús. Jesús Mota de Suarez. In Oaxaca and the rest of Mexico, it is a quite common name. Here in Brazil, nobody has heard of Chucho, but they like the sound if it. It's what they would expect a Mexican to be called. What they don't accept so easily is the fact that someone would have the name Jesús. Here in Brazil, there is only one, and he never roamed anywhere near Rio. I learned quickly that it's easier just to say my name is Chucho. But inevitably, when anyone looks at my passport they're somewhat put off about it, and I can see the '*oh, really!*' attitude on their faces. My new wife, Zully, joked in the taxi that we were going under the feet of Chucho when we entered the André Rebouças tunnel between the Botafogo and the Lagoa Rodrigo de Freitas neighborhoods in Rio. It passes below a mountain, atop which stands the Redemptor Statue. I laughed, but knew it would not be funny to the driver.

Our stay has been better than I could have dreamed. This city is romantic to say the least. It's the most sexually exuberant place on earth. Or at least, that I've ever experienced. Sexuality is celebrated. It isn't just the exotic setting; the people of Rio exude femininity or masculinity without giving it a thought. A Speed-O or a thong isn't something that attracts attention. It's just beach attire. However, nudity is not permitted. Yesterday we saw a European woman remove her top on Ipanema Beach. In short order, a father of a nearby family strolled over, and without a word poured his beer on her. When she complained, everyone around stared at her, as if she was from outer space. One can wear as little or as much as you wish, but don't try to go it in the buff. When I walk around here, I notice how the clothes fit the hot climate. They're designed to allow air to circulate. I bought Zully several new outfits that revealed more of her than she was used to in Mexico, especially in Oaxaca. She hesitated to go out in public in the abbreviated attire. Once she tried it, however, it quickly became second nature.

Our ten days in Rio would end tomorrow. We decide to take our rental car down on the highway that traverses the coast along Recreo dos Bandeirantes, a jungle-backed area of rocky cliffs and wild surf pounding endless beaches. We leave at dawn and drive up Atlantic Avenue, beside Copacabana Beach. We pass Ipanema and the road starts uphill in a majestic arc above Leblon Beach. The sun is sparkling, and the ocean is too. The small islands that dot Guanabara Bay offshore are surrounded with a short skirt of sea mist in the rising sun. The blue sky mixes with the gold and orange waters. Inland, lie tropical forest uplands. The lush smells seem like something from another world. We're excited to be here. It's sublime, and yet supercharged with anticipated adventure.

The road twists and turns, exposing a new quixotic scene at each turn. We stop often to soak it all in. The breezes tame the raging sun and bring the Atlantic scent to our faces. Each time we stop, the world we knew in Mexico fades softly into the background; much like the haze that surrounded the islands on the horizon. There are moments when the currents of the rivers of our lives subside and allow us to drift into swirling eddies of time, leaving us on our own, without instance, distance or responsibilities. This was one of them. We knew we were right to have married. We celebrate our great fortune of finding each other with few words spoken. We feel part of something we don't have to understand. At this moment, all is right in our existence. We are aware that we're creating our own spirituality, and have the incredible luck of not wanting to know why or what that means. We're part of all that ever was and ever will be. We not only love each other without limit; we're young, healthy and ready for everything that lies ahead.

We pull over in the town of Recreo dos Bandeirantes, park the car, and head off for a stroll down the beach. The waves here are powerful and only the surfers can handle them. It would be foolhardy to try to swim. However, the wide beach with its cream-colored sand is a delight. At the far end of the long, curved coastline, we come to a massive rocky headland. It has a small trail that ascends up to a rounded promontory that overlooks the ocean. We climb up and find several dozen people taking in the view.

The high waves crash against the stone and sound like explosions. White spume flies far into the air. The mist mixes with the late afternoon sun to form an orange-violet hue in the air. We're bathed in sound, light and scent atop an enchanted boulder. It's a far cry from the Southern Sierra Madre range in Oaxaca. We sit down and silently let nature do its thing to our awareness.

After a while, Zully asks, – You think we might be able to extend our trip?

– I think if we don't, we'll be letting an opportunity slip away that we may never again have.

– Thank you for bringing me to this place. I had no idea it would be like this.

– Neither did I – I laugh. – And thank you for coming with me. If it weren't for your support of my odd ideas, I'd never have the courage to put them into action.

I had met Zully after I escaped a long and pointless relationship at a young age. Why do the young so often trap themselves into senseless dreams? And more importantly, why does society encourage this nonsense?

– ¿Chucho?

– ¿Sí, mijita?

– Do you love me?

I pause and gaze out over the surreal scene before us. I don't just love Zully. I believe in Zully. I'm a Zullist. She is my religion, my center of it all. I know better, but it's true. I've so many centers of light in my life: family, friends, the natural world... and more. However, I've accepted that my soul has a twin, and it is Zully.

– More than I can say, baby.

19
Yoko

When I arrive, Márcia opens the door of her family home in Vila Mariana, a wealthy neighborhood in São Paulo. It's a large house of three stories. Her father is an airline pilot for TAM airlines. The décor is modern, with each room having a theme. She introduces me to her parents who seem mild mannered. They are clearly of Japanese ancestry. Márcia shows me around the spacious home. Her bedroom is the African room, with statues of elephants, paintings of animals on the Serengeti Plains and a bed that stands four feet above the floor. She says it's made from imported Africa Mahogany.

Her mother calls upstairs to let us know that the almoço is ready. We eat in a formal dining room that's decorated in a French Renascence theme. A maid brings out a large Italian meal, complete with antipasto, fettuccine alfredo and Chianti wine. For some reason I had expected Brazilian or Japanese food, but I'm pleased to see that, in this family at least, one does not have to live one's life according to what others might expect.

– Márcia tells me you are hoping to discover if some of your relatives still live in Brazil. – her mother comments.

– That would be nice, but the main reason I came to Brazil is to see what life is like here for people of Japanese descent. To that aim, I've already seen much. Liberdade was amazing.

– Oh, that reminds me! – chimes in Márcia. – My friend at the Japan foundation was able to ascertain that more than twenty families with the name Koga immigrated to São Paulo during the first decades of the twentieth century. Most worked at the coffee plantations in this state, which is also named São Paulo. He was able to find current addresses of five of them, and he phoned all five. Unfortunately, none of them has heard of any family members that emigrated from Brazil to the United States.

I feel relieved. I don't really want to speak with distant relatives who know nothing about me. I'm quite content with the extended family I have in America. It's my mother that wants to have names and photographs of our estranged family in Brazil. My interests here are the beaches and the cities. What I discovered in Liberdade added a different dimension to the trip. My mother and father were excited to hear all about it. I mailed them a stack of postcards yesterday. I'm sure I'll be home before they get to Portland.

– Tell him that I am grateful for all of his efforts. Just knowing that we're not the only Kogas to take the journey from Japan to here is enlightening. My parents will be grateful for the information.

Márcia's mother looks at me and asks – Do you plan to travel anywhere else before you return home?

I reply that I have a return ticket from Rio de Janeiro and that my final five days are scheduled for a visit to Ipanema Beach. I tell her I want to see a place called *Pão de Açucar* while in Rio. Márcia's mother tells me that the name of the place translates to Sugarloaf in English.

– You'll love it! Be sure to hike the nature trails on the backside of the mountain.

Márcia asks if I know anyone in Rio. I tell her that it's my first trip to Rio de Janeiro and that I don't know anybody there. She gives her mother a long look, as though they had already discussed something.

– My daughter speaks very highly of you Yoko. She's a very intelligent woman who is astute when it comes to judging character in others. We have a small summer home in Paraty, in the state of Rio de Janeiro. It's not good to travel alone as a woman in Brazil. I'm not saying that it's particularly dangerous, but, without knowing the language or the culture, it's difficult to know what should be avoided.

Márcia chimes in – Yoko, why don't we take the bus to Paraty, stay there a couple of days, and then take the bus to Rio afterwards? If it works out, we could even fly out of the airport on the same day, you to Oregon and I to São Paulo.

– What's in Paraty? – I wonder aloud.

Márcia's father finally participates in the conversation. – It's an historic town. It was a shipping port for the much of the gold that was taken from Brazil to Portugal. The setting beside the ocean is remarkable.

– And, – a delighted Márcia croons – it has some of the best beaches in Brazil!

I thought about it as I finished up with the meal. What did it matter? I had no serious plans for Rio, just to relax on the beach. I could call the hotel in Ipanema, and inform them I would arrive a couple of days late. I was fortunate to have come upon this family so far from my home.

– When will we leave?

– If we buy the tickets at the rodoviária today, we can leave in the morning and be in Paraty before dark tomorrow.

– What's a rodoviária?

– It's the bus terminal.

A short time later, I thank my hosts for the meal and the kind offer to use their home in Paraty. I tell them that if they ever wish to visit the USA, I would be honored to show them my part of the world.

– Don't be surprised if we take you up on the offer – the father replies.

I give them my parent's address. I feel that Márcia and I have another thing in common; we both have gracious and intelligent parents. Some things are a blessing in whatever culture.

We buy the tickets that afternoon. Márcia thanks me for deciding to go. She really loves to visit Paraty, and was afraid that I'd say no. She's not allowed to go there alone.

– My folks are old fashioned in that way – she remarks, – they still think I need to be chaperoned.

*****

In the morning, I thank the people at the Santa Maria and Márcia picks me up in a taxi. We head straight to the rodoviária and are soon on a bus weaving its way through a seemingly endless maze of roads and tall buildings that make up São Paulo.

The highway to the Atlantic coast passes through many towns and cities. It seems like every ten minutes we stop to pick up or drop off somebody. The scenery is green farms and pastures, backed by tropical forest. We reach the coast and stop for thirty minutes to eat. We buy a meal on the 'self-service' plan. That is, we pay by the kilogram. At the table, Márcia is curious about my life.

– Do you have a boyfriend In Oregon?

– Not really. – I had several while I went to college in Ashland, Oregon, but I never considered any of them as permanent. I was in no rush to tie myself down. Now, I've finished my education and am more open to the idea. How about you? Anyone on your horizons?

She laughs and answers – Horizons? Not even on the radar. My parents want me to find somebody. At the same time, they want to filter all applicants. But, they have started to see that I will be the one to decide. They're coming around. And speaking of the opposite sex, Paraty has some of the best men in Brazil. It's a place that attracts those who are active participants in life, as opposed to some of the other tourist areas that appeal more to the '*take my hand and lead me to somewhere interesting that I'd never find on my own*' crowd that I just can't handle.

The road we follow is perched high above the coast. The views over the ocean include islands in the distance. We pass through fishing ports and small cities. As we near Paraty, we enter broad fields of sugarcane. They plunge precipitously down to the seaside. As the wind blows them like waves, it reminds me of the wheat fields in the Palouse region of Oregon, where the wheat grows on the mountain tops instead of the valleys. Here, in the evening twilight, golden waves of the sugarcane flow down the steep coastal hillsides and bump into the pale purple waves of the Atlantic in the background.

By the time we pull into Paraty, I feel I'm part of an adventure in a place far removed.

20
Yoko

The small summerhouse of Márcia's family turns out to be a bungalow with corners of the roof that turn upwards in Japanese style. It's in a newer subdivision that lies just outside of Paraty and overlooks the ocean. I walk out on the patio and know it's going to be hard to leave this place. We bath and put on shorts and light blouses. It's much warmer here than in São Paulo.

– We can walk to town – Márcia yells to me from the bathroom. – It's only fifteen minutes from here.

We drop down to the small beach below the house, and take off our flip-flops to walk along the beach barefoot. There are a dozen or so small fishing skiffs anchored a short distance offshore. The sun has set, but it's still light. Orange clouds hang above us. Small waves beat against the sand. We reach a river that goes straight inland, revealing lavender mountains in the background.

We follow the river until a bridge allows us to cross into the town. Paraty has streets that are paved with giant flat stones. The architecture is from the nineteenth century and reflects the wealth that the export of gold brought to the area. It reminds me a little of Santa Fe, New Mexico. Instead of the tan and ochre adobe of Santa Fe, the buildings here are white, with various colors of wooden shutters. We ramble without reason, up one street and down another. Near the waterfront, the streets are flooded with seawater, reflecting the structures in a mirror-like manner. This has been going on for centuries at high tide. Originally, it allowed passengers to be ferried in rowboats to their homes from arriving ships. The town literally ebbs and flows with the tides. People stroll aimlessly: tourists looking for a reason to be here. We stop at a restaurant, and after a snack of shrimp sautéed in butter and wine, we head back to the house.

– I say we go out tonight. I know a place that's so chic. – Márcia blurts out, using the Brazilian term for all things ultra-cool.

– It's a club that's on the oceanfront and has a schooner moored outside of it, where you can order dinner or drinks. It's 'the' spot to find men.

– OK – I agree. I'm a little leery of meeting men here in Brazil. This is not the time in my life to start a new relationship, but I opt not to tell Márcia why. – What should I wear?

– Something sexy of course! And remember, it can get a little cold here at night. This is winter in Brazil.

I put on a red velvet dress. Márcia wears one of those Brazilian blouses that have no back and only one shoulder strap. I marvel at how women here can gracefully wear something that requires a balancing act just to keep it from falling off.

We take a taxi to the club. We have to walk the last block on oversized cobblestones. Márcia walks across this rocky obstacle course in high heels, without conscious effort. Refinement among a brutal ambiance. I think of Oregon, where we're trying to demonstrate that, as women, we shouldn't have to present ourselves as feminine figures to achieve what is rightly our place in society. I'm willingly part of that movement, but here, I realize that sexuality need not be destructive of dignity. Latin American women lack certain rights in the workplace and home, but they maintain the power of overt femininity that many in my country mistake for weakness.

The club is located beside the bay, and, as Márcia said, it has a schooner docked alongside. Márcia suggests we start the night at a table on the boat. As we walk the gangplank onto the ship, I read the name painted on the bow: Jane Dourada, the Golden Jane. We take a small table on the prow with a view of city lights mirrored on the harbor water. I imagine how it must have been like when these schooners were the high-tech transports of gold ingots, brought from the interior state of Minas Gerais by way of mule trains to Paraty, and then on to Portugal. I notice a line of smaller schooners lined up along the docks a few hundred yards away.

– What are those boats? – I ask.

– They're for tourists. They take you to other beaches and bays. We're going to take one tomorrow. You'll love it! – she says with an air of pride.

On our table is a lamp of some sort. It's not electric and the flame flickers constantly. I order a glass of Malbec wine and Márcia asks for a Guaraná, a soda pop made from the Amazon fruit from which it takes its name. It contains twice the amount of caffeine as coffee. In the elevated center of the ship, a young woman is singing to the accompaniment of a young man. I can't understand any of the words, but I find the ballads soothing. The music drifts across the bay and, as I stare off into the distance, I notice a chorus of crickets in the background. Above are constellations I've never seen before. Márcia points out the Southern Cross.

An hour or so later, the wind picks up and a light mist drifts across the bay. It's chilly, so we opt to go inside the main building, a refurbished warehouse. A band plays popular music on a stage overlooking a dance floor with disco lights. It's midnight and the place is starting to fill up. Many start dancing, both at their tables and on the dance floor. Within minutes, two men come to our table and try to convince us to dance.

– Come back after we get our order in, OK? – I state without emotion.

Márcia gives me a 'why did you say that?' look.

– Did you want to dance? I'm sorry. I thought you'd want to order first.

– I'm not here for the refreshments – she laughingly declares.

– OK – I say, – feel free to dance any time. I may or may not.

I order more wine and shortly afterwards a young man takes Márcia away to dance. Another comes up to me, but I decide to stay and watch the action from the table.

After dancing for half an hour or more, Márcia returns.

– I saw several men ask you to dance. Don't you like to dance?

– Well, the dancing here is different, and I'm not exactly up for it tonight. We'll see if somebody comes by who interests me

– I saw you chose the red paper in the Festival of Stars in Liberdade. Aren't you looking for love?

– I am, but not in the way you're thinking. – I say in a low voice.

Márcia reaches across the table and touches my hand. – Is there some problem? It's none of my business, but you seem melancholy tonight.

She's right. But, I don't want to talk about it. Or do I? I've had the same issue running through my mind since we pulled into Paraty. Here is someone who doesn't really know me, who could listen and maybe reply without a preconceived notion of who I should be. I don't want to spoil her night. Still, if she knew where I was coming from, it might make the evening less tense.

– Márcia?

– Yes, Yoko.

– I lied to you yesterday. There is a love in my life. But, it's not a happy story.

– Do you want to talk about it?

– Yes, but not tonight. Not here. It can wait.

– OK, maybe on the excursion tomorrow.

– What excursion? – I reply with my face contorted with puzzlement.

– The one I've already arranged with the schooner my family always uses when we're here. Don't worry, it's all arranged.

I laugh aloud. – OK, then I'm free to dance tonight without you expecting me to fall in love with some gorgeous Brazilian?

– That's fine with me, but I hope you don't mind if I do.

– Good luck Márcia!

– I should have written my wish on one of those red papers in Liberdade too – she declares and laughs.

I dance with several men. They teach me a couple of dance forms and I enjoy the night. Márcia ends up giving her phone number to a man from Salvador, Bahia. We leave around 3:00 AM. She says we need to go back to the house early because we need to be at the dock by 9:00 AM. I laugh and tell her that in Oregon, 3:00 AM is not early.

*****

In the morning, we make it to the schooner just before it pulls away.

– I was about to give up on you girls – the captain says. – Welcome aboard.

We cruise away from the docks and leave the bay behind us. The boat has masts, but we sail by motor. Again, there is a man seated in the raised middle section of the boat, playing acoustic guitar and singing. He continues to do so for the entire six hours of the trip, except when we embark at a couple of beaches. The sun is out, and it glides between cumulus clouds that are evenly spaced across the sky. The breeze is gentle and the verdant mountains that line the shores have clouds obscuring their summits. We're navigating an area known for natural pools formed by huge boulders that protect swimmers from the sea's waves.

– Do you still want to talk about your love life? If not, I can understand. – Márcia ventures.

I think I should have kept my mouth shut, but decide to go ahead and spill the beans.

– I haven't told this story to anyone, not even my family. If it's boring, please feel free to stop me at any point, OK? – I feel anxious, but I'm determined to get an opinion, especially one from somebody removed from my small world.

– I'm here to listen. – Márcia says.

I look off across the water, back at the speck that's Paraty in the distance. I concentrate on the boat's wake and begin to tell my tale.

– Before I started college, four years ago, I had a boyfriend. We were completely suited, one for the other. I was twenty-two years old. Ashland, where the college is located, is a five-hour drive from Portland. I rented an apartment there, and at first, I went to Portland almost every other weekend. I enjoyed my studies.

Márcia simply nodded acceptingly.

– Slowly, I began to spend more time away from Portland and Andrew. His name is Andrew.

I glanced at Márcia. She was studying the same wave pattern behind us. She said nothing.

– Anyway, after a year or so, he started to complain that I was becoming more distant in every way. At first, I didn't agree, but it became apparent that he was right. Part of my newfound freedom allowed me to meet so many more people. Some of them were men. At first, I kept my distance. By the second year away, I was informally dating several of them.

Márcia continued to observe the wake without comment. I wished she would say something, but she remained silent.

– By the third year, I was seldom seen in Portland. Andrew tried for almost a year to convince me that what we had was special... something irreplaceable. But, I saw love everywhere at the college. I met men from many cultures and social spectrums. Each had a certain exoticness. I fell in love with a couple of them. Each time, after a couple of months, I encountered something in each of them that confirmed that I could never have a permanent relationship with them.

– Go on. – She urged. – I'm listening.

– By the fourth year, I had lost my curiosity in other men. I concentrated on my academics and graduated Magna cum Laude.

– Excellent! And, Andrew?

– I don't know. I call him from time to time. He always treats me well, but makes it clear that what we had has ended. Márcia, after four years away from home, I returned with enough knowledge to teach others about who we collectively are. Unfortunately, I also came back knowing that I had let the person who I'll eternally love slide from my grasp. I'd become a fool while I became educated.

Márcia looked into my face and spoke. – So, you didn't leave him at one specific point?

– No, I died from a slow cancer of love. I ignored the symptoms until it was too late. I'm twenty-six years old, young enough to start again. But I can't. I wasted his love.

– You're beautiful Yoko. With your green almond eyes and trim body, you'll never have a problem attracting other men.

– It's not that. I simply can't love anyone else. At times, I lay awake on my bed at night and hear two hearts beating in a synchronized pattern. His and mine. I feel ashamed of my sojourns into foolish love. I know it's not logical and not necessary. But, I can't let it go. I feel he'll come back someday... soon.

– Have you sought help? I mean from a professional? – Márcia ventures, a little ill at ease.

– Oh, yes! I spent the last semester visiting with the college shrink and attended support groups every week for months. Eventually, I realized that I understood the problem. But, I came to accept that I'd rather be depressed with his memory intact than be healthy without hope of his return. I consciously accept my error. I don't want to forgive myself.

– I never want a love like that – Márcia replies. – But, I can see why you are not too keen on starting a new relationship. Yoko, I've no advice for you. I see this as like somebody who wants to quit smoking. You need to accept either that you will always smoke, or find the strength to stop. Nobody can do it for you.

– You're right Márcia. As you've seen, I'm a happy person in my day-to-day life. I just feel awkward when I'm near people seeking mates.

– Well, at least I understand your viewpoint. I'll try not to put you in a difficult position.

– Don't worry about it. I enjoy the company of others. I don't wish to avoid men. I just know what the end thoughts will be. I'm fine with partying and everything else. I still live life quite to the limit.

We pull into a small bay outside the natural pools. I give Márcia a quick kiss on her forehead.

– Thanks for listening. I know someday I'll resolve all of this. Now, let's go see what these pools are like. Do you have your bikini under those shorts?

She does and we take the inflatable raft from the schooner to the pools. As we wade to shore, several men are eying us. I feel good about myself.

– Oi! – one of them greets us.

– Oi! Tudo bem? – I shout to him.

Reminiscence

21

Andrew

I had finished a construction job high in the Rockies. The summer was ending and I was young and anxious to return to Oregon, where I had previously worked. I had time to kill, an MG convertible and extra money in my pocket. Is there anything more American for a young person than a road trip?

I drive over Independence Pass and down into Aspen. The town is known for rich people and when I enter the first bar, I realized why. The prices were from another planet. I decide to pay the ridiculous price for a beer and hamburger, but realize that I'll be heading further down the line this first day on the highway. I put the top down on the MG. It's an invigorating drive down the west slope of the Continental Divide. The sun is setting between two snow-topped mountains as I pull off the interstate near Grand Junction. I take a gravel road into the BLM land that surrounds much of GJ. I grew up in the West. There's always a place to pass the night without paying, if you look for it. I find it a few miles from Interstate 70, where traffic whizzes by without a clue that I'm here. I pitch my tent and leave the rain-fly off. No rain tonight and I want to see the stars. I read a couple of pages from Edward Abbey's *The Journey Home*. The nighttime sounds surround me: coyotes, crickets and croaking frogs. Sleep comes easy.

The next day, I put the top down again. Sunshine! Let it shine on me. I drive through the red rock canyonlands of Southern Utah, north along the Wasatch Range near Salt Lake and into Idaho. The land is open and dry. I pass by farming and ranching communities. Where do they get their water? I find a cheap motel in Twin Falls and spend the night drinking beer and watching Marcus Welby on TV. In the morning, I head into Oregon. My destination is Eugene, home of the University of Oregon. My hope is to arrive in the early afternoon, so I'll have plenty of time to set up camp and head into town. I've heard there's construction work in the area. With luck, I'd be able to secure a job.

The map shows a private campground just north of Eugene. I have some money, but no friends in this town. Things are going well. The Cascade Range in central Oregon is much greener than the parched Rockies to the east. Leaving the high Cascades, I follow the McKenzie River down to its junction with the Williamette Valley. It's been a long drive and I look forward to a shower and some conversation with somebody, somewhere. I pull off Interstate 5. Only a mile to go! As I cross over an old iron bridge above the Williamette River, my gaze is directed to the campground on the far side of the river. It has huge and shady oak trees. This is going to be great.

But, fate had something else in store for me. I barely have time to put my foot on the brake pedal when I see the old Chevy Pickup looming a few yards in front of me. The MG wedges under the rusty rear bumper with a violent crunch. My windshield sits a few inches from the same bumper. After several confusing seconds, I hear an old-timer shout through my window,

– Did that wake you up? How can you not see a car in front of you on a bridge?

How indeed? One thousand, three hundred miles only to end up in a crash just yards away from my destination. How can that be?

– Sorry mister. – I manage to say as I try to open the door. It's jammed and when I go to climb over it, I realize that I've sprung my ankle on the brake pedal. One of the front tires is punctured. The aluminum body panels of the front of the car are flattened around the motor. The old man pulls his truck forward a little.

– You're lucky; it only scraped a little rust off my bumper. Good luck young man, and pay more attention in the future. – He drives off.

Several people have stopped to help me pull the fenders away from the motor. The radiator has a small leak. I put the spare tire on and drive to a nearby gas station. I call the only person I know in Oregon. I had previously worked with Kenny at a machine shop. He lived in Beaverton.

– You're kidding! What are you doing in Eugene? Never mind. Can you drive your car up to Beaverton? – He gives me his address and after topping off the radiator, I drive back to the interstate and head up the freeway. People are staring at the mangled front end of my once-cool MG. What an embarrassment! A few hours later, I park in front of Kenny and his girlfriend's house on Hall Street.

Kenny still has his full auburn beard and Diane is a tall, muscular blond. They graciously offer to put me up for a few days. I accept, thinking that it would only take a few days to get my car repaired. However, when I got an estimate on the cost to restore the MG, I found it is well above the value of the car. I sell the MG to the first person with a hundred dollars in his hand.

Kenny and Diane have a roommate who was into drugs. That's not surprising, where I came from everyone smokes pot. But, this household is into whatever happens to be available on any particular day. I have no objection. Hey, it's the big city and I'm here to learn about life. The attic is used by the roommate to grow marijuana. Interesting, but I steer clear of it, and make a note to move on as soon as I get another car.

A few nights after arriving, I'm sitting in the living room with Kenny and some of his friends. It's raining hard outside and the night has a chill, so he decides to build a fire in the fireplace. It's comfortable and we listen to Creedence Clear Water Revival's *Fortunate Son* and talk about the Vietnam War. One of Kenny's friends has returned from Vietnam with both legs missing from the knees down. A joint laced with some strange drug is passed around. It causes me to have problems with distance and balance. It's not pleasant and I'm not sure why I'm smoking it.

Suddenly, the roommate comes into the living room and calmly says

– Wow man, the chimney's on fire!

We look at him, as if he's crazy. Kenny wants to know what he's talking about.

– Seriously dude! Come outside and take a look. There's more than just smoke coming out of the chimney.

We jump up and run out onto the driveway. Sure enough, there's a strong blast of flame shooting out of the chimney. No one is sure what to do. Kenny goes back inside and extinguishes the fire in the fireplace. I stay in the driveway, watching the flames. They don't subside. Then I see the chimney has separated itself from the house by about a foot. Flames are running up the side of the second floor, between it and the chimney. I observe all of this with an altered vision that puts everything at odd angles.

I go back inside and inform Kenny of the worsening situation. The Vietnam veteran is now up on his artificial legs. As we head outside Kenny yells,

– We've have to get the cars out of the drive. The chimney is going to come down!

The last thing I see inside the house is the roommate running up the stairs. He's in a panic and yells – We gotta get them plants out of the attic!

Nobody is listening to him. Kenny backs his pickup out of the drive, just as the first fire truck pulls up in front of the house. He barely misses being hit by it. They're dropping hose as they arrive.

– Get in! – the vet tells me.

I jump in his Volvo sports car. Firemen are rushing to the house and don't pay attention to us. He's having a little trouble getting his legs under the steering column. The flames are now running along most of the side of the house. The light from the fire and the emergency vehicles are mingling in the dark night.

– I don't think we should try to leave. It's too late! – I tell the vet.

– Hang on. – he replies.

– Get back! It's coming down! – one of the firemen shouts.

At that moment, the chimney comes crashing down right in front of our car. We're already peeling out in reverse. The vet's face is strangely calm. A cloud of cinders and sparks appears in front of the Volvo and a brick bounces off the hood. I look back as we run over several hoses, just missing a fireman, and careen across the lawn to avoid the fire truck blocking the driveway. Somehow, we make it away from the scene.

*****

After a few hours, we call Kenny. He tells us to come on back. We return and find the place is still standing. There are several holes in the roof and the remains of the chimney are covering the drive. Apparently, no legal issues surfaced. The landlord gave Kenny permission to stay. He asked if I would remain and help clean up the mess. I agree.

Diane isn't going to stay in the damaged and smoke-filled upstairs bedroom. She has to be at work in the morning and calls a friend for help. Soon, the doorbell rings. Her friend arrives to bring Diane to stay with her until things return to normal.

– Thanks for coming! I can't tell you how much I appreciate you putting me up at your place. – Diane says.

Her friend surveys the damage and just shakes her head in amazement.

– Lilly, this is Andrew. He has the luck of staying with us while our house burns up.

22
Yoko

I awake the next morning to music: *Ticket to Ride* by the Beatles. It reminds me that we leave for Rio today. My mind is still thick from the partying last night after we returned from the coastal cruise. Through the open door, I see Márcia dancing in the living room. She's singing along with the radio. That girl can party!

– Hey! Wake up in there! – she yells. – We have a bus to catch in a couple of hours.

I drag myself out of bed and into the bathroom. Flashbacks from yesterday are running through my brain: snorkeling among orange and black striped fish in the open ocean, dancing with various guys and a midnight ride along the beach in a Volkswagen buggy.

– Come on! Breakfast is ready! – her voice echoes through the house.

After some coffee, I feel better. We clean the house and grab our suitcases. A short taxi ride later, and we're boarding the bus for Rio. It seems like I've been in Brazil far longer than a week. Foreign travel is a long highway.

We pass through landscape as green as spring in the Williamette Valley of Oregon. There are thousands of coconut palms. They always seem exotic to me, no matter how many of them I see. I wonder what Rio will be like. I'm glad Márcia is with me for this leg of the journey. She's fun and her advice and knowledge of Brazil make this trip far more meaningful.

We stop to eat lunch and she calls home.

– Eita! Oh mãe! – she cries out. – What happened? Nossa senhora!

She finishes the call and looks at me with tears flowing down her cheeks.

– My father has had a heart attack.

– Oh god, Márcia! Is he going to be OK?

– They say it's minor, but my mother is frantic. I've got to head home immediately.

Suddenly, the scenery is less stunning. The constant chatter inside the bus fades away. I watch my friend withdraw into a shell.

– What can I do to help? – I venture.

– Nothing, Yoko. I'll have to buy a ticket to São Paulo in the bus depot in Rio. Will you be OK on your own?

– Don't worry about me. Keep your focus on your family. – I say the words, but inside I'm disappointed that my stay in Rio will be a solitary one.

The rodoviária in Rio is huge and bustling with people trying to buy tickets, looking for their departure gates, eating and simply participating in the timeless existence of a traveler waiting to be transported from one reality to another. After getting her ticket, Márcia helps me buy a taxi voucher. I accompany her to the bus and before boarding it she turns to me and says

– Take care of yourself girl. You have my number. Call anytime, for any reason.

We embrace and realize that both of us are crying. Then we break into laughter. Friendship is valuable in any language. The time for talk has ended. She mutters one word as she steps into the bus.

– Call.

*****

I turn away and into the madness of Rio. An excitement grips me. What next?

The taxi ride to my hotel is more thrilling than I'd have preferred, but at least it takes my mind off of being alone. It would be hard to feel alone in this vibrant scene. But, I do. I wonder if Rio has any waterfalls. I need a friend... And then, I think of Andrew.

– Stop that right now! – I mumble aloud.

At my hotel, the Santa Maria, the staff is upbeat and friendly. After freshening up, I head out to visit Copacabana Beach. It is easy to find, only a block away. When I get there, I find thousands of swimsuit-clad people sitting, laying and standing in the hot sun. Only a few feet separate one group from another. I find it intimidating. Nevertheless, the people-watching is excellent. I've arrived in late afternoon. The shadows from the tall buildings on the far side of the Avenida Atlantica have started to cover the beach. I stay an hour or so, until the sun illuminates only the distant ocean. Most everyone has packed up and left by the time I put my shorts on, over my bikini.

When I reach the sidewalk, I wander along it, without any plans. I come to what appears to be a hippie crafts fair on the median that divides the avenue. They're selling all sorts of art, trinkets, musical instruments and who knows what else. I'm drawn to the miniature statues of Jesus standing on top of blue crystal rocks.

– How much is the small one? I ask the vender in one of the stalls.

– Three cruzeiros – she responds.

– I bought one for two yesterday – somebody whispers in my ear.

I turn and find a woman in her thirties smiling at me.

– You have to shop around a little. The prices here vary enormously. Do you speak English?

– Yes, I'm an American.

– Whoa! I thought you were Chinese or something. There are so many people from all over the world here in Rio. – she replies.

– Where are you from? – I ask.

– I'm from Colorado.

She tells me to follow her to another stand. There, I find the same Jesus figurine for the price as she paid yesterday. I buy it and thank her for the advice.

– I was just getting ready to head off to Ipanema for a few beers on the sidewalk. Would you like to come along? – she states.

I don't even know her name. Still, she's obviously American.

– Is it far from here?

– No, and we can grab one of the VW Kombies that run up and down the coast. They're convenient and cheap.

I am hesitant to take off in a strange city with somebody I don't know. But, the thought of returning to my hotel room and watching TV that I can't understand doesn't exactly turn me on either.

I ask her – do you live here?

She laughs, – no, no... I'm on vacation.

– What is your name? – I inquire.

– Lilly. Lilly Ann Wethington. And yours?

– Yoko, Chiyoko Koga.

– Come on – she shouts above the sound of a vender demonstrating various musical instruments and whistles used in Samba music. – Let's go! I'm hungry and need a drink.

We cross the street and she flags down a VW microbus. It's full of people and we can't sit next to each other. I ask how much it costs and she says not to worry; she'll pay as we leave. We follow the beachfront a short distance and then wind up a hill and down the far side, where we emerge alongside another beach.

– This is Ipanema – she shouts to me. – We'll get out in a couple of blocks.

In a few minutes, she says something to the driver and he drops us off on the curbside.

– Obrigada! – Lilly says as the sliding door of the van slams behind us. – Tchau!

– You speak good Portuguese – I tell her.

– Yeah, all ten words of it!

She tells me that she found a beach shack that serves great carne de sol and French fries. We sit down at a plastic table with plastic chairs.

– Do you like beer? – Lilly asks.

I nod affirmatively and the cans of beer arrive with two glasses. In America, I'd drink right from the aluminum can, but here that's considered barbaric. A man sings romantic music and plays an acoustic guitar. Waves break on the beach in the background. After a few glasses of beer, I relax and let the tropical breeze mix with my thoughts. I think of Márcia and hope she's OK. The carne de sol arrives and we dig in. We have to eat with toothpicks, as they don't provide silverware. No problem. But, the sautéed onion pieces are a little hard to spear.

We explain to each other how we ended up in Brazil, and agree that not many women make this trip alone. The third beer comes with a shot of something. Lilly explains that it's cachaça and that I should try it if I'm to say I've experienced Brazil. The beer cans accumulate on the table. They're not removed because our bill will be based on how many are on the table when we leave.

– Where are you staying? – Lilly asks without taking her eyes off the passing parade of bodies.

– A hotel called Santa Maria.

– You've got to be kidding! That's where I'm staying. – she states, turning to me with surprise.

– Small world.

A girl comes up to our table and points to our beer cans, indicating that she would like to take them.

– Leave them alone! – I snarl at her. The girl looks directly at Lilly and runs down the sidewalk. I turn to Lilly and state – I just hate all the begging that goes on down here. I'm not going to be a part of it. Brazil needs to learn to take care of their own.

Lilly jumps up and runs after the girl. – Marina! Marina! Wait!

The girl disappears into the street scene. Lilly returns with an ashen face.

– Do you know her? – I ask.

Lilly tells me she'll explain later and remains silent for a few minutes. Then she orders another round of cachaça for us.

– Do you have any plans for tomorrow? – Lilly eventually asks.

– I thought I might go on an excursion to see the big Jesus statue on the mountain. Why?

– Well, I'm going to a beach that's full of surfers and everyone says it's a great beach, and less crowded than the ones in the city. It's called Recreo dos Bandeirantes. Maybe we could split the cost of a taxi.

– I'm behind on my sleep. Would we have to leave early in the morning? – Yoko asks.

Lilly laughs. – Travel wears you out, doesn't it? We could leave late in the morning and still return before nightfall.

I have several days to spend in Rio before returning to Oregon, so why not?

– I'll go on one condition. – I say.

– What's that? – Lilly inquires.

– You explain how you know the girl that tried to grab our cans off the table. – I demand.

She agrees. We pay our tab and flag down a cab. On the way back to the hotel, Lilly relates her encounter with Marina.

As we enter the hotel, I comment – that is an example of the reason I hate street people and begging. It only leads to more and more suffering. Giving to them only creates more begging and allows them to think it's morally permissible.

– Yes – Lilly replies, – we seldom see the way things are, but we always see things the way we are.

23

Elephant Rock

When Lilly and Yoko arrive in the seaside town of Recreo dos Bandeirantes, they're in high spirits. The afternoon sun is still hot and they hear the sounds of waves exploding on the beach long before they actually saw it. They are hungry and the taxi driver takes them to a group of simple restaurants just outside of town. The sidewalk and eateries on this part of the mile-long beach are shaded from the sun, but the beach and rocky headlands lie basking in the sun and spray. They take a seat at a table just out of the sun, where they could feel the sea mist cooling them. Along with their driver, they order grilled garoupa, a highly popular fish in Brazil. There's nothing quite like fresh catch, eaten beside the ocean.

On the trip to Recreo, the driver agrees it is rare for women to travel in Rio alone. Lilly and Yoko converse most of the way. They find their lifestyles different, but they're equally determination to live their lives to the fullest. Both find Brazil to be unlike their expectations. And, Portuguese is such a different and difficult language!

– I wonder how it came to be that everyone here treats visitors with almost familial kindness. – reflects Yoko. – Is it like that in other countries you have visited Lilly?

– Well, in Mexico, they also treat you well, but it's less personal than here. In Europe, a traveler is like any other person; they're expected to know what they're doing. Sort of like New York City. In Europe, for example, a waiter is paid a decent wage and they don't have to grovel for tips. They're there to provide a service, not to be your mealtime friend. – Lilly continues – one thing I really notice about Brazil, in comparison to Mexico, is that an American is an exotic person. In Mexico, we're a dime a dozen.

– I'm very happy in America. I never thought I'd like being in another culture. – Yoko speaks with her gaze upon the passing surfers. – It surprises me that I found friends in São Paulo so easily.

It's the fifth largest city on the planet and I had no idea of what I was going to find there. To be honest, I sort of dreaded coming. But, after all that I've seen and experienced, I'm ready to see more of the world.

The two women decide to walk along the waterline. Their driver asks if they would like him to accompany them. They tell him it would be better if he waited at the barraca. He says the sun will set in a couple of hours and that they should not walk along the beach alone after dark. He tells them he'll wait for them in a parking area beside a huge rock that separates Recreo from another beach.

– That's Elephant Rock – he states. – It looks like an Elephant from the far side. I will be waiting for you there at 5:30, OK?

– Perfect – they respond in unison.

They drop down the steeply inclined sand dune towards the beach. When she arrives at the ocean, Lilly is amazed at the power of the waves. Yoko has seen this force many times on the Pacific coast in Oregon. They walk along silently. Speech would be useless here. The sounds of nature take over. Lilly inspects the shells, observes the urubus, or vultures that soar far above the seagulls that fly just above their heads. Palm trees appear as illuminated green halos that crown the hill above the ocean. She smiles when she finds herself doing what she has done so many times in life. That is, she imagines herself in a film taken from a satellite far above in space. It starts as a remote shot of the South American continent and slowly closes in on this spot on the beach.

Yoko thinks about beggars. What is it that about them that brings out so much animosity in her? Why can't everything be like this beach, where everything has its place? Nothing is trying to make others do more than their share in life. Nature is always so balanced. Why do some humans always screw up so much of life? She mentally stumbles upon an odd detail about beggars. She has never seen a Japanese beggar. Why would that be? She was bringing questions about herself and her genealogical background back to Oregon.

Both women amble down the beach at their own pace, separated from one another as much by their different lives as the distance on the beach. Each marvels at the present scene, and tries to fit their dreams and doubts into this moment. Like others who find themselves beside the edge of an unknown continent, they filter their thoughts through an unusual climate, geography and culture.

At the end of the beach, they confront a huge stone monolith. They must either go up multiple wooden stairways to the highway or ascend the steep rock.

– This must be Elephant Rock – Lilly says. – What do you think?

– I think we need to climb it silly!

They scramble up and find themselves on top of a viewpoint where one can see for miles up or down the beach. They drop down to the eroded part of the rock beside the ocean. Waves are smashing into the basaltic cliff below and tossing thousands of gallons of water and foam onto Elephant Rock.

– Wow! Let's back off a bit. No wonder everyone is keeping their distance. One slip and you'll never be heard from again. – As she says this, Yoko turns and walks back up the stone surface. Lilly follows.

They walk a short distance and sit down on a natural rock bench. Yoko notes the couple beside her and imagines them to be Amazonian Indians. The sunlight is at a sharp angle. It will set behind the hill within a few minutes. The clouds above look like endless orange peel. The mist and spray from the ocean bounce through the air like illuminated cotton candy. The ocean is royal blue. Everyone's skin takes on the golden hues of the sunset. Nobody speaks. They're hypnotized visitors.

After a few minutes, one says,

– Chucho, I want to remember your face in this place, in this light, at this moment; forever.

– We did well coming to Rio Zully. What a way to start our life together! – He turns to Zully and they stare into each other's eyes.

Lilly notices that they're speaking Spanish. Yoko assumes it's Portuguese.

– Where are you from? – Lilly asks them in Spanish.

– We're from Mexico. It's our honeymoon. – Chucho responds. – Y ustedes?

– We're Americans, Yoko is from Oregon and I'm from Colorado.

– What are you guys talking about? – Yoko says, a little perplexed.

Chucho realizes that Yoko doesn't speak Spanish and he laughs and says in English,

– Here we are, four foreigners in Brazil, and we're speaking English and unable to understand most of what is said in this country. I thought Portuguese would be much more like Spanish, but most of the time I have to use English to be understood.

– What part of Mexico are you from? – Lilly asks.

– We live in Oaxaca. – Chucho returns. Zully remains quiet, barely able to keep up with the conversation with the little English she has. – What brings you two to Brazil? Did you come down together?

– We came separately – Yoko replies. – I came to find if any of my mother's relatives live here and Lilly came because she won money to travel.

Lilly explains the contest back in Durango and asks for their names.

– I am Chucho and this is Zully. And, you guys?

– I'm Lilly and this is Yoko.

Lilly ponders the names a second and asks – Chucho? That's a nickname for Jesús, isn't it?

– Yes, and you're the first American I've met that knows that. Where did you learn it?

– I've traveled a lot in Mexico and I've always had an interest in names and their meanings. In America, for example, it would be considered very odd to name a child Jesus. It would be considered disrespectful of Christian beliefs.

– In Mexico – defends Chucho, – it's just the opposite; it's a form of respect for the same religion. Funny, how we all look at the same things from different viewpoints.

– Interesting. – Yoko says, – Do you know what Zully means?

Chucho talks with Zully and after few minutes he turns back to the Yoko and states – It comes from the name Zulema. It's from the Arabic word salome, which means peace. How about Yoko? Does it have any meaning, other than being the name of John Lennon's lover?

– Well, Yoko means honored child. My real name is Chiyoko. It means child of forever. My parents expect much from me. – She laughs aloud.

– OK – interjects Lilly. – My turn. Lilly is obviously derived from the flower. But, the Lilly is not just any flower. It has been around for at least thirty-six centuries. Each color has a meaning, but since I'm white, I only remember the history of the white lily. It was considered sacred by the ancient Greeks and Romans. The Greeks thought it sprouted from the milk of Hera, the queen of the Gods. The Romans connected it with Juno, also the queen of Gods. In various religions, up until present day, it's known to symbolize virtue and purity. I'm far from pure, but I like my name very much.

The sun had set. Most of the people on the rock had left. Yoko remembers the taxi driver.

– Oh! It's six o'clock! – she shouts, as though the taxi would turn to a pumpkin at any moment. – Lilly, we have to get back to our taxi!

– We have to get going too Zully. I'm not familiar with this highway. In the dark, it'll be worse. We should have left sooner. – Chucho tells Zully, with a look of concern. – Say, ladies, are you heading back to Rio right away?

– Yes, we're going back to our hotel in Copacabana.

– Any chance we might be able to follow your taxi? That way I can keep from getting lost. Rio is so confusing. We're also staying at a hotel in Copacabana. We could pitch in on the taxi fare.

– Sure, no problemo! – Lilly says. – And you don't have to pay anything. It won't cost us any more with or without you following.

Yoko gives her a look that seems to say 'are you sure?' They all head across the dimly lit stone surface and climb the stairways to the highway. The taxi is waiting for them.

– I was getting a little worried – their driver says.

The two women explain that their new acquaintances will be following them back to Copa and instruct him not to lose them on the way. Chucho says they're parked just two spaces away. They load into the cars and start toward Rio, taking the winding route that follows the coast above São Conrado and, eventually, to Copacabana.

As they weave through the curves between São Conrado and Leblon, the headlights reveal cliffs that drop to the rocky coast below. Chucho keeps close to the taxi, tracking the glowing taillights through the dark night, made worse by the ocean mist rising from below.

– Maybe we could invite them to dinner for allowing us to follow them. I'd never have been able to find the way back to Rio. We're lucky to have met them – Chucho tells Zully.

– OK, but could it be tomorrow? I'm tired and want to spend tonight with you. – Zully has her arm around him and puts her hand on his leg.

Before Chucho has a chance to answer, the brake lights on the taxi come on.   A split second after, as he slams on the brakes, something hits the right side of their car and leaves the road, plunging down the Cliffside. Both cars stop. Everyone jumps out and peers over the edge into the darkness. The rocky coast is barely visible hundreds of feet below the sheer drop off.

– What was that? – a shaken Chucho asks.

– It was a guy on a motorcycle! – screams Yoko. – We clipped him and you knocked him over the cliff!

– Shit! – cries Lilly. – What the hell happened? What are we going to do?

– We have to call the police! – Yoko cries with a grim expression.

The taxi driver runs back to his car and drives off without a word.

– Jesus Christ! He left us! – screams Yoko.

– That son of a bitch! That fucking coward! – Lilly yells in the direction of the taxi. – What now?

Cars are driving by, their occupants looking at the four staring into the abyss. Yoko is crying. Zully wraps her arms around her in a motherly manner.

– We can't stay here either – Chucho's strained voice says. – We have no idea what happened or who'll be blamed. The taxi driver left for a reason. Justice in Latin America is based more on who you know, than what the truth is. I know nobody here and don't speak the language. Zully and I are leaving. We can drop you at your hotel if you want.

– We can't just leave! – Yoko sobs – there's somebody down there!

– Whoever it is, he's dead. Nobody survives a fall that far. I can't even see the motorcycle. It must have fallen into the ocean. There's nothing we can do now. – Chucho flatly states. – We're leaving... now!

He and Zully head toward their car. Lilly grabs Yoko by the arm, drags her to the car and throws her in the rear seat. She goes around the car and enters by the other back door. As they leave, Lilly notices a Chevrolet parked across the road. Yoko continues sobbing. They drive the hour to Copacabana and drop Yoko and Lilly off at their hotel.

24
Vovó

When I was born, at the turn of the century, Almadina didn't have electricity or a paved road. Everyone was born in their parent's house. The Almada River starts as a spring that gushes out of a small, rock-lined opening in the Atlantic Rain Forest. Our home was located a short distance away. In fact, my aunt carried me to the spring and washed away the remains of the placenta immediately after my birth. I've always liked to say that I was born of the soil, and washed by the waters of Almadina.

Our lives revolved around cacao. We were prosperous, but without much money. Our prosperity was our physical strength, combined with farm skills that our ancestors had passed on to us. We knew this land, and how to persuade it to provide us with what we needed. We were fortunate to be born into an era when the harvest of cocoa beans meant having what one needed. Still, due to the isolation, we had few material comforts. The lack of health care and education hindered any real progress. I didn't learn to read until my grandson, Severino, taught me.

Everyone here in Almadina calls me Nalva. Dona Nalva. I guess I've become the elder matriarch of the community. Although it's a position of respect, I'd prefer to be young again. Why do we have to get older? What was God thinking?

My husband, Izidorio, was a strong, gentle and caring man when we married. I was seventeen and he was twenty-five. His father gave us a tiny plot of land alongside the place where the Almada River begins, with the condition that we would build and maintain a fence to keep cattle from entering and polluting the spring. Its water was the purest around. For the first five years, I couldn't get pregnant. We went down to Itabuna to see the doctor, and he said that after so long a time trying, I probably would never bear children.

*****

The other day, I was preparing almoço and I heard somebody knocking on my front door.

– Oh de casa! – somebody yells outside, and claps their hands, the standard way to announce an arrival at a house.

I look up and see several men standing outside of the small patio that separates my house from the street. They're from Itabuna, and bring bad news.

– Good morning dona Nalva. We're here to inform you of an accident that involves your grandson, Severino.

– What? – I think that something has happened at the fazenda where Severino is staying. – What are you talking about?

They show me their identification. They're Military Police, who handle what little police work occurs in Almadina.

– We've been contacted by the Rio de Janeiro Police Department. It appears that your grandson has been involved in a mishap there. Unfortunately, he was killed in a motorcycle accident.

– Meu Deus en Céu! What are you saying?

– He failed to negotiate a turn on a coastal highway near Rio and his motorcycle plunged several hundred feet down a cliff beside the ocean. His backpack, with documents that identify him as the owner, was found near the motorcycle that came to a rest a few yards from the shoreline. His body has not been found, but there's a witness, who verifies he fell into the ocean.

– What? That's impossible. He doesn't even own a motorcycle. – I decide not to mention that I know where he is, since Severino has explicitly instructed me to maintain silence about his whereabouts.

– We also have to inform you that he was being sought by military investigators in the bombing and subsequent deaths stemming from a recent incident at the state university in Ilhéus. It appears he fled to Rio to avoid detection in that case. We've verified that he was staying in Copacabana and that he didn't return after the accident. The police in Rio found his belongings in his hotel room.

At that moment, the other agent hands me a small backpack. I recognize it immediately. When I open it, I find several small items that belong to Severino. My heart drops like a stone. I feel their arms support me as things start to fade into darkness.

I awake several seconds later and find myself lying on the sofa. My neighbor arrives and holds my hand. The agents hover above. I sit up. Now what? Funeral arrangements? Without a body?

– Dona Nalva, if we hear anything more about the recovery of your grandson's body, we'll contact you immediately. Somebody will be in contact with you to verify if anyone in your family has information about the bombing in Ilhéus. We extend our condolences and if we can be of further service in the future, please contact our office in Itabuna.

They leave. I'm left with several friends and family members, who have come to be with me. I'm not sure what to think. Severino would never leave town without telling me. For now, I'll try to accept that he was in Rio de Janeiro and that he died there. But, I know there is more to this entire event than I have been told. I'll need help in determining the truth, but I won't be using the military or police in Ilhéus or Itabuna to sort this out. I'll wait a few days for all to settle down and then find out why Severino was in Rio de Janeiro. I'm sure of only one thing; he didn't die in an accident. There's more to this. I won't rest until I know what really happened.

25
Lilly

Each minute of the flight back to Denver puts more distance between the realities of that ugly event last night and my life in Colorado. After arriving at the hotel last night, I had spent an hour trying to calm Yoko. We vowed not to speak with anyone about what had happened on the highway. Then we said our goodbyes and agreed to contact each other back in the states. In all honesty, I doubted if we would ever communicate again. My plan for the moment was to forget the entire incident as soon as possible. Some idiot drove in front of a car in which I was a passenger. So what? Too bad for him. I have a life to live and I'm not going to let somebody else's stupidity ruin it. I tuck the episode into some obscure part of my consciousness. I'll deal with it later.

I had called Aritana after leaving Yoko in her room.

– Everything's fucked up – I blurt out. – Can you come over?

– I'm in Meier. It will take an hour to get there, – he states. – What is going on?

– My trip is over. I've to get out of Brazil.

– Why? What happened?

I tell him that I can't talk about it on the phone. When he arrives, I explain what happened on the highway. He looks at me with apprehension.

– Did you know the person who was hit? Does the taxi driver know anything about you?

– I've no idea who was on the motorcycle. The taxi driver knows I'm in this hotel and he knows my name is Lilly. When he drove off and left us, I had no choice but to leave with the couple we met in Bandeirantes. You're a cop. What should I do?

– The law requires all persons involved in an accident to stop and report it. – Aritana slowly states. – Since you were in a taxi, that responsibility lies with the driver. Still, in Brazil the law sometimes requires everyone, even remotely involved in a crime, to give a sworn deposition at the police station.

– A crime? – I almost shout at him. – I didn't do anything!

– That's true Lilly, but this was a fatal accident. When someone involved in the death of another person leaves the scene, it can cause suspicion. I know you're innocent and the taxi driver knows you're innocent. Still, if the drivers are investigated, you'll probably be called in to testify as to what happened. If so, you'll not be allowed to leave the country.

– I'm not going to stay in Brazil for an unknown amount of time. I have limited funds and just want to forget this whole thing." I watch the walls slowly start to rise around me. Then I realize I'm sitting on the floor. I don't want to deal with this. Aritana sits beside me.

– Are you all right? Is there something I can do for you?

– Any suggestions on what's next? – I ask.

– There's only one way to avoid problems. You have to leave now. – Aritana stands up and pulls me to my feet. We stop for a second, staring into each other's eyes. He adds, – I'd hoped to spend more time with you. I'd hoped to show you Maceió.

He watches me pack and we check out of the hotel and head to the airport. I'm able to change flights and I leave around midnight on a flight to São Paulo, where I'd catch another flight to Denver. He gave me a departing kiss at the boarding gate. He puts a piece of paper in my hand as I leave. It has his phone number and address on it.

– I'm driving up to Maceió tomorrow. Call me when you get a chance.

*****

My sister meets me at Stapleton Airport in Denver. I called when I arrived and she was surprised to hear I was back in Colorado.

– I thought you loved Rio! What brought you back so soon? – she inquires.

– There was some problem with my reservation at the hotel. I was going to have to find another one, and so I decided to cut the trip a little short. I love Rio. – I didn't like lying to my sister, but neither was I up for explaining the whole thing. The image of the canyon near Durango loomed in my mind. I only wanted to get back there and be alone.

I spent two days with family in Denver, promising to send copies of the photos I had taken when I got the film developed. As I drove up Turkey Creek Canyon and left Denver behind, I felt the tension leave my body for the first time since gazing down that precipice into the dark ocean below. It was over now. I'm going home to the world I know and love. Pinyon and juniper. Rock and sky.

I felt better when I reached Wolf Creek Pass. An hour later, I turned off highway 160 and drove onto the Southern Ute Indian Reservation. When I reached Ignacio, I stopped to buy groceries and other supplies. I was going to spend some time alone.

I was tired from the thousands of miles I had of traveled. During the seven-hour drive from Denver, the positive parts of my Brazilian odyssey started outweighing the negative event. I felt my strength coming back. Just being on the Res and so close to home gave me a second wind. I decide to stop for a beer or two. Ignacio has two bars, one predominately Indian, the other Hispanic. I pull over in front of the Teepee. As I sit down at the bar, I notice an acquaintance at one of the tables. He motions me over. I'm always up for a conversation, so what the hell; I take a seat opposite of him.

– I haven't seen you for a while. Where've you been hiding? – he asks.

– Well Eugene, I've been far away. On another continent.

– I heard you won the tourist trap contest, – he laughs. – So, where'd you go?

I'm just getting back from Brazil, – I state.

– Jesus, what did you go there for?

– A change of pace – I reply as I lick the salt off my fist, down the shot of tequila, followed with biting into a slice of lime.

– Did you find it?

I gulp down some beer and tell him– yes, Rio de Janeiro is about as different as it gets from high desert and mountains.

– Does Brazil have any Indians?" Eugene asks.

– Yes, but most have intermarried with other cultures and produced a vastly different human landscape than we have here in the Southwest. In America, the European colonizers brought their wives and even their families with them. Very few of them married the indigenous peoples who already lived here. In Brazil, the

Portuguese and others arrived without wives or families and married the local Indians, thereby producing a mixed ethnicity. You wouldn't believe the variety of people there.

– You white people came to America to take what we Indians had. – He states. I knew where he was going with this. He always does. – Here, the whites only wanted our land. We weren't welcome in their families. Apparently, in Brazil, the whites wanted the land and the women. In Brazil, the Indians were literally getting fucked. – He laughs.

– Well Eugene, life has never been fair. It's always been a game of survival. The strong win. I didn't make the rules and I don't agree with them. But, the arrival of the Europeans was not the beginning, but more like the end of a long drama.

– What the hell are you talking about? – he demands.

– Since when does it take an invitation for family to unite after a long absence? – I reply.

– Family? Your ancestors have nothing in common with us! What drama are you talking about? Some damn comedy that you whites have written to justify your invasion? Christ!

I'm not sure if I really want to take this on right now, but I decide to give it a go. – Well partner, while I was in Brazil, I spoke with several people about the arrival of Europeans to their shores. I also spoke with some new friends from Mexico who were also visiting Rio de Janeiro. Their outlook is different. Care to hear another viewpoint?

– Have at it! Rave on Lilly. You always do.

– OK – I begin. – Studies show that humans on this planet come from an original mother in sub-Saharan Africa. They lived a nomadic life on the African plains for several million years. For some reason, around 50,000 to 60,000 years ago, they started slowly migrating north. When they reached the Middle East, some of them went west to Europe and the Atlantic Ocean where they could go no further.

– Others went east, across Asia. Around 20,000 years ago, this group reached Alaska. As they crossed over the isthmus that separated Asia and Alaska, they became the first immigrants to North America. Of course, they weren't aware of it. Their children were the first Native Americans. Then, about 15,000 years ago, the ice that covered most of the earth started to melt. Sea levels rose, and the land bridge between Asia and Alaska was submerged, leaving them isolated from the rest of the world.

I continued. – These first American colonizers followed the coastlines of the Pacific and the Gulf of Mexico. Eventually they inhabited most of the American continents. The geographical isolation of the different tribes brought about new languages. One of these was the Ute language that some of your tribe still speak.

– Yeah, before the whites forced us off our land and split our families and tribes into three different reservations here in Colorado and Utah." Eugene asserted.

– Can I finish? – I ask.

– Go on, but you're not telling me much I don't already know. Those are facts for you. My existence is not based on the same realities as yours.

– Granted...

– Go on...

– One day, an interesting thing happened. Some large wooden boats pulled up beside a beach in South America. It was the year 1500. Contrary to popular belief, nobody supplicated themselves on a beach before the Europeans. The Indians went out in canoes to check out the new arrivals. The Portuguese weren't about to disembark without permission from the superior-in-numbers indigenous peoples who lined the beach with thousands of bows and poison arrows. The Indians climbed onto the ships to evaluate the new arrivals. At that moment, the same as in North America in 1492, a long-separated family of humankind looked into each other's eyes for the first time in 15,000 years or so.

– And then you started taking everything.

– True, but the Utes also took from others.

– Yes – Eugene says. – Ute raiding parties were possibly the reason the Anasazi Indians left the mesa tops and built fortified cities in Canyon Caves. We also attacked New Mexico towns and Pueblos to get horses. Still, it was you guys that brought about the near ruin of our peoples. Just look what liquor and disease did to us.

– OK Eugene. What about the millions of people that died and continue to die from the effects of tobacco? I've never heard anyone say the whites, blacks, yellows and others of this world should blame Indians for their choice to smoke tobacco.

– You tell a good tale, Lilly. Life isn't fair.

– Don't get me wrong Eugene. I don't deny the inherent unfairness of human history. I find your tribe's survival against oppressors impressive. Chief Ouray, Chief Ignacio and Buckskin Charlie were as good as any leaders in the history of the world. You know from previous conversations that I'm a person without allegiances. I'm like a shaman that has gone insane and my tribe has left me to my own devises.

– Yes, – he mutters. – And you like it that way.

I finish my fourth shot of tequila, down the last of the Coors and take my leave. I drive across the mesa tops and out onto enchanted point. Home! I unlock the chain and put the pickup in four-wheel drive. Nobody has been here but the deer and other critters.

26
Chucho and Zully

– Hijole! Can you believe this Zully? – Chucho asks, more to himself than to his new wife. – We're leaving today, but I don't like the idea of slipping out the back door on our own honeymoon. – He tosses clothes haphazardly into the suitcases on the bed.

– It's OK Chucho. We have lost nothing. We are together. Nothing is ever going to take you from me. We have more than we need in our lives. – Zully calmly pulls Chucho away from the bed and kisses him. – Somebody is watching over us.

– Let's just hope it isn't the Rio cops. Come on Zully, help me with the packing.

– Why would they be looking for us?

– Zully! There were other cars that stopped behind us, remember? Who knows if they took down our license plate? The sooner we're on the flight back to Mexico, the better I'm going to feel.

They leave the Hotel, return the rental car and leave Rio de Janeiro without problem. Their connecting flight from Mexico City to Oaxaca City leaves on time.

*****

When they descend the stairs from the plane in Oaxaca, Chucho's uncle is there to greet them.

– Hola Chucho! Hola Zully! How was the flight home?

– Long. It's good to be home. – Chucho states. – Everything the same here?

– Everything's the same as when you left.

– That's good to hear. Tío Henrique, were you able to get the new bedroom arranged in our apartment?

– We've some surprises for the two of you. – he replies.

– I'm not sure we're up for more surprises at the moment tío.

– More surprises? – Henrique asks.

– I'll explain later. The end of our trip was not quite what we had in mind.

– Anything I should worry about?

– No. All's well now.

As they cross the parking lot, Chucho's gaze drifts over to the surrounding mountains. He hears his own silent voice tell him that this is where life is. The dry and dusty mountains in the distant landscape reach inside of him and draw him up into their clear, cool heights. The parched air fills his lungs with familiarity.

– Tío, it's good to see you!

Henrique stops beside a VW Beetle that has seen better days. He turns to Chucho and hands him some keys.

– It's yours. The whole family pitched in. We want you to start your new life with some wheels. You'll need it when the baby arrives.

Zully laughs and asks – what baby?

– The one that will eventually arrive – Henrique states with a toothy smile.

– Hijole tío! This is so cool! But, I don't have a driver's license!

– You know how to drive and you're back in Oaxaca. We'll deal with the license later. – Henrique gets into the backseat and motions for the others to climb in the front.

The VW bug lurches as Chucho eases the clutch out. He grinds the gears a little, but his grinning face reveals a happy newlywed. Zully puts her light olive-colored hand on his darker one, and the two of them go through the gears together. No past... just the present extending into an endless future. They take turns staring at the road ahead and into each other's eyes. As they pull up in front of Henrique's apartment house, the uncle speaks.

– What are you going to do here?

– The first thing I want to do is get some rest. Alone, with my wife.

–That's fine, but this is my home. – Henrique states with an odd smirk on his face.

– OK! What's going on here? – Chucho demands.

– Well, we figured you'd need a place to park your new car. Let's take a cruise up the road towards Monte Alban.

Zully turns and stares at Henrique. She says nothing. They drive out towards the ruins. Ten minutes later Henrique blurts out – Turn in here!

They find themselves in front of a small adobe house, in the same sad shape as the Volkswagen.

– It's yours. You don't have to pay rent anymore. – Henrique shouts.

The rest of the family comes streaming out of the simple hovel. – Surprise! – they yell in unison. When they go inside, they find only a small table with two chairs. In the corner hangs the Elvis Presley piñata. The house has two tiny bedrooms. One has a simple double bed with a straw mat as the mattress. In the other is a baby crib.

– We figured you'd need the piñata when the little one gets older. – Chucho's sister Chela adds.

They have brought tamales, tacos and guacamole to eat. Most sit outside under the shade of the lone mango tree. They all listen to the tales of Rio de Janeiro. Nothing is mentioned about the final night. The beer flows and the sense of a timeless family permeates the landscape.

– Our time in Rio was magic. – Zully says. – While there, we felt our love mix with the forces of that tropical land. I'm grateful for Chucho and couldn't be happier with your welcome and my new home. I feel like part of your family.

– You are! – Chela says with a laugh.

At sundown, Chucho's family bid the couple goodnight. A number of them have come to the city from San Pedro el Alto to welcome them back to Oaxaca. Zully extends an offer for them to stay the night, but they decline.

– This is your first night together in the new house. You need to become acquainted with it by yourselves. – declares Henrique. – You'll see plenty of us in the future. – The visitors head off for the city below.

The new home sits on several acres of land, bordered by enormous prickly pear cactus, arranged like fencing along the perimeter. They can hear sounds of music far in the distance, but there are no other houses visible.

– Let's walk around the place and see what we have. – states Zully as she walks to the area behind the house. It's crisscrossed by several low, cream-colored rock outcrops. The vegetation is sparse.

After circumnavigating the property, they sit down on one of the low stone walls that once formed a corral. The stars have taken control of the night sky. Oaxaca City sits a mile high, and the nights are crystal clear. They can make out the silhouettes of several Zapotec pyramids, above them, on the mesa rim. The ruins lie several miles away, at the end of a steep road. The road is full of tourists during the day, but now all traffic has ceased. The Milky Way hangs above, silently saying more in a few minutes than most people do in a lifetime.

– I love your family Chucho.

– They're impressed with you too. I wish some of your family could have been here today. You never mention them. In fact, you haven't spoken of them since our prenuptial talk at Yagul. Who is the oldest of your brothers?

– My sister is the oldest. At first, I thought that she was somehow going to keep us together. Later, she acted like the wise one who kept track of everything in the family.

– Zully, she was a victim of stupid parents, the same as you. Why would you expect her to hold your family together? How was she, a young person with wacked-out parents, going to do that?

– That's true. It wasn't right to expect her to fulfill that impossible role, but I did. I hear from her at times. She invites me to come visit her in Guanajuato, but she seldom visits me.

– Why would that bother you so much?

– I don't know. Foolish isn't it?

– Let's see if we can convince her to come down to Oaxaca.

– Good luck! She's a wonderful person, but her life is private.

– Just like yours Zully! My brother says that we all create our own worlds.

They lean against each other, each one immersed in the scene before them, both literally and figuratively. A shooting star dips below the horizon, just above the Palace at Monte Alban.

– Estoy feliz.

27
Yoko

I'm barely able to keep sleep at bay. I keep seeing the face of that motorcyclist, staring intently off into the nothing beyond the cliff. I sit on the couch and each time I start to drift off to sleep, he taps me on the shoulder and I awake.

– Don't touch me! I had nothing to do with any of this.

– At least let my family know that I'm dead.

– Leave me alone. Get out of here!

He leaves the hotel suite, neglecting to close the door behind him. Jerk!

My last hours spent with Lilly were strained. I was trying to control my anxiety and she was trying to convince me to let it go. Great! A Colorado redneck giving me advice. Worse still, I needed it. I'm not good at surprise realities. I was raised to plan for the future, limit the outside effects and adjust to the bumps in life. So, what the hell is a dead man doing in my hotel room? Worse still, Brazil has gone from dreamy escape to an Indiana Jones nightmare. I've to do something.

Through the open door, I hear voices. I go to the door and see a couple stroll down the hall arm in arm. It looks like Lilly, but where would she be going at this hour? I shut the door and sit on the floor. Call home lost one. When my mother answers, I manage to give her a happy greeting.

– Is everything all right? – She asks.

– Couldn't be better mom." I ask to speak with my father.

– OK, I'll put your father on.

Dad, in his eternal *I love you baby* voice, greets me with gentle concern.

– You OK baby?

– Yes dad, I'm fine.

...

– Yoko, what's wrong?

– Nothing dad, I...

– Yoko! Stop it! What's happened?

I think of excuses that would put him off for the moment. Then, I realize to whom I'm speaking and start to let the tears flow. – Dad, something bad has happened.

His voice remains calm. – Sit down and take a moment to get control Yoko. Are you hurt in any way?

– No dad, I'm fine. I was involved in an accident that left us all confused and worried. It involved somebody who I believe is dead, but we could not see anything in the dark coastline.

– Where are you and who are you with?

– Dad! listen! I'm alone. I think I need to come home. Everyone involved is leaving.

– Who was driving? Did the police come?

– I was a passenger in a taxi and we left before anyone came.

– What? You know better than to leave the scene of an accident. Where are you now?

– In my hotel. Dad, I'm not sure what to do now.

– Yoko, you're not alone. We're with you. I want you to do exactly as I say, OK?

– Sure dad. – I mumble while thinking that I shouldn't have called them. What is my father going to do thousands of miles away?

– Stay by the phone. Don't leave your room. I'll call within an hour, at the most. Do you understand?

– OK. I'll wait for your call.

I say goodbye and hang up. I hear somebody moving around in the bathroom. It's the guy from the accident.

– Can I take a shower? I've got blood all over me.

– Do what you want, but if you come out of there, I'm going to call the police.

I hear him laugh long and hard. Then the sound of the shower. Go ahead and clean up! You drove yourself into that black abyss. I felt remorse, but your treatment of me now makes me glad your sorry ass is dead. Listen you third world ghost... you thoughtless idiot. I repeat; you committed suicide. I had nothing to do with it.

– OK – he yells down the hall. – I'm out of here. But remember, I'll be back.

I see the bathroom light go out. When I enter, he's gone. There's only a small amount of blood slowly draining down the shower stall.

– Just stay away from me. – I whisper. – Leave me alone.

*****

The phone call wakes me from my nap on the sofa.
– Yeah dad, it's me. I was sleeping.
– Yoko, I've arranged a ticket for you to leave Rio in the morning. Arrange a wakeup call for six AM and have your bags ready. Take a taxi to the airport and you'll need to show your passport at the Pan American ticket counter. Your plane leaves at 9:00 AM. Don't miss it. If you do, call me immediately. Do you understand all of this?
– Yes dad. And. thanks. I love you.
– I know you do Yoko. Just get ready to leave and try to sleep as much as possible.
I hang up and hurriedly pack my stuff. I lie down on the bed, and wait a few minutes for the dead guy to appear, but he doesn't. I drift off to sleep.
The wakeup call brings me into a sunny day. I remember how beautiful Copacabana beach is at this hour, with the sun rising over the Atlantic. Why did this have to happen? Oh well! It's not Rio's fault. I'm not bitter with Brazil this morning. I won't throw away good memories.
I check out of the hotel. Forty minutes later, I'm entering the Galeão airport. Soon after takeoff, I look out of the plane's window at the white, green and blue of Rio de Janeiro down below. Damn, I like that place. Someday I'll go back.

*****

The green of the Willamette Valley never looked more verdant. As the plane touches down, the rain forms water trails across the window. My face is reflected and it looks like tears are streaming across my face at a crazy pace. But, I'm only crying inside. I'm so happy to be home. I'll never take the abundant Oregon rain for granted again. Let it rain!
Mom and dad are waiting for me as I walk off of the flight. I embrace them both at the same time. The rest of the airport and the world fade into the distance. I'm out of harm's way. My limitations are mine and they feel so much more familiar than when I left.

On the ride back to our house in Beaverton, I relate the final day in Brazil. My folks listen with a few questions, but mostly they let me talk. For some reason, it's a little embarrassing. I'm bringing so much more back home than I had imagined.

– I spoke with our attorney about the legal ramifications of this – my father states. – He's certain that your connection with the accident is not a cause for concern. You are innocent. Under American law, you're not required to report what another person's actions may or may not have brought about.

As we pull into our drive from Hall Street, I remember how much of my world is based on trees. Wood is an essential part of American reality, especially here in the Northwest. I recall how little of it is used in Brazil. Pine and oak. filberts and walnuts; they form the borders of my world. My mind roams off to the mangy coastal range with its massive trees, clear cuts, vineyards and rivers flowing to the Pacific. Life is good here.

Soon, I'm alone in my room. I think of Márcia and her family. The trip was good for me. I remember the friends I met and the trip to Liberdade. Tomorrow I'd let mom and dad know the positive side of my journey.

28
Agents

The two agents sat across from one another. One spoke with a Carioca accent from Rio de Janeiro, the other with a distinctive Bahian inflection. They were in the São Conrado police station, a fortified concrete box. The dark skinned Bahian wore well-tailored jeans, Nike tennis shoes and an upscale polo shirt. He was sweating profusely. The Carioca agent had blue eyes and light skin, dressed in a khaki uniform with a light jacket.

– We don't have much information about the incident. – the Rio agent says. – We were summoned to the scene of an accident out on the coastal literal. It was around 10:00 PM. We found a motorcycle that had tumble at least a hundred meters down a cliff. It came to rest a short distance above the surf line. At dawn the following day, a helicopter was dispatched from the Brazilian Air Force to search the ocean for any possible survivors.

– Survivors? You mean there was more than one person on the motorcycle?

– Actually, we don't know. The witness stated that there was only one person, but it was dark, and you know how faulty witness statements can be.

The Bahian agent smiles and replies – That's a fact. One man can remember with precision everything that happens in a split second, while another one who sees the same event will unconsciously fill in details that never occurred.

– Anyway, no bodies were found. We did find a backpack with identification that showed the motorcycle was registered to a Severino Silva de Soares. We traced the information to a small village in Bahia: Almadina. We sent his possessions to the military police in Itabuna. They found Severino's grandmother, who verified that the belongings were his.

– Is the case still open?

– Officially, yes. We don't close a case for at least 12 months. But, we have no body, and the only witness appears not to be involved, other than seeing the young man drive off the roadside. We found tire tracks, and it seems to be a simple case of a motorcyclist who lost control of his bike, and ended up drowning in the ocean.

– You say the information is based on one witness. Could you give me his name and address?

– Sure. – the agent walks over to a metal file cabinet and takes out a manila folder. – His name is Daniel Oliveira Sanz. Here's his address and phone number. – The agent hands the Bahian a piece of paper.

– Anything else you can remember that might help me get a lead on finding out what Severino was doing in Rio? His family would like to put this matter to a rest, but nobody can understand what he was doing here in Rio.

– Look, I'm working with you on this because you're a fellow detective. However, if you expect me to spend more time on the case, forget it. I've several dozen active cases that involve murderers, rapists and all forms of depravation that this monster of a city endlessly produces. You're on your own. And, remember, your jurisdiction doesn't include Rio.

– Yes, I'm aware of that. Thank you for all your help. If I do find anything new, I'll let you know.

The two men shake hands and the Bahian walks out into the sun. It's winter in Rio, but he's soaked in sweat. He grabs a taxi back to his hotel, where he calls Daniel.

– Alo? – Daniel answers.

– Mr. Oliveira Sanz?

– Yes. Who's speaking?

– I'm an agent investigating the disappearance of Severino Silva de Soares. Are you available to discuss the matter today?

Daniel's heart rate doubles and he searches for an excuse to put the matter off. – Today's not good for me.

– Tomorrow then?

– No! The truth is I can't remember much about the accident. I observed a man drive off the highway, nothing more. I only reported it because I thought somebody might be able to save his life. Apparently, that was not the case.

– Mr. Oliveira Sanz, we can make this a short conversation today, or I can do some background work on you. Please don't force me to use my position to pressure you. It could be quite unpleasant. We can speak informally, or I can get the São Conrado police chief to bring you in for a formal deposition. Make up your mind now. I haven't time to waste. I need to verify a couple of things, and then you can go on with your life.

Daniel feels gravity pulling him down, as it so often does.

– OK, let's talk today.

– How about right now? I can be at your place in thirty minutes.

Jesus Christ, Daniel thinks. But, what the hell! Just tell the same story as before.

– OK, I'll wait here for you.

The Bahian agent hangs up, leaves his hotel and flags down a taxi. He arrives at Daniel's condominium in Ipanema in less than fifteen minutes. He uses the intercom to page Daniel, who buzzes the door open. The Bahian goes up the six flights of stairs, asking himself why the Cariocas still haven't grasped the need to install more elevators. He's again soaked in sweat when Daniel opens the door.

– Come in. Have a seat.

The agent takes a seat on the couch and Daniel sits on a swivel rocker to his side.

– I want to get right to the point Daniel. Severino's family has hired me to find out what really happened that night... or, at least to find out why Severino was in Rio. They feel this whole affair is much more than an accident.

– I already told the police everything I know.

– If that's everything you know, then you're in for some extended trouble. I'm going to level with you Daniel. I'm working outside of the legal system. If need be, additional pressure will be applied. – He raises his shirt, revealing a 38 special in a shoulder holster.

– Look Mister. What is your name?

– That's none of your business. You are going to tell me what you really know, or you and I are going to take a trip to where Severino took his final swim, and you are going to join him.

– Wait a minute! I never thought things would get out of hand.

– What got out of hand? – He stands up and puts his hand on the pistol.

– OK, I'll tell you what I know about the stupid escapade. I met Severino during a visit to Ilhéus. He later came to me and asked for help with a stunt he was working on. I never asked why. I should have, but I didn't.

– Keep talking.

Daniel wasn't going to spill the beans.

– Severino wanted to scare some of his friends. At least, that's what I think his motive was. He planned to make them think he was killed when their car forced him off the road. Unfortunately, the trick went terribly wrong, and he was killed. I was there to give him a ride home. But, he never came back after the plunge into the dark waters.

– You say he had specific people in mind? Who were they? What could Severino hope to achieve with this stunt?

– I don't know. He didn't say.

– Daniel, I've no intention of playing games. I'm capable of eliminating clowns like you without giving it a second thought. Tell me what you know, while you still can.

Shit! Daniel thinks this is not going to end well.

– Look, I have one piece of information that I didn't give to the police. There were two cars involved. They both stopped. One was a taxi and it left before I could get any information. The other was a small sedan. I took down the license plate number.

– Well, give it to me! If you are hiding anything else, you'll regret it. If I return, you won't know what hit you. You'll simply drop like a brick one day on the sidewalk. You'll be dead before your neck snaps on the curb.

Daniel goes into his bedroom with the Bahian a few steps behind. He takes out a notebook and shows it to the agent, who tears a page out and puts it in his pocket.

The Bahian returns to his hotel and phones the agent in São Conrado. A half hour later, he has the information he needs. He goes to the Galeão Airport. At the Hertz rental counter, a woman greets him with a smile.

– Good afternoon. How can I be of service to you today?

– Good afternoon. I'm here on official police business. – He flashes a badge in a leather identification pouch.

– What's the problem officer? – the woman asks. Her demeanor has changed from cheerful to serious.

– We traced the license plates of a car involved in a crime to your agency. I'd appreciate it if you could check you records for this vehicle on this date.

He gives the rental agent a piece of paper with the information. She pulls out a ledger and opens to the date indicated.

– That vehicle was rented for a week, and was returned the morning after the date you specified. It was rented by a Jesús Mota de Suarez.

– Can you let me have his home address and phone number?

– Yes, but it's in Mexico.

The agent leaves the airport with a blank look on his face. – This is going to be more complicated than I had thought – he mumbles to himself.

29
Lilly

Remnants from the first atomic bomb and the Virgin of Guadalupe have watched over everything while Lilly was away. A Mexican woodcarving of the Virgin hangs in a hollow of a tree on one side of the road that Lilly built by hand. On the other side, a Mexican tin and glass box hold some radioactive trinitite rocks that she picked up at the site of the first atomic explosion, a four-hour drive to the south in New Mexico. Although Lilly leaves the place unguarded for months at times, nothing has ever disappeared.

The truck stops and Lilly hops out. There is no moon and a gazillion stars cover the night sky above. They provide enough light for her to open the door of the camper that is Lilly's home. She lifts the refrigerator out and enters. She takes a candle out of a drawer and lights it.

– The setup can wait until tomorrow. – she says to nobody.

Lilly climbs up on the elevated bed and slips in below the unzipped sleeping bag. In the distance, she can barely make out the muffled sound of the wellhead machinery. Before she left, this was a nuisance. Now, she welcomes its familiarity. The night air is dry and cool. She hears herself whisper something before she falls into a deep and welcome sleep.

– It's good to be home.

The call of a pinyon jay wakes her in the morning. Out the window, she sees the sun is shining above the scrub oak. The sunlight through the glass window is starting to heat her small abode. She drops to the floor and goes outside. The high and dry Colorado air awaken her physically and mentally. She wanders off to the west and urinates under an ancient juniper.

Then it's back to the camper to prepare coffee. She tries the radio and finds the batteries are still charged. An announcer is speaking in Navajo, with a few English phrases mixed in. KNDN: all Navajo, all the time.

– I'm back in my world.

Lilly pulls on jeans and a shirt, and heads out to the storage shed, hidden a few hundred yards away. She opens it, and lets it air out for a while, just in case some mice have left enough droppings to be inhaled and cause Hantavirus. As she waits, she sits on one of the rock ledges that are scattered everywhere on the mesa top. Thank God for the Chimney Rock formation she thinks, laughing within. She drinks the strong black coffee. When the mug is empty, she enters the shed and grabs a heavy bundle of long extension cords.

Over the next hour, Lilly activates the solar array, connects the various electrical components and sets up the shower tent and the dry toilet. Then she wanders down to the deck that overlooks the canyon. In the distance, highway 550 can barely be made out. She can see the cars, but they can't see her. The tarps she brought are strung up to keep the strong afternoon sun at bay. It's cool now, but that won't last long.

There is no phone service out here. She's used to being totally on her own. From the deck, she can see the top of the ladder that she made from some abandoned teepee poles. It's the starting point for one of the numerous trails she has built throughout the canyon. Lilly feels the urge to drop down into the canyon while the morning breezes and shadows cool the rocks below. Instead, she marches back up the winding path to connect the generator. In the heat of summer, she'll need the small air conditioner, and the solar system handles everything except the few hours of extreme heat in the late afternoon.

When everything has been connected and ready for occupancy, Lilly gets in the Pickup and drives the quarter mile to the wellhead, and continues on the gravel road for a mile to the county road. Another mile and she reaches the paved road that leads to Durango. Half an hour later, in Durango, she buys gas for the truck and the generator. Then it's off to the water station, where she pumps several hundred gallons of water into the tank she loaded in the bed of the truck before leaving the canyon. Each rain brings thousands of gallons of clean water to the canyon, but it's too far below to do her any good.

Lilly parks her rig on a side street and walks down Main Street. The tourist season is in full swing and the sidewalks are full of folks who have come to find the Wild West.

– You missed it by about eighty years – she mutters under her breath.

She harbors no animosity towards the hordes of visitors. Everyone is looking for something, and she hopes they find it. But, Lilly is looking for something rather easy to encounter: a cold beer. Durango has more than enough to go around. She heads into the El Ranch and orders a pint of beer and a hamburger with green chile.

– Haven't seen you for a while Lilly. Where you been hanging out? – the bartender asks.

– In tropical South America.

– Oh yeah! I forgot about your prize money. How'd it go?

– Super. Brazil's a trip, man! I'll bring some pictures in when I get them developed.

After a few pints, Lilly heads down to Kangaroo Express where she has a mail account. No mail is delivered in the canyon.

– Hi Lilly! Looking for your mail?

– Yep.

The woman at the counter hands Lilly a small bundle of mail. She takes it and goes to a counter where she starts tossing most of it into a trashcan.

– Somebody was in, and wanted to know if I could tell him how to get to your place. I told him that nobody knows exactly where you live.

– Thanks. The last thing I need is salespeople looking for me. Or, worse yet: bill collectors. Did he say what he wanted?

– No. Actually, he was a little strange.

– In what way?

– Well, he didn't want to say who he was or what he wanted. It's none of my business, but I frankly didn't think he was acting normal.

– What did he look like?

– He looked like a Mexican, but he had some other kind of accent, like from Europe or something.

– If he comes in again, try to get a phone number, OK?

– Sure thing Lilly!

Lilly gets in her truck and heads back towards the canyon. An hour later, she's pumping water into various barrels on the land that she uses for bathing, drinking and fire control. From above, a red-tailed hawk eyes this woman who chooses to live alone among the wildlife and pinyon-juniper woodlands. Her blond hair bounces as she weaves among the trees, doing the chores that accompany her odd existence.

*****

A few weeks later, Lilly passes the afternoon on the deck, writing her mystical poetry that nobody cares to read. A Turkey vulture silently circles on air currents in the canyon below, its wings reflecting the evening sun. At this hour, the angle of the sunlight turns any surface into golden mirrors: wings of raptors, human skin, clouds. She finishes a solitary barbeque on the deck. Winds blow softly from the west. At night, the cooler temperatures produce down-canyon currents. When the morning sun heats the ground, the up-canyon breezes begin. She likes to drop into the canyon during the sundown lull, when breezes disappear, sounds become muffled and time briefly stops.

An afternoon thunderstorm rolls in from the west. It fills the air with an electrical charge, leaving Lilly's golden hair floating at odd angles from her head. She's the link between the positively charged atmosphere and the negatively charged stone of the canyon.

'Stay low to the ground' she thinks as she descends the rimrock, and weaves her way between the hobgoblin stone formations. A familiar thought creeps into her mind. Why is she always so disconnected from almost everyone else on this planet? She loves to talk with others and is known for endless conversation. So, why this incessant need for existing within nature? Even before her days as a Denver hippy, she had enjoyed hiking into the Front Range and leaving everything behind, especially people.

The sound of her boots alternate between clomping on stone, and the muffled thumping of her footsteps as she crosses beds of accumulated pine needles. The canyon is an oddity of nature itself. Most canyons in the American West run from north to south. Here, the canyon runs east to west. This produces a reverse temperature incline. As the winter sun hangs low in the southern sky, the canyon's north-facing cliff receives very little sunshine during these cold months. This leads to extra accumulation of snow on this shaded side of the canyon. The snow provides more water than normal in the spring, and allows a forest of Ponderosa Pines and Doug firs to thrive at an elevation much lower than normal. Here, the high plains, the high desert and the lower mountain ecologies overlap, with an astounding mix of plants and wildlife.

She has left the mesa top a little late, and to avoid the darkening far side of the canyon, she turns east on Artisan Trail. Lilly built several miles of trails on this land. One runs across the rock border of the mesa top. Another skirts the streambed, weaving among the pools that provide much needed water for wildlife in this dry country. On the far side, a track leads below the larger pines and canyon rim. Others connect the mesa tops with lateral trails below. Artisan Trail skirts a rock wall that contains many niches and small grottos that Lilly has filled with items that she brought back from Mexico and Central America. As she approaches, she sees that several are already illuminated by the small solar operated lights. She is the only one who has ever walked this path. The illuminated Virgin of Guadalupe glows red within the cream-colored alcove in the sandstone wall. As she passes by, she mentally crosses herself.

– Buenas noches querida.

Lilly was raised catholic. Then came the Buddhist years. Now she's spiritually on her own. God is nature, and that's that.

The sun had already set when she reached Grammy's Grotto. This serene and tiny parkland of tall Ponderosa Pines and centuries of accumulated pine needles sits just below the mesa top. It's where Lilly encountered her long deceased grandmother one evening, just like this one.

All of a sudden, she hears something land on a nearby boulder. Her first thought is of the puma. A female puma hunts on the mesa top and passes through the canyon with regularity. Lilly has only seen it once. Generally, it leaves only tracks, sometimes accompanied by yearly offspring. As Lilly turns towards the sound, she hopes to see the cougar. Last time, she had barely glimpsed the animal. As soon as they saw each other, they both turned and ran. This time, she was going to look it in the eyes.

– Just sit down right there miss!

Christ on a cracker! Lilly was stunned. She has never encountered anybody on these trails. The man appears to be some sort of game ranger or something. He wears a khaki uniform. If he thinks he's going to be welcome on her land, he has another thought coming.

– Just who the hell are you, and what are you doing on my property? – Lilly shouts.

– I said sit down. – He places his hand on a holster on his hip. – I'm not here for games. If you wish to end your life right here and right now, just make one false move.

– Who are you? Show me some identification!

The stranger pulls out the pistol, points it at her and says – this is the only ID you're going to see. – He then turns and fires a round into a Ponderosa beside Lilly.

Lilly's mind starts racing wildly. She keeps a gun handy, but it's up in the camper. She studies the face of the intruder. He is calm: almost without expression.

She sits down on a sandstone ledge. – What do you want?

– Somebody important in my life has been murdered. I know you are involved. If you value your pathetic life out here on the rocks, you'd better cooperate with me.

– Mister, you're mistaken. I know nothing of any murder. I don't know who you're looking for, but I'm not the person you want. I live a simple life and leave others to themselves.

– Look Lilly, I already know more about you than anyone around here. You recently came back from a trip to Brazil. While down there, you were involved in the murder of a motorcyclist on a road near Rio de Janeiro.

Lilly is silenced by this revelation. How could he know about the accident? Who is he and how did he come to know where I am?

– You're going to fill me in on the details of the set up to kill the young man. I know you were working in unison with a woman from Oregon. I also know that you were paid or blackmailed into helping with the ambush on the highway. You're going to reveal your connection to the Brazilian military, or you'll meet the same fate you arranged for my friend. You'll die in this desolate wasteland.

– Look partner, I had nothing to do with that accident, other than being in the wrong place at the wrong time. As far as the woman in Oregon, I had just met her the night before. You're mistaken. There is no conspiracy. I'm sorry about your friend, but I was just a passenger in the taxi that hit him.

– Funny! Everyone has an excuse for their participation. Lilly, it's just a matter of time before I get all of the information. I promise you this; I'm going to eliminate anyone who doesn't cooperate. I'm not sure how a trip you won in a contest ended up being connected to a murder for hire, but I'm going to find out.

– How did you know about my trip? I have absolutely no idea of what you're talking about!

– Durango is a small town and a few drinks and a couple of meals go a long way towards getting information. I know about your family in Denver. I have no scruples. I also have little time. Tell me about the other woman: Yoko.

How would he know all of this? Lilly thinks. – I'm sure you know more about her than I do. Honestly, we only knew each other for a couple of days. Yoko had nothing to do with any conspiracy, I'm sure of that.

The thought that Yoko could have been involved in a murder plan and had manipulated Lilly in order to have an alibi started seeping into Lilly's consciousness. And, just who were those Mexicans? How is it that they ended up together on that dark highway? Could I have been involved in something illegal without knowing it?

– As I stated, those responsible are going to pay, one way or the other. Tell me exactly what happened that night.

Lilly relates the incident in minute detail. She has nothing to hide. As she speaks, she mentally tries to determine if, indeed, she could have been witness to a premeditated murder. She remembers the Chevrolet that was parked on the other side of the road. Was that coincidence?

The man takes notes while she talks. It's now dark and he's using a flashlight.

– I'm going to continue with this investigation. When I'm certain of your role in it, I'll return. For your sake, I hope you're telling me everything. If not, you'll be as dead as that pinyon tree behind you. Stay seated on that rock for thirty minutes. If I see you following, at any distance, I'll finish you off. Believe me, I'm a good shot.

Lilly watches the beam from the flashlight dance among the boulders and canyon walls. The man is obviously having problems finding a way to get back onto the mesa. 'Too bad I don't have a weapon. I would finish you off as easily as the puma kills the deer that get trapped by the same canyon rim,' she thinks. When the light disappears, Lilly backtracks to the deck. She knows the trail well and the starlight provides enough illumination. When she reaches the deck, she sits down and listens. Nothing. She grabs her flashlight from the camper and finds his footprints coming and going on the sandy road. She follows them up to the wellhead, where they stop at some car tracks in the dirt.

A shooting star draws her attention to the heavens. Now what?

30
Chucho

In the Zócalo, Chucho was drinking an espresso and conversing with several friends who also made their living by guiding tourists to the local ruins and villages. Having the Volkswagen had opened an entirely new set of opportunities for him. He could now provide services to the tourists who didn't have a vehicle or the money to rent one. Moreover, he could offer tours to the more inaccessible areas surrounding Oaxaca City.

– We hardly see you anymore Chucho. – states Manuel, one of the friends. – You only show up at night and always with gringos.

– My life has changed, and completely for the better – says Chucho. – My income has more than tripled. My home life couldn't be better. Zully is more than any man could want. God has smiled on me.

– Next thing you know, you are going to tell us that the baby is on the way.

Chucho laughs and adds – And why not? We're more than ready. Both of you have children. Would you give them up for anything?

– I'd let my wife go before my children – comments Lalo, the other man at the table. – They changed my life. Without them, I'd have long ago left Margarita. To remain with my kids, I stay with a woman I don't love.

– I find that hard to believe – Manuel states.

– I stay loyal to the family. I don't want to complicate or compromise my relationship with my children. After they leave home, we'll see what happens.

– So, Lalo, how is business going? – asks Chucho.

– Well, it's fairly steady. It pays the bills and I feel good about sharing our history and culture with most of the visitors. Some are assholes. They seem to think the pre-Columbian sites are some sort of Disney World created just for them.

Manuel smiles and asks him – Is there a difference between the reasons for constructing Monte Alban and those for building Disney World?

– What a dumb question!

–Really? – adds Manuel. – Disney World was created to attract people from near and far to participate in the American cultural experience. Admittedly, it's a fantasy world. Still, there are those who actually believe that the American culture is protecting and projecting a concept of God and truth.

– Interesting point Manuel. – Chucho says. – You really believe that both represent centers of spirituality?

– I'm not sure about spirituality. Disney World displays cutting edge technologies. Monte Alban did the same. Disney World displays a fantasy world that reflects the expectations and hopes of the Americans. I think Monte Alban did the same for the Zapotecs.

– Jesus Manuel! – Lalo spits out. – I can't believe you're comparing the bullshit American cartoon land with a sacred Zapotec city!

– I'm just throwing out ideas. It was a French couple that I was guiding through Mitla, who mentioned the comparison. At first, I thought they were insulting my ancestors. Later, I thought it over and I can see that the analogy works to a certain point.

– It figures that some Europeans would come up with some crap like that. They didn't build Disney World in Europe, so why would they say something so absurd?

At that moment, a man crosses the cobblestone road from the plaza and stops beside the table. In English, he asks if one of the men at the table is Chucho.

– That would be me. – responds Chucho. – How can I help you?

– I've been told you give tours.

– You heard right. What do you have in mind?

– I'm interested in visiting some of the smaller communities in the Sierra Madre between here and the coast. Is that something you could facilitate?

– That area is my homeland. How much time do you want to spend and what specifically are your interests?

– I want to do some short interviews and take photos for a class I teach in Latin American Culture. I only have one day for the project.

– We could visit Amatlán and Ozoltepec in one day, if we left at daybreak. When are you thinking of doing the trip?

– As soon as possible – the man adds. – What will it cost?

– I charge fifty dollars a day and you pay for all gasoline, food and drink.

– OK – the man answers. Would it be possible to go tomorrow?

– Wow! That's pushing it. I guess I could get everything together this afternoon. Where are you staying and what's your name?

– My name is Estefan and I'm staying at a small guesthouse near here. Any chance you could pick me up here, in front of this restaurant, at 6:00 AM?

– Do you have a phone number where you could be reached?

– No, but if you give me yours, I can call if any problem arises.

– Ha ha... I don't have one either. Let's just count on meeting here at six in the morning. Bring a jacket, as it gets cold up in the highlands.

– OK, I'll be here. Hasta luego.

– Oh, by the way, where are you from?

– I'm an American.

*****

They meet at the Zócalo the next morning at dawn. No stores or restaurants are open yet. Chucho has brought sweet rolls and coffee. The two men hold the swaying cups of coffee in front of them as the VW bug weaves through the narrow streets of colonial Oaxaca City. They leave the city behind and head up the Valley of Oaxaca. It is illuminated by the sun that peeks over the surrounding mountains. The ocotillo cactuses glow and the dessert birds shout and soar, looking for their breakfast among the flying insects that are also splattering their brains on our windshield.

The car passes through Ocotlan de Morelos and Miajuatlán before starting the steep climb up the hairpin curves that lead to the pine-covered highlands. The paved road ends abruptly. Chucho downshifts and says,

– Amatlán is about forty minutes from here and the road is twisting and steep all the way.

Estefan leans back into his seat and stares out the window at the passing pine trees.

– How long have you been running tours?

– For about five years.

– Where do most of your clients come from?

– Mostly, they're Europeans, but a few Americans contract me at times. – Chucho looks over at Estefan and says – You don't look American. What is your family background?

– My ancestors are South American. Have you ever been there?

– Actually, I just got back from a honeymoon in Rio de Janeiro.

– How did you like it?

– I loved it!

– O shit! – Estefan cries out. – I've to go to the bathroom right now!

Chucho is used to tourists who have bowel problems in Oaxaca. He wheels the VW off the road and parks in a narrow space between some towering pines.

– There's toilet paper in the glove box.

I've some in my backpack. – Estefan replies as he reaches for his small pack in the back seat. He pulls out a pistol, and points it at Chucho.

– Please take what you want, but don't shoot – Chucho begs. – I was just married and I'll give you anything you want.

– That's good, because there is something I need from you. Let's go for a walk.

They exit the VW and Estefan motions away from the road with his head.

– Walk slowly in front of me. Don't try anything or it'll be your last act on this earth.

After a few minutes of walking, he announces – Stop. Sit down.

Chucho obeys and asks – What can I possibly give you out here in the woods?

– Look, I know you were in Rio. I know about the accident with the motorcycle. You killed somebody very important to me. If you want to leave this forest alive, you'll tell me who paid you to kill him and why.

– Kill somebody? I have no idea who you are talking about!

– The one you ran off the road that night in Rio. Don't play games with me. – Estefan fires a round into the air above Chucho's head. – The next one will be between your eyes.

– For god's sake, I've no idea what you are talking about. Yes, there was an accident on the highway. Somebody on a motorcycle pulled in front of a taxi that I was following. When he left the highway, he clipped our rental car. We barely touched him. In fact, there wasn't enough damage for the rental agent to notice when she inspected it at the airport in Rio. I swear. I have no idea who was on that bike. I never saw the person before or after.

– Who was with you in the car?

– I was with my wife.

Estefan fires another round into the tree beside Chucho. – I'm not going to ask you more than once. Who was with you? Two other women were with you when you left the scene.

– That's right. There were two women. They were in the taxi ahead of us, but the taxi driver abandoned them beside the road. We had met them earlier in the day and gave them a ride to their hotel. I never saw them again.

– They were in the taxi that initially ran the motorcycle off the road?

– Yes... they were in the taxi that the motorcyclist barely missed. That's all I know. Your information is wrong. There was no conspiracy to harm anyone.

– You say you had just met the two women? If that's so, how do you know what they were up to, or not?

– OK, I don't know if something had been arranged or whatever. I can only say that my wife and I had absolutely nothing to do with any plan. I find it hard to believe that anybody was out to get the motorcyclist.

– What are the names of the two women?

– One was called Lilly and the other Yoko.

– I'm going to give you one chance to set yourself free Chucho. Don't fuck with me. I need to know where I can contact Yoko and Lilly.

– They live in the United States. I haven't heard from them since that night.

– Do you have their addresses or phone numbers? If so, you have your ticket out of this mess. That is... for now. If I find anything that contradicts what you have told me, I'll be back. If I need to return, you'll not be the only one who'll be paying the price. Your wife, Zully, will also be on the list.

– How do you know her name?

– That's none of your business. Do you have the information or not?

Chucho feels the world starting to sway in front of him. He has no doubt about the conviction of Estefan. He thinks of Zully and decides the best thing to do is to cooperate.

– If I give you the information, will you just leave us alone?

– As long as it checks out, you'll not see me again. But, I'll be verifying the addresses before I leave Oaxaca. If you go to the police, I have others here in Oaxaca who will deal with you and that pretty lady waiting for you in that shack you call home.

– OK, but I don't have the information with me. It's at my house.

– Let's get going then.

They return to the car and drive to Chucho's house.

– Remember, I have a gun. Don't try anything stupid.

They enter the house and Zully asks,

– What are you doing home already? I thought you guys would be gone all day.

– Zully, this is a client of mine. Would you get him a glass of water? We need to exchange some information. He has an emergency at home.

Zully heads off to the kitchen and Chucho pulls out his address book and gives Estefan the phone numbers of Yoko and Lilly.

– Do you know their last names?

– No. We're not really friends, especially after the incident in Rio. We were supposedly going to call each other, but I think we were all too traumatized for that.

Zully returns with the water and Estefan drinks it.

– Well, it was nice while it lasted. – says Estefan. Zully extends her hand and he shakes it. – Adios!

Chucho and Estefan leave the house and drive into town. They stop beside the Zócalo.

– Remember our agreement Chucho. If you contact the police there will be hell to pay.

Estefan exits the car, and is quickly absorbed into the daytime mob of tourists and businessmen around the plaza.

31
Yoko

Yoko's parent's home on Hall Street in Beaverton resembles most others on the block. It's built of wood, with rock accents. Her mother and father are returning from a visit to the Saturday Market in downtown Portland.

– I can't believe you paid that much for this tiny bonsai plant. – Yoko's mother complains. – It just isn't worth fifty dollars!

– What is worth fifty dollars at our age dear? – her husband asks.

– What is that supposed to mean?

– I've worked for over thirty years. I've raised my children, paid off our house and have no outstanding bills. Why shouldn't I be able to spend a couple of bucks on whatever I want?

– You know we're not going to be able to bring in an income forever. I just think the money could be better used by putting it into retirement.

– I can enjoy the bonsai now, who knows if I'll live long enough to retire.

They pull into the driveway and the garage door opens. They park and enter the house. The mother goes upstairs to bathe and change into her nightgown. Yoko's father takes the bonsai into the kitchen, sets it on the table and sits down to admire it.

– There's more beauty in this plant than fifty dollars in the bank.

– I agree.

Yoko's father is startled by the voice from behind him. He turns to find a man in a beige suit with a bright red tie.

– Relax fellow! You don't want to upset your wife, as that could bring unpleasant circumstances for all of us.

The father calmly replies – What is your purpose here?

– My purpose is to get some information. I'm here to speak with Yoko, your daughter.

– She doesn't live here.

– Where does she live?

– What do you want from my daughter?

The man sits down across the kitchen table from the father. As he does so, he quietly lifts a flap of his suit to reveal the holstered gun.

– You won't need that. Neither I, nor my wife, will give you any resistance. Just what is this about?

– Your daughter has recently returned from Brazil. Am I right?

– I assume you wouldn't have asked such a specific question if you didn't already know the answer. Yes, she was in Brazil.

– Yoko is involved in a scheme to kill a Brazilian friend of mine. I'm here to find the reason for his death. I need information that only she has.

– You're mistaken sir. Our daughter has been raised properly. It's virtually impossible that she's involved in any plot to kill anybody.

– I'd like to believe you. Everything I've found out about you leads me to believe you are an honest man. Unfortunately, that may not be the case with Yoko. She was at the scene of a murder. Are you telling me that she didn't mention anything?

– Look mister, I'm aware of the accident that occurred in Rio. Yoko revealed all of that to us. In fact, we related the whole incident to our attorney. He assures us that she was, in no way, legally responsible for anything other than not reporting an accident that she didn't cause. She'll not be returning to Brazil and the matter is closed as far as we are concerned.

– Not as far as I'm concerned. I'm here for facts and retribution. I want to speak to Yoko. When will she be home?

– Yoko doesn't live here anymore.

– I'm aware she teaches in another city. I need to know where. I need her address.

– Well sir, you won't get it from me. You can do what you want, but I'll not help you. You should go to the police if you think there is some link between my daughter and some supposed murder plot. Your mannerisms are not those of a common criminal. What is it you're really after?

– The truth. And, I'm going to get it one way or the other.

– If you are threatening me with physical violence, it will do you no good. I will not give you any information about Yoko, other than to repeat; she's not guilty of what you are implying.

– Look. Your wife is upstairs. She might not be quite so brave about keeping silent.

– I wouldn't sell her short. She's one tough woman and she loves Yoko as much as I do. Why don't you just let the police in Brazil do the investigation?

– You apparently don't know much about Brazilian police investigations. I tell you what. I know you and your wife are innocent in all of this. Nevertheless, I'm going to speak with Yoko. You can count on that. She's not as innocent as you seem to believe. If you love your daughter, convince her to tell me the truth. It's only a matter of time before I find where she's located.

With that, the man stands up. Yoko's father does the same.

– Remain seated for twenty minutes after I leave.

The father sits down again.

– OK, you'll have your twenty minutes. Just, don't return.

– I'll be back if the situation requires it. Hopefully, I'll not need to bother you again. That depends on Yoko.

The man nonchalantly walks out of the kitchen, out the front door, and down the block.

Yoko's mother descends the stairs and asks – Who were you talking to? – She then sees her husband's face. – What's wrong? What happened?

– Sit down for a couple of minutes. Something has come up.

He explains the encounter with the stranger.

– For God's sake, let's call the police! – she insists.

– Not yet! We need to speak with Yoko first.

*****

When Yoko answers the call, she knows immediately that something is wrong in Portland. Her father details the visit. She denies any connection with a crime. Her father wants to know if there could have been any ulterior motive behind the accident.

– Dad! It was just a freak accident. The people I was with were just tourists like me.

– Yoko, I want you to come home this weekend. I've hired a private detective. This is not the time to bring in the police. I will explain more when we speak in person. Can you be here on Friday night?

    – OK dad! I'm sorry you've been brought into this crazy situation. I have no idea what this whole thing is all about.

    – Don't worry about it now, baby. We'll get to the bottom of it together.

    – I love you dad.

    – We love you too. When we know more, we can take action to confront the matter. We'll see you in a couple of days.

    Yoko hangs up. She stares at the sandwich she made before the call. She had been hungry, but it now had no flavor.

    Yoko walks into the bathroom. When she washes her hands, the water swirls blood red around the basin.

    – I told you to stay away from me!

32
Lilly

Lilly wakes up with the cold Colorado morning surrounding her. It's early and she hasn't slept much. She grabs a cassette and plays her personal anthem, *Hang Fire* by the Rolling Stones. The beat starts her feet moving. Money never means much to Lilly, but the underlying pulse of life certainly does.

– That son of a bitch! I should go into Durango and report this.

She doesn't. What could she tell them? She had no idea of who that guy is, or why he was after her. The last thing she needed was somebody from the county snooping around her place. She kept the place clean: no trash, sewage or anything else accumulated there. She was adamant in her belief that the place belonged more to nature than to her. Lilly didn't pay much attention to local ordinances that control the manner in which land can be occupied. For that matter, she held no fondness for government in general. Lilly the anarchist. She paid the taxes. That's enough.

Lilly often speaks aloud when alone at the canyon.

– I'm not afraid of him. I'm not ready to die, but I'm not afraid of death either. I'm a part of forever. You can kill part of nature, but you can't kill nature. Humans! They'll never get it right. The sooner we evolve into something else, the better.

She decides it would be better to leave the canyon for a while. She grabs her pack, tosses some other gear into the pickup and drives through Durango, heading towards Telluride. She worked seasonally for the Uncompahgre National Forest for years. Her job was trail construction and maintenance and she knows many places to get away from everyone. A few hours later, Lilly turns off at the road to Ophir. A few miles further, she puts the truck in four-wheel drive and takes an old mining road that ends just below timberline, and not far from the continental divide. She sets up camp in a few minutes. Much of her life has been spent outside. In the high mountain air, far from the canyon, she feels the stress of the recent events lighten a little.

She hikes a short distance and sits down on a blue spruce log. She peers into a small, fast flowing and snow-fed brook. Sunlight shimmers on the aspen leaves that line the bottom of it.

– My life is like this stream. I am iridescent. I won't let anybody take the light out of my life.

After two days in the high elevation, away from the human world, she decides to seek a friend's opinion.

She breaks camp and returns to the canyon. There, she loads the camper onto her pickup. Hopefully, she won't need it. She has plans to stay with a friend until she figures out what her next moves will be.

The lizards are darting around as she takes a last look from the deck. A red-tailed hawk dips its wing and gives out a cry.

– Yep. I know it's sort of copping out, but I don't see you hanging around when the going's not so hot. I'll be back before your little ones take flight.

A cottontail crosses the path as she returns to the camper.

– What are you doing out at midday? Something got you spooked?

Lilly drives off, headed in her favorite direction: south. She crosses the state line into New Mexico, continues through Aztec, Cuba and Albuquerque. At Socorro, she turns west, winding up into the mountains. She's looking for her friend's place in Magdalena. As she enters the village, she stops at the only pay phone in town. Nobody answers, so she rings Audrey's father's house.

– Audrey?

...

–Yeah, I'm in Magdalena.

...

– Oh great! I was hoping to spend a few days at your place. Maybe a few weeks.

...

– Wow, that would be great! How do I get through the gate? Is it locked?

...

– Oh, OK. I really appreciate it. I guess we'll see each other when you get back. You know you're going to have to get up to Durango one of these days.

...
– That's true; it's a tourist trap. But, the canyon is another world. Anyway, I'll give you a ring in a few days. Give my best to your dad. Tell him he's my favorite crazy ole miner.

...
– That's for sure. Take care and thanks again. Bye.

Lilly hangs up the phone. She should have called from Socorro. She drives on through town and up towards South Baldy Peak. She turns into a dirt drive, stops to find the key under a rock and opens the gate. She parks beside an old adobe house. Once again, she starts thinking aloud.

– Audrey lives my other life.

Lilly loves adobe structures. She helped restore this tiny three-room casita, years ago. It dated from the late nineteenth century. The walls are almost two feet thick. As she enters, she notes the temperature inside is well below that outside. July in New Mexico is no joke. Inside, the adobe keeps things cool.

She returns to her truck and brings in some supplies, along with her cassette deck. Songs from Judy Collins fill the house. She looks out the window. Below the pine trees, she can make out the Plains of San Augustine in the distance.

– God! The light is so clear here.

That night, Lilly sits on the hardwood floor beside the adobe fireplace that's built into the corner of the small living room. The smell of burning pinyon and juniper logs fills the room. She ponders her options in the situation with the stranger on her land. She has never let anyone force her to do what she didn't want to do. Since leaving home at the age of seventeen, she's pretty much done things in her own way. At times, her stubbornness has cost her plenty.

Her marriage at a young age was disastrous. When it was over, she threw the baby out with the bathwater. Young and stupid. She knew that someday it would catch up with her and she would pay the price. Still, she always played the game as it was dealt. When it was her turn to deal, she often sat the hand out. Until she bought the canyon, her manner of dealing with almost everything was fight or flight. Generally, she chose to flee. She was over thirty years old before she learned that the easy path seldom leads anywhere one would want to be. From an early age, Lilly had learned to deal with extended periods of isolation. She accepted it, and loneliness was one of her most constant companions. It's the price of going one's own way.

This present threat was different. She doubted it would just go away. She thought about her options. It's sink or swim, she believes. She starts a conversation with the flames dancing on top of the logs.

– I'm not going to let a stranger decide my life for me.

Lilly keeps several weapons at the canyon and sometimes in the pickup. One of her favorites was a thirty-two caliber six-shooter that an old friend had given her. It wasn't the most effective in stopping a person in their tracks, but she was well practiced with it. She goes out to the truck and brings the pistol into the house, and returns to her position on the floor. The light from the fire falls on the leather of the holster, giving it a burnt orange glow. She takes the pistol out, opens the cylinder and ejects the shells.

– Hollow point, magnum. That should do fine for my purposes. At least it should in combination with the twelve-gauge shotgun.

When Lilly makes her mind up to do something, nothing can stop her. She's going to head back to Ignacio and live her life as always, but with one change. When she first moved onto the mesa, she had checked on solar powered security systems. It would require very little effort to put infrared sensors on the entry road. Anyone crossing the invisible line of light would trigger a buzzer that she could wear on her belt or just leave in the camper. The intruder at the canyon had entered by the road. If he returned, he would do the same.

– Let's see how he fares when the surprise is on the other foot.

All of a sudden, Lilly feels relieved. She remembers her grandmother's words. 'Always be true to yourself, especially when it's difficult. Stand up for yourself.'

– That bastard is going to regret ever learning my name.

In the morning, she's warmed by the New Mexican sun as she enters the Magnolia cafe in Magdalena.

– ¡Buenos Días mijita! ¿Cómo estás?

Lilly sees Audrey's mother in one of the booths and sits down beside her.

– When did you get into town?

– I pulled in late yesterday.

– You missed Audrey. She's in Albuquerque visiting her father.

– Yes, she told me about the trip. I should have given her a little more notice.

– How long are you in town for?

– I was planning on spending a week or two, but something's come up in Colorado. I'm heading back after breakfast.

– Must be something urgent. I've never seen you in such a hurry.

– It is. I left something unfinished. I should have dealt with it before coming down.

– Well, at least we can have breakfast together and you can tell me what's going on in that eccentric life of yours. Lilly, are you ever going to settle down and be like everyone else?

– Nobody wakes up one morning and says to herself, 'I think I'm going to be different than others.' I just ended up that way. I am settled down. It just doesn't seem that way to some folks.

33
Chucho

As Chucho and Zully pass through Miajuatlán, Chucho remembers driving this same route a few days earlier with the threatening stranger. After the gangster guy had left, he and Zully had talked throughout the night. They came to agreement on two things: they didn't believe that Lilly or Yoko was involved in any conspiracy, and it would be best if Zully stayed with Chucho's family in San Pedro de Alto for a while.

Chucho had tried to call Yoko, but when he dialed the number, a recording said that it was no longer in service. Yoko had said she was moving and that the number would be disconnected soon. Lilly didn't have a phone number and Chucho didn't want to wait another day for the post office to open. He would write when he got back to Oaxaca.

– You know, there's always the chance that Yoko or Lilly could shed some light on this whole thing. – he states as they start the endless curves that wind up to San Pedro de Alto.

– How are they going to do that? I can't believe you haven't called the police. This thing is way over our heads, Chucho.

He keeps his eyes on the ever-changing road. The VW kicks up a continuous cloud of dust. All vegetation for five yards from the highway is covered with a powdery layer of dirt.

– I've got a strong suspicion that fellow isn't going to be satisfied with phoning those two women. There's a certain air of desperation about him. Worse yet, Yoko's number is disconnected. He said he'd be back if the addresses didn't check out. How can he verify that from Mexico? We need to be prepared Zully.

– Do you think the taxi driver was in on a plan to kill that man on the motorcycle? – Zully asks.

– I don't know. The whole thing seems crazy now. Try as I may, I can't come up with a scenario of how that taxi driver could have purposely planned to run that motorcycle off the road.

Remember, Lilly and Yoko said they were running late when we returned to the parking lot in Recreo de Bandeirantes. It would have been impossible for anyone to know the exact time we'd arrive on that stretch of highway.

– Maybe he was looking for the motorcycle the whole time.

– How would he have known when and where the guy would drive by?

– I don't know Chucho, but we're the ones that knocked him over the edge.

– Only after the taxi swerved into the other lane! I thought it was to miss the motorcyclist, but I'm not so sure now. Why would he leave without a word?

– That would be normal in Mexico. We don't have insurance. What would you have done if you were in his shoes?

– OK Zully, maybe I'd have done the same thing. How do you explain the guy with the gun? He's convinced we're involved. Where's he from? His accent is different from the other Americans I've worked with.

– Chucho, I don't like the idea of being apart from you, especially knowing that he could come back to our house. Why don't you stay with me in San Pedro? That weirdo knows how to get a hold of you!

– We've been over this a dozen times! I have to work. We need money. Besides, I won't be alone. I'll be staying with my uncle. We'll be armed and ready.

– You said he's an expert. What good is being ready, if he simply shoots you from behind or something? Chucho, please go to the police.

– Sorry, that's not an option. Trust me Zully.

– Trust you? No problem. I don't trust him!

Both of them look out opposite windows of the VW beetle. Their uncertainty is palpable. A unique bond is being challenged. This marriage could end with death. How they handle the doubt and conflict could have lasting consequences.

– Chucho, I trust your judgment. I love you.

– I won't let you down. This will pass with time.

They enter the pine forests of the highlands. Several hours later, they arrive in San Pedro. Chucho's father is waiting for them in the small town plaza. The air here is cool.

– ¡Hola queridos! It's good to see you.

– It's always good to be back home, dad.

Chucho's father climbs into the back seat. They leave the mountainside town, drive a few hundred yards up one of the omnipresent dirt roads of Oaxaca and pull up to a stick and thatch house. Two of these structures and a large concrete barn make up the hacienda of Chucho's family.

This will be a place of refuge for Zully. Chucho remembers the first time he spoke with a Gringo. It was in this same shack. He was ten years old, and in the wee hours of dawn, an American couple had arrived at the door. Air, sound and light pass easily through these stick walls. The Americans had bought a ticket to San Pedro, thinking the town had a hotel that would be open when they arrived. However, there were none, at that time. They got off the bus and found themselves alone at three AM. The town was silent, dark and locked down. They wandered up the road and came to Chucho's home.

His mother spoke little Spanish; her native language is Zapotec. The gringos spoke very little Spanish. Still, the sight of the couple shivering in the dark night brought about a natural response in Chucho's mother. She opened up a thatch hut and gave them a couple of Oaxacan blankets. In the morning, she fed them. As they ate, Chucho learned his first words of English. Now, the same hut will be a temporary home for Zully.

Chucho spends several days with his family. There is something mystically nostalgic about the air, the light and the smell of pines in these highlands. Here, Chucho speaks his native Zapotec language. The simple and clean life in these mountains is forever etched into his *self*. Zully is treated like a long-lost daughter, who has returned home. She basks in the attention.

*****

A week later, as Chucho prepares to leave; Zully wraps her arms around him and says

– Chucho, why don't we live here and forget the rest of the world?

– I do live here baby. This is where my soul resides. We've joined our spirits together, and you're now a part of this place. My roots are here. I only leave on a series of journeys to the lowlands, like a tourist.

– Chucho... Stay with me please.

– Zully, you said you'd trust me on this.

– I do. But, it seems so safe here.

– That's good, and we'll spend part of our lives here. But for now, I have work to do. This is a place of poverty. Please don't make it any harder than it already is. I love you, and you know that.

– Cuídate Chucho! If I lose you, I've lost everything.

– Don't worry. Everything will be fine.

Chucho hops in the VW and is soon winding his way down the dusty highway. When he enters Oaxaca City, he's confident the stranger won't return.

34
Yoko

Yoko is leaving La Grande for the weekend in Portland. She packs her suitcase, locks her apartment and drives down Spring Street to I-84. On the last part of the trip, the interstate follows the Columbia River. The dry desert highlands drop down to the lush rainforests of Western Oregon. She turns off the interstate and follows the Columbia River Highway that twists through the forest above the giant river. Along the roadway, waterfalls tumble hundreds of feet off volcanic highlands that line the river gorge.

– I need a few moments to prepare myself for what awaits me at home. – she states emotionlessly to the windshield. – This life can't be mine.

She parks in the lot below Horsetail falls. It's a short hike to the falls. On the way, she stops beside a rhododendron plant. The flowers are a personal symbol of her life in Oregon. Looking beyond it, she sees the inverse V of the top of Mount Hood in the distance. She has missed the green of Portland. La Grande is in dry pine forestland. Where could she use the webbed fingers she'd grown in Portland?

– I'm coming home to a place I need to avoid. – she tells the rhododendron. – My life has gone to hell, along with that idiot on the motorcycle.

Yoko hikes to the thundering falls. Rainbows of mist are arranged like shrubbery around the cool, crystal-clear pool at the base of the falls. There aren't many people here today. She sits on a black volcanic rock where the mist engulfs her. It's a hot summer day, and it feels good. Yoko has visited the falls in this gorge many times in her life. As a child, her father would laugh when she spoke with the other thundering waterfalls in this canyon. He teased her that she could speak harshly and cruelly here without being scolded. Actually, she would deal with her deepest secrets and fears. It was liberating. Yoko isn't Christian. She believes we all carry a certain spark of spirituality within us, wherever we go. Below these falls, she felt it surface and illuminate her pale Japanese skin.

Looking up from the rock where she sits, she begins a conversation with her *self*.

– I've missed you. I've needed to talk, and there's nobody but dad to listen to me. As you know, he won't give me the down and dirty feedback that I need.

– Where've you been and what's the problem now? You only come to speak with me when you have troubles.

– That's not true! You know my most joyous thoughts and aspirations.

– You're here to talk about joy?

– I'm here because of a dilemma that seems to be spiraling out of control. You already know the details.

– Yes, it's a mess.

– Look, I need advice. There's a bloody ghoul hanging out in my bathroom. My parents are being threatened by somebody who wants to get to me. God knows why! If I don't get control of it and myself, I don't know what's going to happen. It could affect my job. My performance this first year as a teacher is important.

– Yep, you're screwed, if you don't get your act together.

– I wish I could talk to Lilly. She might be trying to call me. I had my number unlisted to avoid the hoodlum that visited my folks. I want to know if she has been visited by the man with the gun.

– What could she do?

– I'm not sure. Maybe she knows more about this mess than she let on in Brazil. She may be a tree hugger, but she's street smart.

– Lilly can't help you. You're on your own here, young lady.

– Don't call me young lady. I've left home.

– Oh really? Then why are you heading to your parent's house like a child that's fallen off her bike?

– I'm going there to help them! My misfortune has put them in a precarious position. We need to come up with a plan to deal with this problem.

– Why don't you do the right thing and assume responsibility for your own life? I mean, they're innocent in this matter. Why would you leave them holding the bag?

Yoko stops talking and looks deep in the pool in front of her. Fish swim on the bottom. They serenely whirl around each other, seemingly knowing where they are going and, at the same time, it's obvious that they have no idea where they're going. Just like Yoko and the human race.

– You're right. This is my problem and I have to protect the ones I love.

She stands and takes one last glance up at the bouncing wall of water that descends from the heavens above.

– Don't be a stranger. It's always good to chat with you, Yoko.

As Yoko leaves, she notices a couple watching her open conversation with nobody. They look away when she smiles at them. 'Who cares?' she thinks. She returns to the car and drives into Portland, across the Williamette River and to her parent's house in Beaverton.

Yoko's father greets her at the door. – Hi, baby! How was the drive?

– Just fine dad. It's a scorcher out there. I stopped off at Horsetail Falls.

– To talk with you invisible friend?

– Dad! Don't even go there.

Yoko's mom greets her and gives her a quick kiss. Her father takes her suitcase upstairs. When he returns, they all sit down at the dining room table. Her mother has prepared sandwiches, fruit and lemonade.

– How's the new job? – her mother asks.

– Mom! It's summer. I've only arranged my cubicle in the teacher's suite and met with the administration. I think it's going to be great. To be honest, I'm not thrilled with small town life, but I'm pleased with the situation overall.

They start to eat, and little is said during the meal. As they finish, Yoko's mom serves coffee.

– Well – the father begins, – let's get this whole thing out into the open. You know we had a visitor and that he was armed and threatening. Can you shed any light on this?

– Not really dad. I'm as surprised as you are. What happened? What did he want?

Her father gives a detailed account of the strange encounter.

– Obviously, there's some sort of misunderstanding going on here – Yoko injects. – I have no idea why anyone would think the accident was premeditated. Did he leave any way for me to get in contact with him?

Her mother blurts out – Get in contact with him? No way young lady!

– Mom, don't call me young lady! I've decided to get in touch with him. I want to get this whole thing resolved.

– Yes, but it involves us too – Yoko's father says. – He left no phone number or address.

– Did he tell you his name?

– No baby, nothing. He said he would be getting in contact with you.   I refused to give him any information about your whereabouts.

– Mom... dad. I want you to give him my phone number and address, if he returns. This is my problem. There's been some mistake, and I intend to get this sorted out.

– You could be looking for trouble Yoko.

– Dad, you said you hired a private detective. Did he come up with anything?

– So far, he has nothing. He checked for fingerprints in our home, but found nothing. His partner spends each night in a car down the street, in case the stranger returns.

– Dad, I don't want to bring in the police at this point. I can't lose this chance at a clean start in my career. If they get wind of a dangerous person stalking me, I'll not be allowed to start the school year. That sort of history would stay with me for a long time. Promise me you won't let this become public.

– OK Yoko.   However, the moment we get a chance to apprehend this thug; we'll do so. I expect the same from you in La Grande.

– Logical. Trust me. But remember, I want to meet with him. This is taking a toll on me and it has to end.

The discussion terminates.   Little more is said about the matter over the weekend. That night, Yoko looks out her window and sees the investigator parked down the street. 'At least mom and dad will be safe' she thinks. She spends as little time as possible in the bathroom. When she showers, she keeps her eyes closed.

– I'm not going to give you the opportunity to scare me anymore. – she mumbles to herself as she turns the water off.

On Monday morning, she bids her parents goodbye with a long-lasting hug. Something has changed in their relationship. Yoko isn't sure if it's for better or worse. Time will tell. Her father walks her out to the car. Her mother waits in the doorway, watching them.

– Dad, you know how much you mean to me. The distance between you and me is difficult at this moment. I don't intend to let this incident divide us.

– Baby, nothing is ever going to divide us. Einstein said it best; our separation from each other is an optical illusion of consciousness.

One last embrace and Yoko pulls out of the driveway. In the rear-view mirror, her parents wave goodbye. She doesn't say a word during the four-hour drive back to La Grande.

35
Severino

I wake up confused. But, I soon remember the recent events of my life. Just a month ago, I was finishing my first year as a teacher in Malhado. Everyone was happy with my work, but nobody was more pleased than I was. My future was helping others, while doing what I love.

Today, that's all history. Tomorrow won't be different. These few acres of land below the hot Brazilian sun are my future now. Somewhere down inside of me, I'm OK with this reality. I can't say why. After a quick breakfast of coffee and cheese rolls, I walk out of the hut and start to inspect the cocoa trees that occupy most of the land. They've overgrown the original orchard-like spacing and now haphazardly compete for nutrients in the soil. I gather several types of the cocoa pods. The pods are about the size of a cantaloupe, but have an elongated shape, like an American football. Inside, the cocoa beans are surrounded by a sweet white gelatinous substance.

I open one of the pods and taste the white "honey" that separates the cocoa beans. This is often strained, and cooked-down into a syrup that has no chocolate taste whatsoever.   It's used to make juice, and as a base for liquors that are produced by combining it with cachaça.

When the cocoa pods are harvested, the beans are placed on screens. The gel slowly drips through to waiting tanks and the beans go through a period of fermentation. It is during this fermentation process that the familiar chocolate smell emerges. Afterwards, the beans are spread in the sun to dry. This ritual has gone on in numerous small and large fazendas around here for more than four hundred years. When the beans reach a certain degree of dryness, they are taken to cocoa wholesalers in Ilhéus. A tiny percentage of them are refined into chocolate in Ilhéus, but the majority is shipped throughout the world, mostly to Europe and the United States. The boom and bust economic cycles in this part of Bahia has always been determined by the price that cocoa brings.

As I examine the fruits of this land, I notice an old man walking up the trail to my place. He appears to be around seventy years old, with white hair that accentuates his dark chocolate-colored skin. He moves at a slow pace and leans on a cane as he works his way up the trail. I watch as he approaches me. He says nothing and his gaze is more on the patch of road in front of him than on me. When he's only a yard or so away, he raises his head and our eyes meet.

–Bom dia filho! – He says in a soft, but steady voice. – Tudo bem?

– Tudo! – I reply.

– I've noticed you pass by my place several times. Do you know the owner of this property?

I try to imagine where he could live. I've seen no other houses on the main road, or along the trail that leads up to my place. What could he want? The last thing I need is a neighbor telling others that I'm living here.

– This place has been in my family's possession for many years. – I say, hoping that he will let it go at that.

– You're related to dona Nalva?

Oh no! That's exactly what I didn't want to hear. No way out of the truth now.

– Yes, she's my grandmother. I'm cleaning the place up a little for her. Do you know her well?

– In the past, I was her husband's best friend. Izidorio and dona Nalva raised five children on this spot before his heart attack. Dona Nalva moved into Almadina after that. She had nobody to help with the endless chores this place required. All but one of their children had moved away to Salvador, Rio and São Paulo. Zé Paulo, the one son that remained in Almadina, was a worthless drunk.

– He was my father.

– Oh! I'm sorry for putting it so bluntly, but he had a problem with cachaça and women. Eventually, he moved up here and tried to make a living. He died here, but I guess you already know that.

Suddenly I remember this old man standing in front of me. He often helped us with the cocoa harvest. I grab his shoulders and look him directly in the face. – Dinho! I hardly recognize you. Don't you know who I am?

He studies me with steady eyes. – Meu Deus! You're Severino aren't you? Christ, it's good to see you after so many years!

I feel relief, knowing who he is. My Vovó has maintained contact with him over the years and he's the most trusted of her friends. We embrace like family.

– Have you visited Zé Paulo's grave?

I search my memory, but can recall nothing about my father's death.

– Dinho, where is he buried?

– He's buried up by the high line of this fazenda.

– What? – My grandmother never mentioned his grave. I had visited my mother's grave in Almadina every year, but my father's last place on this earth was never mentioned. When I was younger, Vovó hadn't wanted to talk about it. In time, I had stopped asking. Life's secrets are discovered at unexpected moments.

– Can you show me the location Dinho?

– Let me rest a little, and we can go up there afterwards.

We sit below the cacau trees and both of us gaze off across the valley.

– He loved this land, you know? Unfortunately, he was a complete failure at farming. He would work like there was no tomorrow for up to a month at a time, but each time, he would end up letting the chores and harvests go to hell. He could drink more cachaça than any two men. What little money he managed to bring in, went out to pay for drink and women. I tried to help him... but, time and again, he fell back into his old ways.

– Vovó has told me about his problems. She said he was hopeless.

– Yes, but I tell you this Severino; your father was a good man. He grew to love this fazenda as much as your grandpa Izidorio did. There are people who are born only to dream. They just can't see that they're destined to failure. He believed, until the day he died, that he was going to turn out OK in the end.

– How did he die?

– Dona Nalva never told you? God in heaven! Well, he was trimming the cacau trees one afternoon with his machete. He had returned from a lunch that included plenty of cachaça. I was down in my house, eating lunch, when I heard him call my name. I knew immediately, from the tone of his voice, that something serious had happened. I ran out the door and up this road. I couldn't find him and didn't hear anything else. In his house, I saw that the machete wasn't in its place behind the door. I started searching, and found him a few minutes later. He apparently was running down the road to get to me. He lay face down. I saw he was missing his left hand. He had cleaved it cleanly off. I followed a trail of blood up to where he was working, and found his hand, still holding onto a branch in a cacau tree. We buried him the next day, below the same tree.

– Did you include his hand in the grave? – I ask as though it was important for some reason.

– Yes. We arranged cocoa pods around his body. He always said that he wanted to go out surrounded with cacau. He died doing what he most enjoyed.

We walk up the steep hillside, under the cacau forest. Dinho points out a cupuaçú tree, and pulls one of its fruits off for me to see. I'm quite familiar with it, but was unaware it grew on this land. Its unique and super-sweet fragrance immediately permeates my skin and clothes. I lay the cupuaçú pod on the ground.

– I'll leave it here, and pick it up on the way back – I tell Dinho.

As we continue on, the smell of cupuaçú continues to surround me like an invisible halo, from head to toe. A hundred yards further, Dinho stops. I see a weathered piece of wood hanging from an aged cacau tree. I can barely make out the fading words that are painted on it.

Zé Paulo
Loved by God and Mother

– I painted the marker. Your grandmother only came up here one time. She said she could talk with him better in the church in Almadina. I just thought something should mark his spot. – Dinho reaches out and touches a large branch in the scraggly tree. – This is the branch he was holding onto, when the end came. This old tree doesn't bear fruit anymore, and I'm surprised it's lived this long.

– It's lasted about as long as anyone's memory of him. – I add.

We stand on the ridge that delineates the upper edge of my new place. I look out across the valley. A series of grey and black rocky outcrops rise above undulating forest, with green pastures spreading out below on both sides of the Almada River. My father chose a good spot to spend eternity. I bid him goodbye, and we head back to the house.

When we reach the dirt road, Dinho gives me a departing pat on the shoulder. I tell him to visit me whenever he wished. – I plan to stay here awhile. I can't say exactly for how long.

– I'm willing to help you in any way I can filho. You can count on me. – he states.

– There is one thing that I need from you. I'm in dire need of privacy. Can I count on you not to let anyone, absolutely nobody, know that I'm here? Something has happened in my life and I need a few months of isolation.

Dinho laughs softly, and says to me as he turns to maneuver down the rutted tracks of the road, cane in hand.

– You sound like your father... Don't worry, nobody ever comes up here. I'll guard your secret. You'll be as alone as Zé Paulo was.

*****

That evening, beside the lantern that illuminated the shack on the hillside, Severino decided something. He wasn't only going to stay on this piece of land; he was going to turn it into his sanctuary. It would become what his father had wanted. Maybe his father had already found the spiritual aspect of the fazenda. Severino was going to turn this place into a land of cocoa again.

The problem of how to avoid detection still consumed his consciousness. Although he was sure that the authorities in Itabuna were no longer looking for him, Severino wanted to be alive again. As he lay on his back on the ground, he watched the stars above dissolve into his memories of the escapade in Rio.

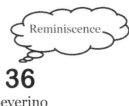

36

Severino

– Nothing like a little practice for perfection. The stunt had worked even better than I expected. I hardly got a scratch. Luck was with me; the bike landed just short of plunging into the ocean.

After the accident, I realized that I was lying on the ledge that a friend and I chose last week. I met Daniel last year in Bahia. He's a stunt director for Mundo Studios in Rio. We were introduced by a mutual friend, who attended the same university as I in Ilhéus. When Daniel visited Bahia, I'd given him a place to stay and he was willing to help with my plan. Better yet, he didn't ask why, although he did ask if whatever was fueling my desire to attempt the stunt was worth possibly losing my life.

The plan was straightforward. I'd ride my motorcycle in front of some unknowing driver, and then over the cliff, into the darkness of night. It was to appear as though I had missed the curve. We had scouted the cliffs for the perfect place. There were many possibilities, as the highway passed for miles along breathtaking drop-offs between Barra de Tijuca and São Conrado. What appears as a near vertical drop-off is actually a series of steeply sloping hillsides with intermittent rock shelves. At night, what stood out when looking down, was the white sea-spray from the waves slamming into the black basalt base far below.

Daniel made the first attempts. After observing him a couple of times, I felt up to the task. From the beginning, I found it much easier than I had expected. I practiced the maneuver more than a dozen times, many during nighttime. I'd bought a beat-up old bicycle, and Daniel loaned me a harness from his business with the studio. It fit like a lifejacket under my windbreaker. We attached a rope to it that had been dyed black, to avoid being seen. During the practice, I rode the bike around a curve and across the oncoming lane, and then sailed off the edge. I kicked the bicycle towards the ocean at the same time I felt the rope go taught. Immediately, I dropped like a stone onto the ledge about ten feet below the roadway. As I fell, the friction between the rope and the edge of the roadside slowed my drop. When I was safely on the ledge, I disconnected the rope and gave the all-clear signal: three tugs on the line. At that moment, Daniel quickly reeled it in. He was positioned in his car on the far side of the highway. If something went wrong, he was to act like a casual observer, and come to my aid. I soon perfected the technique, and felt confident that I was as ready as I was going to be.

– I'm up for it. I'm good to go! – I tell him confidently.

– Remember, it's going to be harder with the motorcycle. You have to make sure that you don't actually get hit by the car, – Daniel advises me.

I practice driving the cycle across the lanes and along the far shoulder of the road numerous times.

– I tell you I'm ready. All systems are go! – I state without a doubt in my mind.

The following night, I look out the window of Daniel's house in Ipanema. It is foggy.

– Let's do it man! – In a flash, I'm in the harness. Daniel grabs the car keys and we head out.

Once positioned, I sit on the motorcycle with its engine idling. I watch car after car come around that curve. Their headlights make it harder than I had thought it would be to see where the road ended and the drop-off began. Daniel had attached his end of the rope to his car and he was silently waiting beside it. A sound like a kitchen timer goes off in my brain. I accelerate... – Tchau!

I'm a little off on timing and the car catches the tail end of the bike sending me on a sideways trajectory. Then I see the second car. Shit! That's not part of the plan! It does little more than correct my angle of departure as I fly off into the darkened nothingness alongside the highway. I have a split second thought of Woody Woodpecker as he runs off a cliff, and realizes there's nothing below. I kick the cycle as far away from me as I can. Simultaneously, I feel the rope tighten, and I hit the rocky ledge with a thud. Not much pain. I hit the quick-release for the rope, give the three tugs and roll into the darkness of the cliff face.

I hear panicked screams from above. Later, Daniel shouts down that it's OK to come up. I walk down the ledge to a spot where it's easy to scamper up the slope to the road.

– Are you all right? – he asks.

– Yes, I'm great. What a thrill!

Daniel's face looks a little strained.

– Both of the cars drove off.

– Damn! – I respond. – Didn't anyone else stop?

– A number of them did, but when the taxi and the other car following it left, the others drove off too. Only those in the cars that clipped you knew what had happened.

– OK – I state. – Then you'll have to make the report to the police.

Daniel doesn't like this idea at all. He protests that he had plans for the night. I tell him that we'll have to repeat the whole thing if he doesn't follow through on this. He concedes, and flags down a passing car. He tells them there has been a fatal accident, and asks them to call the police from the first phone they come across on the highway. I climb up the incline on the far side of the road and hide in some shadows. The police arrive about a half an hour later. I watch as they take Daniel's report and flash their lights on the motorcycle on the rocks below. Eventually, Daniel drives away and I hike over the hillside to where he waits around the curve.

– They're going to send a helicopter to look for your body, – he laughingly says.

– Along with my identification in my backpack – I reply. – Perfect!

– Not really, – Daniel objects. – I didn't really want my name associated with this. There are no other witnesses, and you know how cops have a way of connecting whoever is convenient with a crime.

– This wasn't a crime. There are skid marks on the far side of the road and I saw the police measuring them. Did they try to tie you to the accident in any manner?

Daniel exhales and mumbles – No, not at all. Still, I would have preferred not being associated with this. Don't you think it's time to let me know what this is all about?

– Trust me. It's better that you don't know. – I reply.

We return to Ipanema and I buy dinner for us at an expensive restaurant across from the beach. We celebrate the act with cachaça, beer and Malbec wine. At dawn, we stumble to Daniel´s house, leaving his car at the restaurant.

That afternoon, Daniel drives me to the rodoviária and I buy a ticket to Ilhéus. I thank him for everything. On the ride back to

Bahia, I feel as though a weight is lifted off me. The police will find my identification papers, but not my body. They will notify my family of my death, and the authorities in Ilhéus will no longer have any reason to search for me. The thought of my grandmother receiving the bad news causes my upbeat mood to taper off. Surely, the police have been to speak with her. Then it hits me. Oh god! She's going to think I've killed somebody in the explosion at the university. She didn't do anything to deserve this. At least she won't have to suffer too long. After a decent interval, I'll be able to surface again.

I pay a moto-taxi to take me directly from Ilhéus to the bottom of the hill below the fazenda. It's good to be home. I walk up the path-like road, and see that nobody has been here in my absence.

37

Vovó

Years ago, when my husband and I were trying to start our family, the nearest neighbors, just downstream a little, fell ill with the influenza that was killing millions throughout the world. They died within a month. Their three sons were taken in by several families in the area. We decided to take one of them into our home. His name is Jorge. At the time, he was twelve years old and a great help in the cocoa harvest. His mother had taught him well. He could read and write as if he had attended one of those private schools in Itabuna. At night, he would read the bible for us, using the oil lamp that we had at that time. He even wrote poetry. My husband, Izidorio couldn't read or write and wasn't comfortable around intellectual folks. But, he enjoyed those poems as much as I did. Jorge's words could make things as simple as drying the cocoa beans in the tropical sun seem more important than the news that arrived from the outside world. Through his words, we found value in ourselves, and our lives in this remote corner of the planet.

Jorge was my first son. He was only seven years younger than I, but that didn't matter in the least. The link between us grew strong, as close as the bonds between me and the other children that I eventually brought into this world. I always knew that Jorge was destined to leave Almadina to participate in the outside world. Little did I realize that his outside world would be so distant, and so different. When our other children started to arrive, he grew anxious to move on, to try to use his intelligence to find a place in the outside world. He said he felt like something was waiting for him; he could feel the future talking to him. It wasn't speaking Portuguese.

Soon after he turned eighteen, he packed his few possessions and walked down the dirt road that connected our place with Almadina. I watched him turn around at the first bend in the road. He was smiling and waving to me below the almond trees that were like giant emerald embers, illuminated by the sunrise. He kept walking all the way to Coarací, Itabuna and far beyond. His first letter came a few weeks later. It said he had been hired on a freighter that brought cocoa from Brazil to Europe and the United States. He was leaving the next day. Three months later, another letter came. He was living in California. He decided to stay in that strange land. Over the years, he always wrote me. He went to college and married. After his divorce, he moved to Boise, Idaho. I'm not sure where that is, but he occasionally speaks to me by phone at my daughter's house in Itabuna. He speaks English and has been working as a detective for the state police for over twenty years. Although I've not seen him for forty years, he remains in my heart. He still sends poems and writings to me.

38
Severino and Vovó

A month has passed since Severino returned from Rio. He has been able to re-thatch the roof of his unassuming home. It isn't perfect, but it doesn't leak. He worked in the early morning to avoid the heat of day. He tied the green straw that he cut from the banks of the river into bundles and attached them to the wooden framework, copying the pattern of the ones he removed. He thought he remembered seeing his father do this same chore when he was young. Recently, Severino had been thinking of his father. These memories were limited to a few incidents when he was young. While pondering this incomplete relationship, he started filling in the blanks with histories that never happened, but might have, if things would have been different. It always ended with the same question; why was my father the way he was?

He spent his afternoons in the cacau orchard. He dug up dead tree stumps and removed some of the newer trees, in order to give the remaining ones room to grow and produce. It was slow work and would take months. The forgotten homestead returned, little by little, to resemble its heyday period when his grandparents, Vovó and Izidorio, had raised their family on this plot.

At night, Severino would take out his notebook. During the daytime, he would think of things he wanted to write down. He wasn't sure who might someday read it, and it didn't matter. He would sit with pencil in hand and try to force the words from his feelings onto the paper in front of him. Instead, he imagined words sliding across the dimly lit wall. They seemed to flow in rhythm with the sounds he could hear from the river nearby. He wanted to write what he felt inside, but the notebook remained without words.

Dinho often came to help. His companionship and skills were a godsend. Severino learned his father had fallen in love several times, after his mother's death.

– Severino, your father would fall completely in love with women that were only with him for the good times. Every time he brought them up here and tried to convince them to stay, they would leave him, sometimes without a word spoken. Each time, he would be drunk before the sun went down.

Severino was feeling more confident about not being discovered by the police from Itabuna. A few more weeks and he would contact Vovó.

Dinho bought supplies for Severino. This seemed to be working well, but in a small town, curiosity often provides the day's entertainment. For many years, Dinho had bought most of what he needed for his life from the same store in Almadina. He was well known and they allowed him to purchase whatever he wanted and pay for it when his monthly retirement money came in. It was this monthly accounting that brought attention to him. The owner was not worried about being paid, but noticed that the monthly amount had more than doubled.

–Dinho... did you get married or what? – he laughingly asks.

– Why in God's name would you ask that?

– I noticed your bill has skyrocketed.

– I'm stocking up. The last time I was sick, I almost starved to death before I got into town.

– OK. But, what are you doing with the new tools and construction supplies? You've waited a long time to start remodeling you home.

– Can't a fellow improve his place without somebody meddling into his affairs?

– Sure, but when I delivered those sacks of concrete last weekend, I saw you returning from the old Silva de Soares place. You were carrying a shovel.

– I was killing snakes. They keep working their way down to my place.

– OK. Who was that young man walking alongside of you?

– Look! The activities of my life are none of your business. I'm not a young man anymore. I sometimes hire help to maintain my house and the few cacau trees I still have. If you want to keep me as a customer, you'll stay out of my personal life.

– Relax. I was just curious.

As Dinho left the store, he noticed others were listening to the conversation and staring at him. He knows Almadina all too well.

Once a mystery appeared, there would be no end to speculation until somebody came up with an explanation. It wouldn't matter if it were true or not.

That afternoon, when Severino came down to pick up his supplies, Dinho told him what had occurred in town.

– I came up with excuses for the excess purchases, but I don't think he believed it. He apparently saw you walking down the road with me.

– This is going to be trouble. I'm going to have to do something to head it off. Dinho, can you go back into town and speak with Vovó? Remember, she thinks I'm dead.

– Whatever you wish, Severino. What do you want me to tell dona Nalva?

– Tell her that you have urgent news about me. Let her know that you have reason to believe I might still be alive. Bring her to your house as soon as possible. If she can't come immediately, then arrange a time when she can. With or without her, come back as soon as you can. I'll be waiting here in your house.

Dinho flags down the first bus that passes by. Severino sits in the shade behind Dinho's house. From there, he has a view of his fazenda extending to the horizon above. He mulls over possible actions. He could have Vovó tell everyone that she hired some workers to get the place ready to sell. She could report that squatters had taken over the land, but that would draw attention of others who might also want to occupy the place. He could simply leave, and move to some unnoticed town or city in the interior. The list of possibilities grows to the point that Severino decides to wait until he speaks with Vovó.

The more he thinks about seeing her again, the more his anxiety increases. What will she think? Will she forgive him for his selfish acts?

As those thoughts linger in Severino's mind, a taxi pulls up on the roadway below the house. He knew vovó was with Dinho; if not, he would have returned by bus. He watches the two slowly exit the taxi and help each other walk up the path to the house. Neither of them was getting any younger. Severino felt guilty for having put his welfare above the love of his aging grandmother. He felt the forces of love, gratitude and a pending reunion stir within him. He waits for them to enter and sit down. Dinho is looking around for him.

– OK, you've brought me all the way up here. Now what? It had better be good.

– Nalva, you know me better than to think I'd ask so much of you without a good reason. There's somebody here who wants to see you.

– Well, where is he?

At that moment, Severino walks through the door. He stops a few yards from his grandmother who is looking at him as though she has seen a ghost.

– It's me vovó.

She stares at him in disbelief. Severino quickly closes the gap between them and they meet in a bear hug that starts in silence and ends with both speaking at the same time.

– I missed you so much vovó. Forgive me for what I had to do.

– Thank God! He has brought you back to me!

They each take a step back and look at each other.

– This had better be good young man! I almost died of grief. For the love of God, tell me what this is all about.

– Sit down, and I'll fill you in on everything.

Severino details the entire Rio de Janeiro episode. Then he brings the history up to date by explaining the time he has spent up here on the fazenda.

– Jesus, Severino! Why didn't you just include me in the plan? As far as everyone knows, you're dead. I'm looking at my dearly departed grandson. If it weren't so damn pathetic, it would be funny.

– There's nothing funny about this situation vovó. Things have gone from bad, to worse. If it gets out that I'm still alive, I'll have to flee or face prosecution for something I didn't do.

– Severino. You have no idea of how mistaken you are. Now it's my turn to bring you up to date on what has happened in your absence.

She sits down on the couch and motions him to do the same.

– The last few days have changed my life, and it's going to change yours too. Dona Nalva calmly details the realities that would take Severino a while to absorb.

– First, you are no longer wanted for the deaths in the explosion at the university. It was determined shortly after your disappearance that the cause of the blast was accidental. The soldiers that died in the blast were searching for information on suspected subversives. As they tossed metal drawers from the file cabinets around the room, they cut a hose between a propane tank and a stove used to heat lunches for the staff. Nobody knows what ignited the gas. The case was closed and they notified me soon afterwards.

– I'm not wanted? – Severino felt his spirits soar. – Vovó! This is too good to believe. What a fool I've been! I can return to a normal life.

– It's not that easy Severino.

– Vovó, you don't understand. There was no victim in the Rio accident. It was all faked to convince the police in Itabuna to believe I was dead, so they'd no longer look for me.

– Severino, it's you who don't understand.

Severino sits quietly with a confused look on his face. Dona Nalva tells him she had contacted Jorge, his adopted brother in the United States and told him of her suspicions about Severino's disappearance. They both felt the disappearance was an assassination for Severino's participation in the bombing. Jorge had always wanted to do something for dona Nalva to repay her for taking him in when nobody else could. Unknown to her, he had taken it on himself to find the truth behind the death in Rio. A few days ago, he had phoned from America and revealed the series of investigations he had undertaken in Brazil, Mexico and the United States.

– Jorge went to Rio and those countries in search of your murderer Severino. He used his experience in criminal investigations to collect information on the people involved in your faked death. Severino, he went outside of the law on your account.

– I didn't use anyone else in the accident. The only other person involved was a friend of mine in Rio. Why did he go to those countries?

Dona Nalva repeats the information that Jorge had given her about the two women in the taxi, a certain Daniel in Rio and the Mexican couple.

– Did you tell him that I was no longer wanted?

– Yes, he now knows.

– How did he find those people? I have no idea who they are.

– It's his profession Severino. He felt it was his mission to find out. He did it for you and me.

– Vovó, we have to let him know that I'm alive.

– Yes, but it's not that simple querido.

– What do you mean?

– Severino! He used the threat of violence to attempt to force those innocent people to provide information they didn't have. He left them fearing for their lives from a stranger who was stalking them for unknown reasons. He wanted them to be living in terror of his return, in order to convince them to tell the truth. He now believes they're innocent. They were only witnesses to the accident in Rio. He returned to his job in Idaho after finding you were no longer wanted.

– Why did he do all of this? Nobody asked him to butt into our lives.

– I've already told you why. Severino, he is part of our lives. He was my first son. You have to take my word on his good intentions. Regardless of that, what happened; has happened. We need to think about what we're going to do now.

– There's nothing we can do vovó. We simply go back to our lives here in Bahia and hope for the best for the others.

– Severino, I didn't raise you to let others suffer innocently on your account. Do you really believe we can return to a normal life, knowing the consequences of your actions? I won't leave this life with the suffering of others on my conscience.

You're right vovó. This is entirely my fault. I've thought and acted only to save my skin. Instead, I've lost my dignity and self-worth.

– Querido, there's nothing lost that can't be found again. Sooner or later, everyone has something in their life that they never get over. We're going to think this thing through, and come up with a plan to make things right for ourselves and the others.

– OK. But for now, we have to contact Jorge and let him know I'm still alive. Do you have any way to get a hold of him?

– Yes, we can phone from your sister's house in Itabuna. Come home with me tonight. In the morning, we'll head into Itabuna and phone Jorge. It's going to be quite the shock for him.

– Welcome to the club! That sounds good vovó.

The two head into Almadina. Several other passengers on the bus want to know how he has returned from the dead.

– I was in an accident and had amnesia.

39
Almadina

– At least everything is out in the open. – Severino declares.

– Yes, but the damage remains. Four people's lives are still in limbo. You're going to have to make amends with them and set things right.

– Vovó, do you think Jorge could contact them again and explain the situation?

– Are you crazy? Severino, Jorge has an excellent chance of losing his job, and ending up being prosecuted. He has no intention of revealing who he is, much less returning to the scene of his crimes.

– Well, what do you suggest?

– You must take responsibility for your actions. None of the foreigners participated in anything wrong. They're victims of your poor decisions. You're a casualty of the eternally senseless politics of our country. But, you brought the others into this mess.

Severino and his grandmother had been going round and round with this topic ever since they spoke on the phone with Jorge in Idaho. Even though they had enjoyed hearing Jorge's voice, the conversation had left both of them with a foreboding feeling about the Mexicans and Americans who Jorge had harassed. They knew that the matter was not just going to go away.

– I feel like a new man vovó. The worst of this has passed. I want to start anew. To do so, I'm going to set this matter straight. I know what I'm going to do.

– What do you plan on doing?

– There's only one way to get this thing resolved. I'm going to reveal the truth to all of them. I'm going to visit personally with each of them.

– Have you gone nuts? How are you going to do that?

– I'm going to Mexico and America vovó. It's the only way to set things right.

– Ha ha... Severino – vovó laughs aloud. – You don't have enough money for a bus ride to Salvador, much less to another continent.

– That's true. But, I've something else: an idea that just might work. I'm going to ask all of Almadina to help me in this effort.

– What? OK, now I know you've lost your marbles.

Over the next few days, Severino comes up with a plan to have a town festival. He starts calling it the Festival of Redemption. Most everyone finds the idea absurd, and even embarrassing. Why would anyone want to help Severino go abroad on a harebrained adventure? He convinces the city government to decorate a plaza for the event. A friend of his grandmother has a nephew that's willing to print t-shirts with the motto:

FESTIVAL OF REDEMPTION
HELP SEND SEVERINO AWAY!

The event is to be held with only a week's notice. Everyone knows that it can't possibly produce enough money to get Severino further than São Paulo, but he insists the effort be made. Several cars are equipped with loudspeakers to blare out an announcement of the festival. They are sent to the surrounding villages, to Coarací and down the roads that border the many cacau fazendas around Almadina. Severino persuades the local churches to get involved. Within a couple of days, the entire region is talking about the young man who wants to fulfill his moral obligation by going on a mission of redemption abroad. Everyone finds the idea ridiculous, but momentum builds and when Saturday, the day of the event arrives, there are thousands of people packing the plaza and the surrounding streets.

Two stages have been set up, one on each end of the plaza. On one, forró music rings out over dancing citizens. On the other, Brazilian Popular Music is having the same effect on other revelers. The skies are blue. There are tables of food lining the sidewalks. They offer churrasco, farofa, fejoada, acarajé, beer and other items prepared by volunteers in the community.

People have come from as far away as Olivença and Itacaré. The t-shirts were given to the first fifty who arrived. It didn't matter; the entrance fee was a donation, if one wished. The glass box that received the donations had to be emptied several times.

The event went on until the sun came up over the tabletop mountain that towers over the town. The last song was sung, the last dance finished and the last stragglers departed with the morning songs of tropical birds in the background. All agreed; it had been the largest event of its kind that anyone in Almadina could recall. Many were already thinking that the town should have some sort of annual event.

Severino was the last to leave. Afterwards, he slept for four hours and then went to the city hall, where the proceeds from the festival had been kept. He was anxious to find out how much had been raised.

– You certainly surprised us all with this party Severino. – the mayor tells him when they're alone in his office. – I would never have dreamed you could have come up with so much money.

– How much did it bring in? – Severino asks his anxiety showing in his stern face.

– The festival brought in more than 100 cruzeiros! – the mayor announces. – Congratulations!

Although that's a lot of money in Almadina, Severino knows it will not be enough to buy the tickets to Oaxaca, Colorado and Oregon. And, that was only half of the expenses he would have to cover. He thanks the mayor, who agrees that the best place for the money would be in the local bank. The mayor will deposit it until Severino directs him to use it to purchase tickets.

Severino leaves without letting anyone know that the amount would not be sufficient. He projects a cheerful attitude and nobody guesses his true feelings. At home, he tells vovó of the shortfall.

– Still, it's an impressive start! We can have another event and raise the rest.

– No, that wouldn't be right. The community has already given far more than the cause deserves. I do not intend to become an ongoing beggar.

Over the next few days, the news of the shortfall spreads throughout Almadina. Everyone waited to see what Severino would do next. Severino also wondered what he would do next. He felt himself slipping into a sort of hibernation; he was alive, but not participating in the world.

Severino returned to his small fazenda to be alone. One day, word came. Vovó sent a message for him to come to her house immediately. He flagged a car down on the road, and went directly to vovó's house. There was a couple sitting on the couch. When they were introduced, he found the man was a wealthy American businessman and the woman had been born in Almadina. He didn't know her, however, as she had left for Europe at an early age. It seems that they had attended the festival and were impressed by the community spirit they witnessed.

– Severino, we'd like to donate to your cause. – the Bahian woman says. – We'd like to offer our help in your mission. We want you to stay with us when you arrive in the United States. After you rest up, you can continue your journey to Colorado and Oregon.

Severino is encouraged by this, but continues to think about the insufficient funds he collected. At that point, the husband pulls out an envelope and hands it to Severino. When he opens it, he finds a confusing series of airplane tickets.

– The first flight is from Salvador to Oaxaca, via Mexico City. Then, it's on to our place in Oklahoma. After that, you fly to Durango, Portland and then back to Salvador – the husband blurts out in English, with a big grin on his face. His wife quickly translates to the others.

– God has heard my prayers! – cries vovó.

Severino speaks to the couple. – I'm humbled by this. I'm not sure if it's correct to accept this, but I will. I'll make sure that everyone in Almadina knows of your kindness.

– No! The only thing we ask of you is that you don't let anyone know who has given you the money. – the woman says. – Please respect our privacy.

– Of course we will! – vovó adds. – no one will know.

The couple soon departs. Severino and his grandmother dance in joy around the living room. Before long, however, the reality of the logistics of the trip, the possible dangers and the sheer magnitude of what Severino was going to attempt brings a more somber tone to the household. As usual, word spread quickly through the town. Everyone knew what had happened and who had brought it about. If anyone had wanted to keep something a secret, Almadina was not the place for it.

40
Oaxaca

An afternoon storm is tossing thunderbolts in all directions as Severino's plane starts its descent to Mexico City's Benito Juarez airport. Lightning takes turns illuminating first one side of the jet's fuselage, and then the other. The tense expressions on the passengers' faces turn to an audible sigh of relief when it touches down safely. Severino has never seen a metropolis so large. Although curious, he's glad that he only has to meet a connecting flight connection here. Inside the terminal, he finds a small restaurant and tries to determine what he would like to eat. The problem is; he doesn't understand anything that's listed on the menu. Tacos, burritos, enchiladas? What could they be? When he asks for an explanation of the items, he quickly finds that Spanish is much more different than Portuguese than he had expected. He had thought that written Spanish was easy to decipher. Maybe so, but not when it comes to food items in the world's second oldest cuisine.

He orders huevos rancheros and when the plate arrives, he tries his best to eat only the eggs and tortillas. The salsa that comes on top is spicier than anything he has eaten in Bahia. 'This Mexico trip might be a little more challenging than I had imagined' he thinks. He tries to order a soda pop, but the Portuguese word for it doesn't work in Spanish. So, he settles for a *café com leite*, and is shocked when the waitress brings him a tall glass of hot milk with a jar of Nescafe alongside.

– What have I gotten myself into? – he asks an empty table in front of him.

The last leg of his journey to Oaxaca is through clear skies. Below, he has his first view of Mexico's high sierra, covered with massive pine forests. Mount Orizaba looms out to the right of the plane. Severino marvels at its snow covered peak. It's the first snow he's seen in his life. He tries to imagine what it must be like to walk in it. Does it have a smell? Is it wet? How do you make the snowballs he's seen in the American movies?

Oaxaca City's airport is small. The taxi ride to the city center goes through cactus covered sub-tropical scrubland. The driver tries to make small talk in Spanish, but Severino doesn't understand. When the driver tries his broken English, Severino realizes that his English major in the university in Bahia was going to come in handy in Mexico. English is spoken widely here, especially in the tourist and business areas. Severino informs the taxi driver that he's from Brazil, and shows him the name of his hotel from his reservation.

– No problemo Señor, that's right on the Zócalo.

'Whatever that is!' Severino thinks to himself.

The taxi parks near the point where traffic is not allowed to continue.

– We have to walk the last block. – he states. – cars aren't allowed on the Zócalo.

He grabs Severino's lone suitcase and the two walk below the cloisters of the buildings that surround the plaza. The taxi driver enters the Hotel Oaxaca and Severino follows. He sets the suitcase beside the check-in counter and tells the hotel clerk that Severino is visiting from Brazil and speaks Portuguese.

– I've never heard Portuguese – the woman behind the counter says.

*****

After taking a shower, Severino reviews his notes from the information that Jorge provided. Apparently, Jorge had encountered Chucho on this very plaza, not far from this hotel. The thought of actually approaching Chucho started to weigh heavy on his psyche. Had he really thought this through enough? He hadn't imagined Spanish would be so difficult to understand. He was glad the couple in Oklahoma had given him a toll free number he could call if he encountered problems.

Severino leaves the hotel and wades into the mass of tourists and locals who occupy most of the tables that fill the covered sidewalk areas around the plaza. He hears many languages being spoken and lots of laughter. In the kiosk at the center of the plaza, a band is playing marching music. Venders sell balloons and cotton candy. Children scurry around the fountains and all seems tranquil. After a stroll through the plaza, he walks around the entire circuit of sidewalk cafes, looking for somebody that might know where to find a certain tourist guide.

He decides it would be better to wait until the morning, go to the tourist office and inquire about informal guides. Just before he enters his hotel, he sees a trio of young men at a table that has a small triangular sign in the middle of it that states:

TOURIST INFORMATION
WE SPEAK ENGLISH!

He stops beside them. When they look at him, he states in English:

– Hello. I'm looking for a guide. Are any of you familiar with a person called Chucho?

They have trouble understanding him, but when he mentions the name, they all perk up and pay attention.

– He's a friend of ours. – says one of them. – What do you want to know about him?

– I need to get in contact with him. Can you help me?

– Sure. You need a guide, right?

– Yes.

– Where are you from?

– I'm from Brazil.

– I tell you what mister. Come with us to a payphone not far from here and we can give him a ring. Do you have any coins?

They pay their bill and get some change for the phone from the waiter.

– You're lucky you ran into us. – one says. – Chucho is one of the most popular guides in Oaxaca and can be hard to find.

The four men walk away from the plaza and down a darkened street. About the time that Severino starts to have doubts about the men's' intentions, two of them grab him from behind, twisting his arms so hard he thinks they're going to break or dislocate. The other man stands in front of him with a hateful expression.

– Look, take what you want! My wallet's in my back pocket.

– So, you want to talk to Chucho, eh? Well, start talking. – Chucho snarls as his spits the words into Severino's face. – I assume you're a friend of the asshole that left my wife and I terrorized a couple of weeks ago.

Severino utters a string of Bahian expressions. He can't believe that he has come across Chucho without even knowing it.

– Speak imbecile, or you're going to wish you had.

– OK. Wait a minute. My identification is in my wallet. Yes, I'm associated with the man that wrongly accosted you before. It was all a mistake and I'm here to make it right.

– Make it right? What kind of shit is that? – Chucho moves so close that both men can only see each other's eyes. – Just what kind of fool do you take me to be?

– My name is Severino. I was the one on the motorcycle that went over the edge of the highway on that night you were driving in Rio de Janeiro.

– So, now I'm talking to a dead man? Mister you'd better start making some sense. If not, you're going to end up in the slammer.

– I know it seems impossible, but I really am the one that was on the bike. It was a staged incident, done to fake my death.

– Sure, everyone fakes their death by driving over a cliff hundreds of feet above the surf crashing on rocks below. Listen you sorry excuse for a man, this is the last chance I'm going to give you to tell me who you are. Who sent you, and what is this all about?

– Please, take my wallet and see who I am. I know about the guy who threatened you before. It was all a mistake and I've come to explain the regrettable situation.

– Get his wallet and let me see it.

The two others keep their grip on Severino while one grabs the wallet and hands it to Chucho. Inside, Chucho finds a Brazilian driver's license with the name Severino Pindoba Jucá printed on it.

– I know this whole thing seems strange. If you'll let me, I can explain everything. I'm here to clarify and calm the fears that the other man caused you and your family.

– Who is the other man?

– I can't tell you his name. Please, let's go back to the plaza and I can explain everything. It's complicated and in a public place, we can both feel assured that neither is going to do anything violent or foolish.

Chucho thinks for a few seconds. He's not a violent man and this whole scene is leaving him uneasy. He's not going to do anything to Severino, other than maybe turning him in to the police. He asks his friends if they would mind staying with him while the man reveals what he has to say. They agree.

– If you try anything, and I mean anything, we're going to make sure you end up in a Oaxacan jail. Believe me; that's not a pretty place to be. With your lack of Spanish, you'll not get out anytime soon.

The four of them walk back to the Zócalo, with Chucho in front of Severino and the other two behind him. They sit down at the same table they had left a short time earlier.

– This may take a while. Can I buy you guys a drink or something?

Chucho orders a round of beers for them, but not for Severino. The Bahian starts the long explanation of the bizarre history that starts at the university in Ilhéus and ends at the Redemption Festival in Almadina. Every once in a while, Chucho asks specific questions. Severino talks for over half an hour.

– You can call the city hall in Almadina or the American couple in Oklahoma for verification.

– Waiter, bring another round, and give this guy one too. – Chucho tells the waiter. – Your name is Severino, right? OK Severino, I want you to allow us to go with you up to your room and look through your luggage. That should help substantiate your claims.

– Sure thing. No problem. Better yet, I'll stay down here and you can go up and search the suitcase and room without me. I want you to believe me, and I'm willing to trust you. – As he speaks, Severino hands the room key to Chucho.

Chucho takes the key, leaves both friends with Severino and goes up to the room alone. He searches the suitcase, the bathroom and everywhere else. He finds nothing, other than simple travel items. He returns to the others.

– Nothing there. Listen, Severino. I hope what you say is true, for your sake as well as mine. I'm going to verify your story with the city hall in Almadina. It will be interesting to see if the number you gave me is real. I won't just call the number. I'll go through the operator. I'll also call the gringos in America. I want you to stay in your hotel or this café until I return tomorrow morning. If you leave, I'll know that you are lying and I'll go to the authorities to make an official denunciation.

– Don't worry. The only reason I'm here is to set this matter to rest. I'll be awaiting your return.

– OK, we'll see you in the morning.

Chucho leaves with the other men. One of them invites him to go to his house for the night, just to be sure that the stranger doesn't try to find him.

– We have a phone you can use to make those calls.

They hop into the VW and drive the short distance through the old colonial city.

*****

The next morning, Chucho finds Severino drinking cappuccino at the cafe outside of the hotel.

– ¡Buenos días!

– Bom dia Chucho! Were you able to confirm what I told you last night?

– Yes. I still find it hard to accept, but there's no doubt that you're here with good intentions. It's too bad you didn't think of the consequences of your actions before causing so many people so much agony. Your unknown friend won't be forgiven. He should be locked up.

– Perhaps that's true – Severino responds. – However, he's also a casualty of my stupidity. He meant well, and did what he did for the love of my grandmother.

– Oh! Speaking of your grandmother, the mayor of Almadina wanted me to be sure to tell you that she sends her best and wants to remind you to call your sister.

– I called last night.

The two converse in English, sip cappuccino and watch the morning parade of tourists, indigenous families and businessmen pass between them and the plaza. They discover they have more in common than they would have imagined. They compare their rural roots. Both had come from backwater villages and both had moved to a nearby city to find employment. Both hold their bonds to family and nature in high regard.

– How'd you like to go up to Monte Alban with me?

– What's that?

Chucho laughs. – You're the only person on the Zócalo that doesn't know what Monte Alban is. I tell you what; let me surprise you.

The two men are soon heading up the steep drive to the Zapotec ruins. Severino spends hours roaming the ancient city. Chucho explains everything.

– It's funny speaking to you in English. You're Hispanic, but can't speak Spanish. I'm not used to using English with others who come from Hispanic America.

– Actually, I'm Luso-Brazilian. We didn't have the Spaniards ruling us like you guys.

– Yeah, I know. It was the Portuguese. Regardless, we in the Americas all come from colonial roots of one form or another.

On the way back to the hotel, Chucho tells Severino that he would be going to pick up Zully in the morning. He would have to get her approval that evening, but he'd like Severino to come to San Pedro with him.

– I think she would get over this whole thing better if she could hear you personally explain... and apologize. How many days do you plan to stay in Oaxaca?

– Five days.

– I'll give you a call tonight. I'm sure you'd find it interesting.

– I don't want to be any bother. My intentions weren't to impose myself on your lives.

– Relax man. Let me talk to Zully and I'll get back in touch tonight.

*****

The next morning, as the VW bug starts up the winding road from Miajuatlán, Chucho feels uneasy as he recalls the incident on the roadside with Jorge. As they pass the spot below the pines where Jorge had threatened him, Chucho points out the window.

– There's where your mystery man revealed his true nature. I still can't quite grasp why you would let him off the hook.

– Chucho, I'm not trying to excuse his behavior. It's part of the whole series of events that spun out of control. I can tell you this; I had no idea of what he was doing until well after it ended. If I could have stopped it, I would have.

They pull into San Pedro el Alto. Severino had never seen skies so blue. The air at that high altitude was thin and clear. He marveled at the tall pines.

– The forest here is so different than where I come from.

– I know, I was there, remember?

At his family's place, Chucho goes inside. Severino stays in the car until he returns, with Zully at his side.

– Zully, this is Chucho. I'll let him explain his mission of redemption.

Chucho spends the next hour or so explaining everything again to Zully and the others. They find his accent and appearance exotic. Severino finds the Zapotec mannerisms and culture fascinating. North America meets South America in a manner that seldom happens. He learns how tortillas are cooked on a comal, hears Zapotec spoken by most of the family and notes how simple and antiquated their lifestyle is.

In the morning, Chucho and Zully have a surprise for him.

–We're going down to the coast at Zipolite. You'll love it!

The three of them, along with two of Zully's cousins, pile into the VW and they drive down the long and winding road to the coast. As they approach the sea, the temperature rises significantly and the humidity and tropical forest reminds Severino of Brazil. The final few miles are on a twisty, bumpy path that passes for a road in these parts. In Zipolite, they stop at Susana's place. There is no electricity. Here, backpackers from the world over hang hammocks and pretend to be removed from the modern world.

– The beach here is beautiful. – says Severino. – The waves are higher than any I've ever seen in Brazil.

– In January, this place has some of the highest waves in the world, second only to Hawaii. – replies Chucho. – And, it's a great spot to meet people and practice English.

They wander along the beach. None of them knows how to swim, so they settle for wading a little in the surf. That night, Chucho brings them up to a spot on the steep hillside above Susana's.

– When I first started coming here, I'd hike up here and hang my hammock between these two trees each night, sometimes for weeks at a time.

The half moon illuminated the ocean in the distance. The beach itself is not visible, but the waves hitting the shore sounded like explosions. The five of them sit awhile on the huge boulders that tumble down the hillside.

– Life is good again – Zully says.

The next day they drive on to Puerto Escondido. Chucho takes them to a small hotel overlooking the Playa del Amor.

– Tonight, something different is going to happen. – he states with a big grin.

– And what would that be? – Zully asks.

– You'll see.

That evening, Chucho takes them to a street that parallels the beach. It's closed to traffic, and full of tourists looking for whatever this tiny city has to offer. That's not much. After they wander up and down, checking out the other folks in town, Chucho leads them into a pizza place. He chooses a table that's separated from the roadway by a waist-high wall.

– The action will begin soon – he states.

– What action? – Severino and Zully both ask.

– I'll explain when it starts.

The pizzas arrive. As they all grab pieces of it, they hear people yelling and laughing up the street. A group of people, each wearing masks, and some with costumes, are dancing down the street, handing out bottles from several wheelbarrows that are following them. Behind them are children and other stragglers. Most appear to be inebriated, or something. They're offering their wares to anyone and everyone.

– Take what you wish! – one man cries out in Spanish. – He and the others hand out beer, mescal, marijuana and psychedelic mushrooms.

– Holy shit man! – a tourist shouts. – they're getting everybody stoned.

– It's the *Escandalosos*! – yells one of the shop owners. – They're back!

The gang of masked merry-makers moves on fast. They're gone before most of the tourists know what's going on.

– They come once a year. – states Chucho. – It has been going on since an English rock band came through here a few years ago. Some say it was the Rolling Stones. I'm not sure, but ever since, a group of masked men and women descend on Puerto Escondido every year and attempt to get the whole town wasted. Eat up! We'll want to either get back to our hotel, or let ourselves go and participate. There'll be dancing in the streets until dawn.

– We have to get my cousins home tomorrow and Severino needs to make it back to Oaxaca by tomorrow night also. We're not going to be getting drunk or anything else tonight Chucho. Just how did you know that the *Escandalosos* would be coming around tonight?

Chucho just smiles and says – No comment.

*****

Two days later, Zully and Chucho bring Severino to the airport.

– Take care, my friend. I'm sorry we weren't able to get in contact with Lilly in Colorado. Be sure to tell her we think of her from time to time. Our honeymoon was magical up until that last night. Now we can again focus on the good times in Brazil. You were wrong to do what you did Severino, but we thank you for restoring the innocence in our memories. ¡Adiós!

Zully adds – I wish you well, Severino. ¡Que le vaya bien!

41
Durango

On the flight from Oklahoma, Severino stares out the window at the farmland below. He's amazed at the vast flatlands of this part of America. His visit with the wealthy heartland couple had given him time to rest. They're gracious people. He still marveled at the standard of living in the United States. He's not impressed so much by the huge cars and houses, but rather, by the little things he never imagined: fans in every bathroom, closets and screens on all windows.

Below the grasslands abruptly change into mountains. He expected a gradual change in gradient. Instead, the mountains ascend out of the flatlands as though God had drawn a line on the Earth, declaring:

– This is horizontal; this is vertical.

Severino sees a snow-topped range of mountains. He wonders why the pine forests end at a certain point on the flanks of the high peaks. Another line drawn by God?

At the La Plata County Airport, Severino picks up the rental car that the Americans in Oklahoma have arranged for him. He laughs when he sees it's a VW beetle, but this one is new. He gets directions to Durango, and thirty minutes later, he's in his room at the Strater Hotel. That evening Severino roams the saloons and bars from another epoch. This place is like the far west movies he's seen in Ilhéus. He's glad he knows English, but it's still a struggle, as everyone is constantly using slang terms that he doesn't understand. He thinks about the way it must have been for Jorge when he got to America, without any previous English.

In the morning, Severino goes to the county tax office and asks for assistance in locating the property of a Lilly Ann Wethington. The young woman helping him quickly finds the property.

– It's undeveloped land – she stays. – So, nobody actually lives there.

– Do you know where she lives?

– I haven't a clue. But, she does have a Denver address where we send her tax billings.

Severino takes down the address, but he already knows where to find her. Jorge has already explained how to locate Lilly.

– Can you show me on a map where the property is located?

– It's on the Southern Ute Indian Reservation.

She shows him the location on the county property map.

– I can make a copy of this part of the county if you'd like. It'll cost a dollar, though.

Severino leaves with map in hand and written instructions on how to get to the point on a county road nearest to the property. He returns to his hotel and gathers the documents he hopes will convince Lilly of the legitimacy of his mission: his letter from the mayor of Almadina, a letter written in English from Chucho that describes his visit in Oaxaca and another letter from the couple in Oklahoma.

His experience as a guide has given Severino map reading skills. After leaving US highway 550, he drives up County Road 318. The road winds up a canyon, through sandstone walls and ponderosa pines. He stops to examine the strange scene. The pines have long needles and he doesn't recognize any of the other plants. He returns to his task of finding Lilly's place. It takes him several attempts, but he eventually located the natural gas wellhead that sits beside her land. A crude road leads down from it, but a locked chain blocks the entrance.

He follows the narrow road through the pinyon-juniper woodlands and soon comes to a metal gate. It blocks the road, and is locked.

– Why would anybody put up a gate where there are no fences and you can just walk around it? – he asks himself. He smiles when he reads the sign posted beside the gate.

No Trespassing!
No Hunting!
No Nothing!
This means you!

'The point of no return' he thinks. 'I haven't come this far just to turn back.' He walks around the gate and on down the road. He crosses several sandy draws, slowly gaining elevation. The beauty of the place causes him to stop several times and examine the trees, plants and rocks he has never seen. He tries to guess what animals have produced the footprints he finds everywhere in the sandy soil. Lizards scurry. The sun beats down hot.

Suddenly something large bolts across the road in front of him. He has startled a large mule deer, and as it crosses the road, their eyes meet. Severino has never seen an animal this large in the wild. At first, he's frightened. Then, curiosity gets the best of him and he follows it into the forest. He's able to keep up with it for a while, but then loses sight of it. He decides to return to the road, but soon realizes that he has no idea which direction he should go to find the road. He follows his instinct and makes a beeline in the direction he thinks it will be found. Five minutes later, he comes to the edge of a canyon.

Jorge had spoken of this canyon, and said that Severino should avoid it. What now? He decides to follow the canyon rim. Maybe it would lead to Lilly's place. Looking down into the abyss, he sees a hawk flying below. It soon notices him and starts screaming at him. It's easy walking along the almost seamless rock rim of the canyon. A breeze blows onto the mesa top from below. He stops in the shade of a large Juniper. The smell of pine needles in the hot sun reminds him he's in a strange land.

All of a sudden, he sees movement. Something has darted from the rimrock into the woodland. He assumes it's the deer and hunkers down, hoping to get a close-up look at the animal.

– Don't move! Stand up slowly! I've got my gun trained on you! Put your hands on the back of your head!

Lilly is impressed with how well the alarm system had worked. After the buzzer on her belt sounded, she had cautiously followed the road. She found the intruder's footprints, and it had been easy to track him across the mesa top. When she saw him attempt to hide from her under the juniper, Lilly decided to take action.

– Easy lady! You're Lilly, right?

– Listen buddy! If you want to live to see another day, put your hands where I can see them.

Severino reaches for the documents that he has tucked into his back pocket as he says,

– If you'll just look at...

At that moment, the sound of a gunshot echoes across the mesa and down the canyon. The papers in Severino's hand fly into the air and land on the dried pinyon needles. They're stained with blood. Severino drops to his knees.

– You shot me!

He holds his right hand. Blood is flowing freely.

– I told you not to do anything. – Lilly yells.

– I'm unarmed! I was just going to show you the letter from Chucho and Zully. Shit, I'm bleeding to death. I'm going to die out here in this godforsaken nowhere-land!

Lilly comes to his side. Severino is kneeling and she sees he's also bleeding from his right leg.

– Stand up! I need to search you for weapons.

She helps him to his feet. A quick pat-down reveals he's unarmed. She examines the hand. The shot had separated the thumb from the hand. It's still attached by bone, but the skin and muscle between are ripped apart.

– Oh fuck! Why didn't you just do as I said?

– I couldn't understand what you were saying. You were screaming and I only understood not to move. Those papers show who I am and why I'm here. Oh god, you shot my leg too!

– Look, we have to get you to a doctor. Can you walk?

She helps Severino up and he leans on her as the two of them amble like two drunken ducks towards Lilly's truck. She grabs a pillowcase, and makes a quick bandage for the hand. Then, she wads up a tee shirt and puts it on the leg wound.

– Keep pressure on this with your left hand. Keep your other hand elevated above your head. She loads him into the truck and they take off for Durango. On the way, she notes his pale appearance and the fear in his eyes.

– Shit man! – Lilly blurts out. – Why didn't you just leave me in peace? I can get over anything with a little time. Just what I didn't need: a ghost from the accident in Rio that's come back to haunt me. Fuck!

– O sinto. Não foi minha intençao fazer nada assim.

At Mercy Medical in Durango, Severino is taken into the emergency room and attended by an intern. Lilly waits on a bench outside of the curtained cubicle. A nurse comes by and tells her that it's requiring quite a few stitches, but that he'll be OK. Later the doctor brings him out in a wheelchair.

– He's a lucky guy. The bullet passed through the hand without breaking any bones before grazing his leg. He has eighteen stitches in his hand and four in his leg. We're going to keep him here overnight for observation, but I expect him to be up and about by tomorrow. He says he has no insurance, so we'll have to limit his stay to the minimum required to insure his safety. He's going to need physical therapy. That hand will never function like before. Nonetheless, he will have some use of his thumb.

– Thanks doctor.

– You're going to have to file a report on the accident with the police, as I'm required to report any injuries that involve a weapon.

– The accident? – Lilly asks.

– Yes, he told me about you tripping as you were showing him how to load a pistol. I guess he's one Mexican that'll have a little more respect for firearms in the future. And, you should too. Have you taken the firearms safety course?

– Yes, years ago. And he's not a Mexican. He's from Brazil.

Lilly stays with Severino until he's wheeled into a hospital room. When they're alone she states,

– I'm going to have to file a police report. Thanks for saying it was an accident. I had no idea that you were unarmed. You had no legal right to be on my property. Still, it would be hard for me to explain why I was expecting trouble when I never reported the first invasion out at the canyon. I have many questions for you, not the least of which is: just who is this Jorge that came to my place? For now, get some rest. I'm going to the police station. The doctor reported the shooting, and I hope the matter won't lead to further problems.

– Lilly, we tried to get in contact with you ahead of time.

– Let's not talk about this now. I'll be back before I drive home.

– You can stay at my hotel for the night if you want. Somebody may as well use it; it's paid for. It's room 202 at the Strater.

– Let me see what happens with the cops first. I'll see you after I file the report. I need you to tell me exactly what you told the doctor in the emergency room about the shooting.

– I told him that I'd never actually held a gun in my hand, and that you wanted to show me your pistol. When you went to give it to me, you tripped, and the gun went off. I told him it hit my hand because I was holding it out to for you to give me the pistol.

– Good thinking.

– Lilly. Did you get the letters off the ground?

– Yes, and I read them while they were stitching you up. For now, just relax. Get some sleep, if you can.

*****

The accident report at the police station is accomplished with minimal stress. Lilly is questioned about the circumstances and they want to know why Severino is in Colorado. She says he's on vacation and mutual friends had recommended Durango. The whole matter is finished in less than twenty minutes.

– You'll have to be available for questions, should something come up.

– Like what?

– Like, if the man you shot doesn't collaborate your story.

– He already did, at the hospital.

– Yes, but I'll go by in the morning to have him give me his version of the incident. I don't expect a problem, but it's a departmental requirement that all parties to an injury with a firearm be interviewed.

Lilly gives him the phone number of a friend who lives up on Missionary Ridge. She also provides him with a list of people who can verify she's never had a violent run-in with anyone.

After leaving the station, she gives Severino a call from a pay phone. She decides to stay at the Strater. Severino says he'll call the front desk to instruct them to give her the room key. They agree to meet in the morning, after the detective interviews Severino. He'll give her a call at the hotel.

Lilly's main purpose in staying in town is to call Chucho and Zully. She has the reception desk make the call and she takes it in the room. They're both glad to hear her and, at first, they're in high spirits. But, when Lilly tells them about the shooting, there is a long silence on the other end of the phone call.

– You've got to be kidding! How did that happen? – Chucho asks.

– Oh, it was sort of natural. Until I found out that he was unarmed and meant no harm, I was actually enjoying it. I thought he was the same guy who scared the shit out of me the last time.

Lilly explains about Jorge's visit. They tell her that Severino had clarified the ugly encounters with the American stranger when he was in Oaxaca. She also lets them know that Severino will recover with minimal problems.

– So, you guys took him to your folk's home in the mountains and to the Pacific Ocean? What was that all about?

– Lilly, he's actually a decent guy. With being shot and all, he's suffered as much as anyone for his mistake. He's gone to extremes to make things right. He could've just let it be.

– Maybe he should have.

– I'm personally glad he made the trip. – Chucho interjects. – It's odd to look him in the face and realize he went over that cliff that night in Rio.

– Yeah, I want to talk to him about that tomorrow. It still seems far-fetched to me.

– It is. But, it's a part of us, and I for one am glad he gave Zully and I the chance to bring this thing to an end. We consider him a friend. I know that sounds bizarre, but it's true. Do you want to say hi to Zully?

– Just for a second, I'm charging this call to his hotel room.

They both laugh and Chucho puts the phone down. She hears Zully laughing as she gets on the line.

– ¡Hola Lilly! ¿Cómo estás? – Zully almost shouts into the receiver. – Can you believe this whole thing? Life is strange at times.

– Tell me about it! How are you and Chucho doing? I mean, how's married life treating you?

– I love it. My marriage was the start of a form of happiness that I never dreamed of in my life. Then that thing in Rio ruined the end of a perfect honeymoon, and lingered in the background. I'm glad it was all a misunderstanding.

– Well, I can't call it only a misunderstanding. At least, not yet.

– Lilly, we've been thinking of inviting you down to Oaxaca sometime.

– That would be great. Let's keep it in mind in the coming months. For now, I'm just trying to cope with all that has happened in the last month or so.

– I think when you talk to Severino; you'll find he's sincere.
– I hope so. Zully, I'm going to have to let you go. Take good care of yourselves.
– Cuídate Lilly. Nos vemos.

*****

The next day, Severino calls to tell her that the questioning went well. Lilly picks him up at the hospital. They go for lunch in the Diamond Bell bar at the hotel. Severino is much more lucid, although he has pain in his hand. They gave him some pain pills, but he insists on taking only half of what they prescribed.

Lilly asks him to explain everything that happened before and after the incident in Rio. Severino fills in all the gaps. She finds herself staring into his face and trying to imagine what he was thinking that dark night when he drove himself off a cliff.

– You could have easily died that night, you know. – she says.
– At the time, I felt it wouldn't have made much of a difference.
– Are all Brazilians as crazy as you?
– Most of them – he says with a big smirk.
– So, what's next? Going on to see Yoko?
– Yes, but I'd like to see this place called Mesa Verde. My friends in Oklahoma told me all about an ancient culture that lived in cities in caves.
– Yes, the Anasazi. Their ruins are impressive. In the summer, Mesa Verde has thousands of visitors. Hey, do you think you could hike in the heat of summer, here in the high desert?
– What do you mean?
– The best place to see the culture you speak of is in the heartland of their ancient civilization. That's Chaco Canyon. It's located a hundred miles south of here. I haven't been there in a few years and I'd like to take you to see it if you think you could handle the trip. I mean, with your injury and all.
– Lilly, you are kind, but I don't want to impose. It's funny; Chucho and Zully also took me on a trip.
– Yes, I spoke with them last night. They think highly of you. You're never going to get another chance to see a place like Chaco. It's magical. We could head out in the morning and spend the night

at the campground in Chaco Canyon. What do you say? It would give me the chance to make up for shooting you.

Lilly starts laughing. She laughs so hard that she ends up crying. – Christ! Forgive me, but the whole thing, the accident in Rio and shooting somebody is just too much for me to incorporate at this moment.

Severino looks into Lilly's eyes and replies, almost without emotion – I'd love to see this Chaco canyon place. What time will we leave?

It's a long drive, so I'll pick you up at seven in the morning, OK?

– Perfect.

They finish eating and Severino heads up to his room. Lilly goes to City Market and buys the supplies they'll need for the next two days. Then, it's back to the canyon. As she stands to unlock the chain at the entrance to her land, she stares out across the distant mesa tops, to the HD Mountains beyond. She hears herself quietly mouth these words:

– He's good looking.

*****

The air is still cool and the sun low on the western horizon as their pickup sails along Highway 44, south of Bloomfield, New Mexico. The high desert is just starting to come alive. The top of Angel Peak glows bright orange to the east. The distant canyons are still a lavender color, between the sunlit mesa tops. Lilly is driving eighty miles an hour. The cassette deck plays *Honky Tonk Woman* by the Rolling Stones.

– Hey! Look at that crazy bird. Man, it can really run! – Severino abruptly says while pointing to the road ahead.

– That's a roadrunner – Lilly replies. – they can't fly, but they can sure as hell run down their prey. They're sort of like desert penguins; they go through life as a bird, but they never get to see the ground from above.

– Who knows what God was thinking when he came up with them – Severino states.

– Yeah, an animal that doesn't know how to act like others in its order in the animal kingdom. As she finishes the words, Lilly realizes that she could be talking about herself.

– This is a strange land. It's so dry and empty, but I keep seeing more and more life – Severino adds.

They pull off on a gravel road that leads to the ruins, twenty-three miles away. They bounce over ruts and ridges for an hour before entering the national monument. Just beyond the entrance, Lilly stops the car near the rock wall of the canyon they have entered.

– Come check this out!

She leads him down a trail. The face of the cliff is still in the morning shadow. At first Severino notices nothing. Then his eyes adjust to the limited light.

– This is amazing! Who painted these odd pictures?

– Actually, they're not paintings. They're petroglyphs. They were etched into the stone at least seven hundred years ago. The Chaco Canyon area has thousands of them.

Severino studies the glyphs. Some are obviously animals. But, most are symbolic representations that are hard to decipher.

– What do they mean? What were they trying to say?

– Most are still mysteries. It's one of the reasons I always like to return here; the best, brightest and most educated minds in the world can't tell any more about them than we can. In the passage of almost a millennium, these shapes reach out to us as humans. As we attempt to put meaning to them, we search within ourselves for meanings to our own precarious lives. The only thing I've come up with in the times I've studied the glyphs here and at other places in the Four-corners is that they're stating what artists always do: that life's an enigma.

– And they lived out here, disconnected from the rest of the world? – Severino inquires.

– Not exactly. Back then; this was the center of civilization in the region. They had roads and methods of communicating across vast stretches of mountain and desert. They were great observers of the sun, moon and stars too. Let's go to the visitor center and you can get some idea of what's ahead for today.

They spend an hour at the center. While there, Lilly registers for a spot in the campground. Then they drive down one of the monument's few roads to Pueblo de Arroyo, one of the cities that were built in this remote canyon system. They spend the day roaming through ruins of cities, large and small. As the late afternoon sun casts long shadows over everything, they hike up on the mesa that overlooks Pueblo bonito, the largest of the cities.

– God, from above it's obvious that this entire city was built with one master plan from the beginning. How long did they take to construct this place?

– The guidebook says it took over 200 years.

– I would never have imagined finding a place like this in the United States, Lilly. You're right; this place holds magic. This isn't the America we think of in Brazil.

– Ha ha... – Lilly laughs. – Nobody really knows America, least of all the Americans.

*****

That night, they roast wieners over a campfire. Lilly shows Severino how to make smores. The stars form a celestial star-dome: that high desert nighttime show that has entertained so many for so long. They talk about their fates crossing, about their families and their lifestyles.

Lilly has pitched her tent without the rain-fly, so that the stars could be seen from within it. The time comes to turn in. Severino has never actually camped out. His lifestyle could be said to be a form of camping, but he has never slept in a tent. He mentions this to Lilly.

– Well, in fact, I'd been thinking that you would sleep on the picnic table. But, since you've never slept in a tent, you can tonight.

Severino looks at her with an unsure expression.

– No. Forget that! I'm sleeping on the table.

*****

In the morning, before leaving the canyon, Lilly stops her truck just inside the park boundaries. They hike up Fajada Butte. She leads him to a petroglyph. It is a spiraling line etched into a rock that's somewhat hidden by two other large, angular boulders.

– On the longest day of the year, the summer solstice, a blade of light is formed by the sun passing between those two stones – she says as she motions to two angular boulders behind them. – It descends to exactly the center of this spiral. It only happens on that day, each year.

From the top of the Butte, they can see most of the canyon system: a maze of sub-canyons, all eventually connecting with the larger Chaco Canyon.

– It looks like a vast wasteland from up here. I'd never have guessed this environment could have produced such a civilized culture.

– Civilized? Severino, they were humans. We always try to put a veneer of civilization over ourselves. That way we can ignore our strange relationship with nature. We can disregard our natural selves.

– I wonder what ended it all.

– Who knows exactly? There are lots of theories. You read some of them in the visitor center. Personally, I think they destroyed their own environment by cutting the mesa top forests and cultivating more corn than the limited resources here could handle. A simple theme that repeats, over and over, on this planet: overpopulation. When things got bad, the inevitable cruelty of human nature simple took its course. We humans are so stupid; I'm surprised we've lasted as long as we have.

*****

A few days later, Lilly stands beside Severino as he prepares to board a plane to Denver and then on to Portland. They're standing face-to-face and somewhat oblivious to the surroundings.

– Thank you for everything Lilly.

– Everything? For shooting you? – Lilly laughs.

– Well, almost everything. And, hey... it's getting better already.

– Yeah, sure. Thanks for trying to make me feel better. Not just about your hand, but about the whole thing in Rio. You're a good man Severino. I wish our first encounter had been under different circumstances. But then, I might've never gotten to know the real you. Speaking of getting to know you, I'm not sure why Yoko's father seemed so aloof and distant when we called him yesterday. I had expected him to be at least somewhat relieved by the news we gave him.

– Well, I haven't exactly been welcomed in Mexico or Colorado either – Severino says with a soft laugh.

– You are now.

– Lilly, you've showed me that my preconceptions of America were mistaken. I've only heard about the war mongering politicians and egotistical wealthy gringos here. I'm glad to understand another side of this country.

– Those negative things are a definitely a part of my country. You can count on that. But, they're not a part of my life. At least, I try to avoid that part of American realities. I believe most Americans do the same. At least, most would like to. Many get swept up with the endlessly hopeful and futile events of our times.

The small plane arrives and the boarding announcement is made. The other passengers file out the gate towards the plane.

– Take care, Severino. Good luck in Oregon!

– Call me in Oaxaca! Thanks for everything. I'll never forget you Lilly.

The two embrace, the gate attendant gives the last call and Severino turns and walks onto the tarmac. He doesn't look back.

42

Portland

Severino calls Mr. Koga from Stapleton Airport in Denver. He again finds Yoko's father tightlipped. They arrange for Severino to come to their house at noon the following day.

– Will Yoko be there?

– Just come at noon, and we'll end this whole situation.

Severino attempts to get more information, but Mr. Koga cuts the conversation short and hangs up. By the time Severino gets to Portland, he's full of doubts. That night, in the motel on the Capital highway, his misgivings continue to grow. He starts to ask himself questions. 'If Yoko was there, why didn't she get on the phone? Am I walking into a trap of some sort?' He wakes frequently throughout the night. 'Maybe it would be better to head back to Brazil in the morning. They already have the facts and that's why I'm here. Why should I risk more than is necessary? The trip has been more successful than I had expected. Maybe I should just quit while I'm ahead.'

By the time Severino finishes breakfast in the morning, he again feels he's doing the right thing by going to Yoko's home. As the taxi drops him off in front of the house, he notes there are no police vehicles nearby. 'At least they don't have the cops waiting for me.'

Yoko's father answers the door.

– Mr. Koga?

– Yes, and from your appearance I assume you are Mr. Pindoba.

– Yes, but most people call me Severino.

Yoko's father escorts him into the living room, where he is introduced to Mrs. Koga. Yoko is not in the room. A man in a plain beige suit is also sitting with the parents.

– I was hoping to get to speak with Yoko directly, Mr. Koga.

– And I believe you shall. However, we must first know the entire nature of you visit and the information that you bring.

– Of course, that's why I'm here. Wouldn't it just be simpler to have Yoko in on the explanation of the events in Rio de Janeiro? Do you harbor doubts about my reason for coming?

No Mr. Pindoba, we've checked you out thoroughly, including your background and your progress across America since you entered the country. You're trying to correct the foolish mistakes that you made in Brazil. If I thought that putting you in jail would be beneficial for Yoko, I wouldn't hesitate for a second.

The word jail echoes in Severino's mind. 'Maybe I shouldn't have come after all.'

– I haven't done anything illegal in this country Mr. Koga.

– That's debatable. Regardless, you have information about somebody who has. It wouldn't be difficult to convince the authorities of your involvement in a conspiracy to extort information from several women in the US. You have crossed international and state borders in what could be perceived as an attempt to circumvent justice.

Severino mentally makes note that there is no one between him and the door.

– Relax young man. We've no intention of causing you harm. But remember, the reason for that is the well-being of Yoko. Your personal situation is of no interest to us. We are going to do what is necessary to bring about the recovery of our daughter.

– Recovery? From what? Nobody was hurt in the accident on the highway in Rio. That's why I'm here; to verify that fact.

– Actually, somebody was damaged in the accident Mr. Pindoba. That's why this gentleman is here today. This is Dr. Holland. He's a psychiatrist. I've asked him to explain Yoko's condition to you.

Severino feels the adrenaline rush in his body. 'Shit, what now?'

– Good afternoon Mr. Pindoba. I'm going to describe the condition that Yoko is experiencing, but I will limit the conversation to a general description of the personal affects that she suffers; more than that would be a breach of patient confidentiality.

Severino stares blankly at the short, stout man in the too-tight beige suit. This is not what he'd imagined would happen in Oregon, especially after Mexico and Colorado.

– Yoko suffers what many of our young soldiers returning from Vietnam are experiencing: posttraumatic stress disorder. She apparently suffered a distressing incident in Brazil. Upon returning, her inability to accept the event as over and finished has created, in her psyche, an ongoing fantasy about a fictitious character that's neither dead nor alive.

– Jesus! I never dreamed of something like this – Severino states. – Is there anything I can do to help?

– Possibly. That's why we asked you to come here today. These cases usually respond to therapy over time. It often helps to be able to confront a concrete reality that opposes the internalized fantasies. On the other hand, sometimes it can have the opposite effect and bring about a further relapse into the mental isolation that many who suffer this symptom create internally.

– Severino – Yoko's father interjects. – Yoko appears normal in ninety-nine percent of her everyday interactions. Most of the time, she's not aware of her problem in determining reality from fantasy. She's especially adept at hiding her problem while with her parents. This difficulty of adapting to negative realities has been a reoccurring problem since her childhood.

– That's fairly common in these cases – interjects Dr. Holland. – It also adds to the problem of treatment, as the very ones who can be supportive, are the ones in whom the patient doesn't wish to confide.

– God, I feel so guilty – Severino says. – I had no idea what my plan would bring about. I was only trying to get free of my own psychological fears.

– Severino, I think now would be a good time for you to explain everything that occurred that night in Rio – Mr. Koga calmly says. – Please, be specific.

Severino relates the entire episode of the night he drove off the edge of the highway in Rio. Dr. Holland asks several questions about Yoko's specific response to the accident. He discovers that she was the one most bothered by leaving the victim without doing anything to help, or even call the police.

– She was crying and wanted to stay at the scene of the accident? – the psychiatrist asks.

– Yes, she appeared to be terrified about leaving a person down below in the dark ocean. The others were more concerned with avoiding legal problems, but Yoko didn't display any fear of the law. She was only interested in the wellbeing of the person on the motorcycle.

– That would be your wellbeing, Severino! – adds Mrs. Koga.

– Yes, she was worried about me.

– It's too late to change things, and your repentance might possibly help Yoko heal from this condition. Time will tell. – Mr. Koga says. – I respect the importance of doing the right thing Severino, but in this case, my daughter's health comes before my forgiveness of you. I appreciate your coming here, but I'm not ready to just forgive and forget. Not yet.

– I understand Mr. Koga.

– There are some things that might help with the healing process Mr. Pindoba – the psychiatrist says. He looks Severino directly in the eyes. – We want you to explain to Yoko how you arranged the stunt before that night. Concentrate on the aspects of the physical preparations, and exactly how you accomplished the trick of staying alive. Don't mention anything about Yoko's obsession with you or your body after the event. Clearly admit your purposeful attempt to deceive, and that she was not an intentional victim.

– When will I be able to speak with her?

– My daughter is upstairs, waiting for us to invite her down to speak with you – Mrs. Koga replies. – She's quite eager to meet you.

– Then, she knows about me coming?

– Of course – say Yoko's father. – Why wouldn't she?

– But I thought you just said....

Dr. Holland interrupts. – As I stated, Yoko is stable most of the time. Her psychotic episodes generally occur when she's alone. This is symptomatic of the illness. Treat her the same way you did the others you have visited. Clear the air, and whatever you do, don't mention our conversation about her condition. For all you know, everything is fine.

The doctor stands and tells the Kogas that he must leave now. They thank him for coming and agree to make an appointment to see him in the near future.

– I believe it would be in our interest to have a session with both of you and Yoko as soon as possible.

– The earliest time will be a week from next Saturday. Yoko will be home for the Labor Day weekend. Can you arrange a Saturday meeting Doctor?

– Yes, as a professional courtesy, I'll accommodate your request. Mr. Pindoba, can you accompany me to my car?

– We'll bring Yoko downstairs to meet you Mr. Pindoba–
adds Yoko's father.

As they walk to the car, the psychiatrist tells Severino to keep
the meeting positive. He requests that Severino follow up the visit
with letters from Brazil that show he's living a good life and not
suffering any adverse effects from the incident in Rio. This,
combined with collaborating statements from Lilly, Chucho and Zully
have a high probability of diminishing the degree and duration of
Yoko's symptoms.

– You can count on me doctor.

Dr. Holland gives Severino his business card and asks
Severino to keep in touch. He then gets in his car, and drives away.
Severino returns to the front door, where Mr. Koga awaits.

– My wife is bringing Yoko down. Have a seat.

Yoko enters the living room and her father introduces her to
Severino. She studies him with interest, but maintains several yards
between them.

– Let's sit down and find out what Mr. Pindoba has to say,
Yoko – Mr. Koga says.

– You've already heard what he has to say Dad. I still don't
understand why I had to wait until you grilled him about everything.
You can be so overly protective!

Severino again details the night in Rio. This time he
concentrates more on how the illusion was produced, than the
outcome of it. Yoko has a few questions, but mostly lets him talk.

– Were you injured in any manner Mr. Pindoba?

– Not at all. Please call me Severino, Yoko.

– OK. Severino, you mention you were a teacher before the
explosion in Itabuna. Will you be returning to teaching?

– That's a good question Yoko. I've yet to decide my next
career move. Strangely enough, the series of odd events have opened
up other possibilities that I had never considered. But, my future
looks bright. I've learned that my actions are part of a larger plan, or,
part of a bigger human picture. My hope is that you, and the others
that I affected negatively, will find peace in your lives again.
Forgiveness is secondary.

– I forgive you Severino. I forgave you soon after I heard the
truth about the whole fiasco from my father. That's how I was raised.

She looks at her father, who has kept a neutral face during the
entire conversation. Severino reads Mr. Koga's expression as silent

anger, but Yoko and her mother knew it was his way of showing acceptance.

The conversation draws to an end. A long silence leaves Severino uneasy. Mrs. Koga asks if he would like to stay for lunch, but Severino declines. Yoko's father stands up and says

– It's been very enlightening Mr. Pindoba. We thank you for coming so far to clarify your role in the incident that should have never happened, and to a degree, never did.

– Thank you for allowing me this opportunity Mr. and Mrs. Koga. Feel free to contact me in the future.

Severino asks to use the telephone to call a taxi, but Yoko's father insists on driving him to his hotel. Severino says goodbye to Yoko's mother. Yoko and her father escort him out to the car parked in the driveway. She walks beside him, making sure not to touch him.

– Severino, I'm pleased you came personally to speak with me.

She reaches out and touches Severino's shoulder, as if to verify that he really exists.

– Have a safe trip home.

Yoko's father and Severino drive off, with Yoko watching the car disappear around the corner.

*****

Severino's flight leaves the Portland airport at dawn the next morning. As the plane gains altitude above the Columbia River Gorge, the pilot points out Multnomah Falls. From this altitude, the waterfall with the longest vertical drop in North America seems like a tiny trickle of water dropping off the green-forested canyon rim far below. His thoughts are on Almadina and home. This America certainly is different from his America. He is returning a different person. He feels young. He's free and life is his again.

Below, Yoko is on her way back to La Grande. She has stopped at the same falls that Severino views from above. She has always spoken with the smaller falls in the gorge. This time, she's speaking with the giant she has always feared. Multnomah was too overpowering. This morning, however, it was different. She found a spot on the volcanic rocks alongside the long and silent freefall of millions of gallons of water before they crashed with a sound like thunder on the rocks and pools far below.

– He's alive.

– Yes, I know. He always was.

– Thanks for not telling me sooner! You could have saved me a lot of trouble.

– I'm not here to save you.

– Then, why are you here?

– To keep the clockworks in motion.

43
Posthumous

Severino returned to Almadina with a new status in the community. He was the world traveler and would henceforth be considered an expert in any conversation that involved North America or any other foreign country. His knowledge of English was now recognized as legitimate; he had used it to achieve results in America.

In the first weeks after his return, the whole town wanted to know everything about the trip. Severino was quick to oblige them. He savored his experiences abroad. His tales of Mexico inspired envy among his friends. The wilderness of Colorado was not what anyone in Almadina had imagined when thinking about the United States. When his photos were developed, it was the Zapotec lifestyle that most captivated his viewers. Severino basked in the popularity. Vovó was the proud grandmother of a prodigal son who had returned to his birthplace with new respect for everything.

His fame had spread as far as Ilhéus. The director of the school in Malhado where Severino had taught came to Almadina to hear about his transformation from outcast to icon. He offered the English teacher position to him, should Severino care to return the following year.

– I need a while to consider it. I loved the work I started there. Can I have a while to think it over?

– Of course. Just remember that your students have been clamoring for your return since you left. I've been in this profession for most of my life, Severino. I feel that nobody can learn to teach. It's either in your genes or not. I've never seen a teacher make such an impression on our students, in such a short time. Consider the offer, young man. We'd sure like to see you come back.

Over the following months, Severino's life returned to normal. That is, he was no longer the center of attraction in the community.

Other small town intrigues and trances passed from mouth to mouth in Almadina.

Severino stopped going into town with regularity. The fazenda became his place of physical dedication and mental contemplation. He adjusted his life's rhythms to those of the revolving planet and its interaction with the sun and moon. His love of his grandmother brought him to see her several times a month. Other than that, he stayed up on the hillside with the cacau trees. They were now producing enough cocoa beans to bring in a small income. It wasn't much, just enough to pay for what he needed and nothing extra. He felt prosperous. Dinho handled his commercial transactions. Each day brought Severino closer to the natural rhythms of his land. He gave his watch to Dinho. He gave his heart to his writing. He gave his love to all things.

One day, the late afternoon sun hovered above the forested crest of the hillside on the opposite side of the valley. Its light flickered like a mottled green net over Severino, who stood beside a tree he had just finished planting. He had spent the previous day hauling water, sand and cement up to the highline of his property, where he constructed a stone vault alongside an old and dying cacau tree. Today had been an emotional day. He transplanted his father's remains to the hillside tomb. Above them, he planted the healthiest young cacau tree he could find on the fazenda. On top of the new gravesite, around the opening for the young tree, he shoveled fresh concrete. After he had smoothed the surface, he inscribed this into it:

Zé Paulo
Loved by God, Mother and Son

He finishes the project as the first stars come out. The tangerine skyline is quickly melting into the purple-black night sky. Severino sits on the ground and lets his thoughts drift off, as though conversing with someone by way of the quiet winds that flow from his land over the valley below. He looks out across the darkening valley below, and sees the lights of the distant fazendas up and down the valley. This is a peaceful place. Sounds of far-off traffic and an occasional donkey braying are overshadowed by the sound of the wind, as it weaves its way down the hillside, through the cacau trees, along the Almada River and flows out over the Atlantic. Severino turns and puts his hand on the cool and still moist cement on top of his father.

 – You doin' OK in there dad? I made sure to include your hand. I knew you'd want it with you.

The author has taught at the University of New Mexico, the University of Kentucky, Southern Oregon University and Fort Hays State University. He holds a PhD in Spanish Literatures and Linguistics. He has lived in the United States, Mexico and Brazil. He currently resides in Bahia.

Made in the USA
Las Vegas, NV
21 September 2023

77887071R00132